CARL PERKINS' CADILLAC

I t all went to shit when the dork with the pissant mustache found me. I was sitting in Zeek's Place, a blues bar in Memphis with cold beer, hot waitresses, and a clientele that didn't intrude on a man's God-given right to get drunk in peace. I wasn't drunk, though. It takes a lot to get me there, even with Zeek's high-octane enhanced beer, and I needed to keep my wits about me. I was working, after all.

This night, "working" meant sitting at a small table in the rear of the bar with my back wedged into a corner and a clear view of the whole place laid out in front of me. Zeek's wasn't a huge joint, exactly fifteen round tables bolted to the floor in very specific placements to make three pentacles around the bar, each with five chairs around them. You had to be in the place for a while and be seriously attuned to magical energy to see the pattern of the tables, and even more perceptive to catch the fact that the ceiling lamps were situated precisely above the tables, duplicating the lines of power on the floor.

The layout, along with the silver filigree on the crown molding, the salt sprinkled along the baseboards, and the building's placement on the end of a pier sticking out over the Mississippi River all combined to make Zeek's one of the most magically inert places I'd ever been outside of a binding circle. I liked it that way. I'd had plenty of magic in my life for a while and was looking for someplace to decompress. When an imp in Georgia who owed me a favor told me about this blues joint in Memphis where nobody could cast spells, I decided it had been too long since I had some cool blues and smoking ribs, so I rolled north to Tennessee.

Zeek knew who I was the second I walked in his silver-clad door, of course. It's been a minute since I didn't get recognized by most of the supernatural community, at least the power players. He glared at me the whole walk from the door to the barstool, then slid a mug of dark foamy beer in front of me.

"You're the one they call Reaper."

"Yeah, that's been said once or twice."

"You planning on causing any trouble in my bar?"

"No."

I didn't say anything else, and he didn't ask. That became one of my favorite things about Zeek: his ability to leave it the fuck alone. I sat on that barstool drinking his homebrew like it was my job, and when the night came to a close, I paid my tab and asked if he knew anyplace warded that had vacancies.

"How long you looking to stay?"

"I don't know yet. Going to depend on if I find work and some-place to stay."

"I thought you were loaded?"

"Circumstances change." I didn't feel like telling this guy I just met that after returning from Hell I walked away from my money, my friends, my family, and the woman I loved because I was Number One on Lucifer's shit list and every demon in the material plane was going to be after me for the rest of my unnaturally long life. Even if he was a good bartender, I didn't unburden that easy.

"I could use a bouncer," Zeek said, drying a pint glass with the towel hanging from his waist. I'd been watching him clean the bar with that same towel for about six hours, so I really questioned the efficacy of his dishwashing at that point but held my tongue.

"Hey!" protested a werewolf walking up behind my right shoulder. "You got a bouncer. Me!"

I raised a fist, bloodying the pup's nose, then got off my stool. I kicked him in the balls while his hands were clapped to his face, then planted a right on his temple when he doubled over. The werewolf dropped like a sack of flour and lay on the sawdust-covered floor, snoring little blood bubbles into the dirt.

"I'll take it," I said. "Job come with a room?"

Zeek grinned at me. "Downstairs. Door on the back wall of the storeroom. It ain't much, just a bed, a dresser, and a bathroom. But it's even more warded than the rest of the place, and there's a trapdoor that drops out into the river if things go sideways." He reached for a key ring hanging on a post behind the bar and tossed it to me. "We open at four. Be sober by then."

"I'm sober now," I said, picking up my backpack from the floor beside me. "Thanks."

"Thank me after you live through a Saturday night," Zeek said with a grin. "Some of the scraps in here are hell."

"Pretty sure they're not," I said. I gave him a little wave over my shoulder as I walked to the stairs.

He wasn't lying. The apartment was about as barebones as anything I'd ever seen, but I'd slept in worse. The bed wasn't too lumpy, and while my feet hung off the end a little, and it wasn't my California King, it was fine. Zeek wasn't lying about the wards, either. The key granted me passage, but when I let my Sight drop over my eyes like a veil, the whole room glowed with lines of red, green, and black. Anything coming into this room without a key would have to either be patient, with a real talent for complex spellcraft, or more powerful than anything I'd ever faced. Well, almost anything.

I sat on the bed and reached into my backpack, pulling out a cell phone and a folded picture. I double-checked the battery was still out of the phone and set it on the small dresser. "Dresser" was a pretty kind word for a stack of pressboard drawers that made IKEA look like Chippendale furniture, but it was enough to hold my spare pair of

3

jeans, four pairs of socks, four shirts, and four pairs of underwear. Then I kicked off my Doc Marten boots, sat on the bed with my back and shoulders pressed to the wall, and stared at the picture of the dark-skinned woman with long brown curls, regretting every life choice that took me away from her until sleep finally claimed me around dawn.

Since that night, I'd been a fixture at Zeek's. Busting heads when I needed to, smoothing ruffled feathers when that was called for, making a dumb joke to defuse a fight when that worked better. I was enjoying the work, enjoying the music, and even enjoying the people.

Well, employees. "People" might be a bit of a strong word. Zeek's was a Sanctuary, a place where all types of humans, monsters, and interdimensional beings could come in, have a drink, and be protected by the rule of "Don't start nothing, won't be nothing." That meant you have a lot of supernaturals on the payroll. There was me, with my part-vampire, sliver of a demon origin. There was Zeek, and I wasn't sure what exactly he was, but I had a sneaking suspicion there was a pair of white wings tucked away somewhere under his faded AC/DC t-shirt. Angelique was the succubus waitress, who let her tail snake out from under her miniskirt and wasn't shy about using it to slap patrons who let their hands wander from their longnecks to her long legs.

The house band were all were-cats of one breed or another, from housecat to tiger. Their hearing and reflexes made them the perfect group to improvise together, and they made a game out of trying to push somebody off the beat. I'd never seen anyone win so much as a point. Then there was Henry, the werewolf I decked to get my job. He turned into a pretty good second once his nose healed, but since I didn't need much backup, he spent most nights hauling kegs up the stairs for Zeek.

As far as anybody but Zeek and the rest of the staff knew, I was Eddie Nolen, a half-fae from Manchester hiding out from the Winter Court. I grew out my hair and beard, and worked pretty hard at burying Quincy Harker deep in my past. It was the best way I could come up with to protect the people I loved back in North Carolina.

It only took me one fight to prove that I was enough of a badass to bounce at the preeminent bar for monsters, demons, and angels in West Tennessee, even without my spells. Yeah, my magic wouldn't work in the bar. With all the wards, silver, and salt in the room, it was hard to touch any magic at all, then being over running water completely cut me off from being able to tap a leyline or anything else. The good news was that nobody else could conjure so much as a sparkler, either, so at least we were on pretty even footing.

I was standing at one end of the U-shaped bar, keeping an eye on the place, when I saw Angelique spin around and belt a big bastard in the face with her tail. The point of the appendage left a long red line down the dude's face, so I could tell from across the room that she was *pissed*. Angie has incredible fine motor skills, even with her tail, so if she drew blood, she meant to. And that meant that Big Boy had crossed a line.

I pushed off the wall and waved Henry off. Now that I saw the guy on his feet, I pegged him for a low-level Soldier Demon, no deeper than Third Circle. He'd be strong, but stupid, and not fast enough to be a real problem. Unless he was, then I'd want Henry to be able to jump in and back me up. I hoped he could get all that from a hand wave and a head shake, but I wasn't holding my breath. Henry's strong, but he ain't the sharpest knife in the drawer.

I heard Angie cursing the guy in poorly pronounced Enochian as I walked up, which sounds a lot like someone gargling with lava while skipping rope. I held up a hand to stave off the flow of profanity before she managed to accidentally curse one of us, and she pointed up at the guy.

"This asshole decided to run his hand up my skirt!"

The demon looked down at me, which doesn't happen all that often. But this behemoth was taking full advantage of Zeek's high ceilings with his seven-foot frame. He flashed me a grin, showing me a couple of short fangs in the process. "I just wanted to see if the tail was real, or if she was just a poseur."

"You couldn't have just asked?" I stopped in front of him and hooked my thumbs in the front pockets of my jeans.

"She might lie."

"Or you might see the yellow eyes with vertical pupils and see she's really got abyssal parentage. Or you could try for a free ass-grab and hope she just let it slide. That's not how it works." I turned to Angie. "How much is his tab?"

"Thirty-six. That's his third Patrón with a Corona back."

I looked back to the dumbass demon. "Drop fifty bucks on the table and get out. You're out for a week."

"Fuck you." He didn't move. I didn't expect him to.

"So you're the guy, huh?"

"What guy?"

"The guy the regulars decided should try out the new bouncer and see if I'm as tough as Henry. Fine. I knew it was coming. Just kinda hoped it wouldn't be on my first night. But let's get it out of the way." I didn't bother talking any more; I just made a knife edge out of my fingers and jabbed them into his solar plexus.

The great thing about demons taking on human physiognomy is that they have all the human weak points, too. He doubled over, clutching his gut, and I swung for the fences, putting everything I had into an uppercut meant to end the fight in one massive punch.

It didn't. It broke a couple of bones in my hand and turned Dumbass's nose into paste, but he just sat down on his ass in the floor, shook his head twice, blew a giant bloody booger onto the floor, then grinned up at me.

"Let's dance, motherfucker," he said, springing to his feet like I'd never laid a finger on him. Looked like my new job wasn't going to be all glitz and glamour after all.

2

―――――

The demon lowered his head and charged at me, obviously intending to break my ribs against the bar. I disappointed him by being somewhere else when he got to where I was standing. I look human. If you run into me in the streets, I just look like a normal guy. Maybe a little more world-weary around the eyes, and my hair never really stays put, but an average-looking tall guy with a fair amount of lean muscle packed onto his frame. Nothing about the picture says that I'm way faster than a human, and a lot stronger, and since I haven't been to Memphis in a long time, it's no surprise most of the folks in the bar, including Dumbass, had no idea who I was.

Dumbass slammed into the bar head-first, rattling a few glasses and dumping a couple of empty beer bottles onto the floor. None of the patrons spilled so much as a drop, having all picked up their drinks when they saw the scrap starting up. Zeek attracts a certain clientele, and if you're of that clientele, you expect that two out of three visits are going to end up with a fight.

"If you lay there for a couple minutes pretending to be knocked out, you can fake a concussion when you get up. Then you can leave without the shame of a human kicking your ass, because you knocked

7

yourself out." I've never seen a bear that didn't need poking, and this one was no exception. Sometimes, when I set outside myself and look at my behavior objectively, I wonder how the hell I've lived this long. Shit like that is why I don't look at myself objectively very often.

Dumbass didn't answer, but he didn't stay down, either. He backed out from under the bar and stood up as he turned to face me. There was a little trickle of blood running down his forehead where he busted himself open on the bar, but that didn't seem to bother him in the least. "I'm going to kill you, asshole," he growled, his voice low and scary. At least, scary if you haven't heard *really* scary shit in your life. Like friggin' Lucifer. Since coming back from Hell, I've found I'm pretty scare-proof.

He took a step closer, cracking his knuckles. "I'm going to rip off your head and shit down your neck while I skull-fuck your throat, you worthless piece of human excrement. I'm going to feed you your own spleen and then shove your teeth up your ass one by one with my big toe. I'm going to—"

I held up a hand. "Look, buddy. As absolutely poetic as your imagery is, are you gonna throw a punch so I can beat your head in, or are you just going to talk about what a badass you are? Because I've got the Sunday *Times* crossword puzzle over on the bar, and I'm really struggling with a five-letter word that means 'two-in-one utensil.' So if you're gonna do something, fucking do it already or get the fuck out of here."

That did the trick. His eyes went red, and that's not a metaphor. His eyes literally turned red and started to glow. That's how I knew he was pissed off beyond all reason, which is exactly where I needed him to be. This time he came at me straight up, with his arms low and out to the sides. He was looking for a bear hug, which would do lots of unpleasant things to my organs. The natural thing to do in that kind of fight is to go low and try to get under his arm, then attack from behind.

So I did the unnatural thing and ran right at him. I had about ten feet to get up to speed, and I came straight at him full tilt, leaping from six feet away to slam a knee right into his already busted forehead. That trickle of blood was like a bullseye, and after I planted my knee in his face and vaulted over his head to land on the bar, I dropped an elbow that would make Dusty Rhodes proud right on the crown of his head.

Dumbass dropped to one knee but didn't go all the way down. That was fine with me, because now I was on the floor behind him, so I just wrapped my arms around his throat in a sleeper hold, trying to pinch off the carotid arteries and put him out in a matter of seconds.

Unfortunately, this put me once again between an angry demon and a thousand pounds of highly polished oak. The demon reared back, slamming my spine right into the edge of the bar, and my arms flew off his neck. He spun around and threw a punch that would absolutely have laid me out cold if I hadn't dropped straight down to my knees when I bounced off the bar. I heard the solid *WHUNK* as his fist hit the bar, then a howl as the pain in his fist registered.

Normally in a fight like this, I'd use magic to make a shield, or transmute my skin into living metal, or just throw a fireball at the demon. But magic didn't work in Zeek's, so I was on my own.

Well, mostly on my own. I still had the brass knuckles in my back pocket, which I slipped on right before I punched Dumbass right in the side of the knee. The *crunch* that came from the joint was satisfying, but the hammer blow to my shoulders that followed it was definitely not.

He dropped both fists onto my shoulder blades with enough force to hammer a fence post home in one shot, and I sprawled face-first onto the scuffed wooden floor. I smacked my nose a good one when I hit, and as I scurried away from Dumbass's grasping mitts, I noticed what a good job the sawdust did soaking up the blood. Guess that's why Zeek bought the shit in two-hundred-pound drums.

I scooted through the demon's legs, racking my brain for a next move, but I wasn't quite fast enough. He grabbed one ankle and pulled me backward, and as I moved through his legs from back to front, my next move presented itself. Dangled itself right in front of me, as it were.

Yeah, I punched the demon in the balls. What the hell else was I supposed to do? He was bigger than me, stronger than me, and it looked a lot like he was a better fighter than me. Something about thousands of years in the Pits being better combat training than a little more than a century fighting humans and monsters on Earth. I didn't have a lot of mustard on my punch, but it didn't take much, because I slammed my brass-encased fist up into the junction between his legs, and I felt something soft get a lot softer when I hit it.

Dumbass screamed this horrific high-pitched sound that reminded me of the lambs in that Hannibal Lector movie. He let go of my ankle and clapped both huge hands to his junk, then dropped straight down to his knees.

Right on top of my face. I went from having a demon beating the hell out of me, to having a demon's taint writhing on my chin, and I seriously wasn't sure which was worse. I managed to heave the screeching demon off me and stagger to my feet, swearing silently that I was going to boil my face before I went to bed.

"You give up, fuckwit?" I gasped.

Dumbass looked up at me, then a corner of his mouth twitched up and he held up his right hand. With a grin spreading across his blood-covered face, he extended his middle finger to me, then rocked forward onto his toes and sprang to his feet. "You think that's the first time I've been hit in the balls, human? In the Pits, they used to slam our dicks with spiked hammers every morning just to see who would cry."

"That...that's... Shit, dude, I'm sorry."

A puzzled look crossed his face, and he cocked his head to the side, like a confused puppy. "Huh?"

"I said I'm sorry. I didn't know anything about what you went through growing up. That's awful, man. No wonder you can't keep your hands to yourself. You never had any positive male role models growing up, so you never learned how to treat women. Or anyone, for that matter. I bet you've never even had a real friend, have you?" The sadness in my eyes radiated through the room as I channeled every tiny bit of empathy I could dig up for the behemoth in front of me.

"Friend?"

"Yeah," I said, smiling a little. "You know, somebody you can just hang out with. Have a beer with, go to a game with, that kind of thing."

I saw a glimmer of hope spark in the demon's eyes. "Y-you want to be my...friend? You want to...hang?"

"Fuck no, asshole. I don't hang out with demons." His guard and his hands were both down, so I threw every single thing I had into a huge right hook and slammed my brass-wrapped fist into the side of his jaw. I heard the bone *crack* like a rifle shot and watched as Dumbass spun in a full circle before sitting straight down on his ass right in front of me. His eyes spun in lazy circles for a second before they focused on me. I leaned down and grabbed him by the throat. "In case you missed the memo, I'm Goddamn Eddie Nolen, and I'm the new bouncer. Now keep your goddamn hands off the wait staff, don't start shit with the other patrons, and don't be a dick to the bartender. That way we don't ever have to have this conversation again."

Then I took a step back and kicked Dumbass in the side of the head as hard as I could. He was unconscious before he hit the floor. I straightened up and looked around the room. "Everybody hear that shit?"

Nobody said anything.

"I asked you motherfuckers if you heard my name!"

A few mumbled affirmatives and a bunch of nodding.

"Good. Now you just saw what I can do in here, without my weapons, and without my magic. So if any of the rest of you want to step up like Dumbass here and learn exactly why Zeek hired me to keep the peace in this shithole, now's your fucking chance." I stood there looking around the crowd, but nobody looked like they felt particularly froggy.

"Good," I said, turning to the bar. "Henry, haul this dumb bag of shit out the back door and leave him in the alley to sleep it off. Take fifty bucks out of his pocket to cover his tab, but not a dollar more." I raised my voice a little to make sure it carried through the room. "I find out anybody from in here rolled him while he was out, they'll get

11

the same treatment. He got his ass kicked. He doesn't need to get robbed, too."

I slipped onto a barstool, keeping my face turned to the front so only Zeek could see the wince as I bent around my broken ribs. "Everclear. In a pint glass."

Zeek stared at me.

"It's medicinal," I said. "My fucking ribs are killing me."

"Okay." He poured me a pint of straight grain alcohol. It tasted like jet fuel, but after the first three gulps, the edge came off the razor blades in my midsection.

I looked up at Zeek. "Anybody looking like they want to start anything?"

"Nope. Everybody's on their best behavior."

"Good. I don't know if I could do that again tonight."

I didn't have to. Not that night. There were plenty of people who stepped up wanting a piece of the Reaper, but that came in time. All in all, it was a pretty good gig. Not good enough to make me forget about what I walked away from, but good enough that I could go to sleep without a liter of liquor or half a dozen Xanax.

Until it all went to shit. Like it always does.

3

The dork looked shit-scared when he walked into Zeek's, spinning around like his own shadow was going to take a bite out of his ass. He was a skinny little guy, mid-forties, with his tie loosened and sweat staining the armpits of the pale blue dress shirt he wore. His khakis and loafers looked as out of place in Zeek's as a priest's cassock, but after a cursory glance to evaluate the potential threat, everybody in the bar went back to quietly ignoring the rest of the room.

Dork made it to the bar unmolested, managing to step over the outstretched foot of the twenty-something imp who liked to start shit for no reason. I was glad the new guy made his dexterity check because I was just getting into a new chapter in the John Scalzi audiobook I had playing on my phone and didn't feel like breaking up a fight in the middle of a space battle.

Of course, all my hopes for an easy night went out the window when Dork walked right up to me. He stared at me with hope written across his face in letters almost as big as the giant "Fuck Me" written on his forehead. He motioned for me to take out my earbuds, and I motioned for him to suck my dick. His brow furrowed, he repeated his mime of pulling my earbuds out, and I repeated sticking my tongue into the side of my cheek while moving my fist back and forth toward my chin.

"I need to talk to you," he said, his nasally voice drowning out Wil Wheaton's dulcet narration. Figuring my audiobook was well and truly shitted at this point, I took my time pulling my phone out of my pocket, pressing pause, and taking my headphones out. I slipped the phone and earbuds into a pocket and glared down at the man.

"What the fuck do you want?"

His jaw trembled a little, which was almost the response I wanted. It wasn't as good as him turning around and leaving, but if he insisted on sticking around, being terrified of me was a good second option. A little bead of sweat appeared at his left temple and traced a line down the side of his face, making it all the way to his jaw before he spoke.

"I hear you're the guy around here who can fix things."

I raised an eyebrow. "Like a toaster? Call Home Depot, fuckwad." I turned to the bar. "Zeek? Hook me up with a Ciroc and cranberry, will ya?"

Dork leaned in closer to me than I really want anyone I don't know to be and whispered, "I need help."

I put a hand in the middle of his forehead and pushed him back, gently for the first offense. "You get that close to me again without an express invitation, and you're going to need medical attention. I don't know what you've heard, and I don't know who you've heard it from, but I'm a bouncer. People start shit, I finish it. People paw at the wait staff, I break their hands. People come in with fake IDs, I throw them into the Mississippi. That's it. I'm not a mercenary. I'm not a body-guard, and I'm sure as hell not the fucking Equalizer. Now go away before you really irritate me."

The dumping kids into the river bit was true. Zeek built a trap-door in the back wall of the bar that opened out onto the water, and I tossed out anyone who came in with a fake ID. It also made a handy escape route for more than one of our sketchier customers when the local constabulary came looking for them. Too bad for said sketchy customers that Memphis PD knew about the bolt hole and often stationed a boat cop right under it when they came by to serve a warrant.

Dork looked up at me and said, "You might not be a mercenary, but you are the Reaper. You're the deadliest thing in Tennessee next to cancer, and I need that kind of badass. I've got money, and I'm not afraid to spend it." He pulled a roll of cash out of his pocket and flashed it in my face. I saw the "100" in the corner of one bill but covered his hand with my own in a flash.

"Don't flash that much cash in here if you want to make it back to your car, jackass. This might be a Sanctuary, but the pier outside isn't. Now I don't know what the fuck you're talking about with this Reaper shit, but my name's Eddie, and I just came over here because shite got a little too hot back home with the Seelie court. It was bugger out of Manchester for a century or two, or end up with a cold iron Prince Albert, so I picked America. Now piss off before I get annoyed." I reached out to the bar and took a long sip of my vodka cranberry, looking at Dork over the rim of my glass the whole time. Holding onto the accent after all these years wasn't easy, but I still managed a passable one when I had to.

He didn't leave, but he did take a step back and put his cash away. He motioned over to Zeek. "Another one for my friend here, and a Macallan Eighteen for me. Neat."

"Only way to drink it," Zeek said. "Thirty bucks."

The little man's eyes bulged, and he coughed like something was caught in his throat. "Thirty dollars? Are you fucking high?"

"I assume you're buying both of Eddie's drinks, and Macallan isn't cheap, *friend*." The stress Zeek put on the word "friend" made it clear they weren't.

"Oh. Um, yeah, that's fine. Keep the change." He dropped two twenties on the bar and turned back to me. "Do two drinks buy me five minutes?"

"You keep buying drinks, you can sit on that stool all night for all I care," I said, pushing my earbuds back in and pulling my phone out of my pocket. "But I'm done listening to your ass." I knocked the last of my drink back and pushed off the wall where I'd been leaning. I looked over at Zeek and said, "I gotta piss. Try not to start World War Three before I get back."

"No promises," Zeek said without looking up from where he was drying glasses with his dirty bar rag. One day I was going to introduce him to the concept of bacteria, but this wasn't that day.

I walked into the bathroom and made a quick scan of the room. Empty. I didn't bother trying to take a piss, just leaned against the wall and waited. Sure enough, not twenty seconds after I got there, the door opened and Dork walked in, his head on a swivel. His eyes bugged out when he saw me standing there, arms folded and my best "I'm going to murder you" glare fixed to my face.

"Look, I didn't mean anything by saying who you are out there. I just wanted you to know that I'm legit, that I know stuff, and I'm not just some random asshole who wandered in off the street."

I unfolded my arms and held my hands out to my sides, channeling power into them to make tiny globes of purple fire appear. Dork didn't need to know that was pretty much the best I could do inside Zeek's, and only that because the bathrooms were less warded than the rest of the bar. It was still everything I could do to pull off a parlor trick, but this asshole didn't need to know that.

"Legit? You want legit, motherfucker? I'll give you legit. You turn around and get the fuck out of here before I legitimately burn you alive from the inside out. I'll start with the organs you don't need, so it won't kill you, just hurt like hell. Then I'll move on to the shit you can live without for an hour or two, like your liver and kidneys. By the time I run lightning through your bowels, you'll be in such agony that you won't just beg me to kill you, you'll beg me to kill you and everybody you've ever met. I don't know who the fuck you think I am, but I'm not. And even if I was, don't you think there's a good reason I'd be hiding out here pretending to be somebody else?"

He turned even more pale than before and took another step back, pressing his shoulders against the wall and activating the automatic paper towel dispenser. "I'm sorry! I just...I don't know what else to do. I've tried everything. Bargaining, money, drugs, he won't take anything except exactly what was in the contract, and I can't do it! I thought I could, you know? It didn't seem like such a big deal. But now? I just...can't. You gotta help me!" He was almost in tears now, and I stood there watching him have a meltdown in the men's room of a dive bar for almost a minute before I opened my mouth to speak.

And, of course, that's exactly when the door opened, and some werewolf walked in doing the pee-pee dance. I stepped back, let him take care of his business, and watched him walk to the door.

"Wash your hands, you nasty bastard," I snarled at him. He froze, then turned around to the sink.

"What are you now, Eddie, bathroom monitor?" The wolf said, his voice more snarl than words.

"I'm the guy who doesn't have a lycanthrope's disease resistance. And you're gross. So wash your hands."

He did as he was told, then reached over Dork's shoulder to grab a paper towel, then walked out the door. I turned my attention back to the trembling dork with a paper towel dangling over his shoulder. "I'm gonna regret this," I said, then took a deep breath. "Okay, asshole. Who's after you?"

"Oh, thank you! I can't believe you'll actually help me. I'll pay you whatever it costs, just—" His words cut off at my upraised hand.

"I never said I'd help you. I said I'd listen to you. So tell me a story. But first, tell me your name. I can't keep just thinking of you as 'Dork' if I'm supposed to give a shit about you."

"Um, okay. My name is Mark Robbins. I'm an actuary. That's someone who—"

"I know what an actuary is, Mark. Now get to the part where I give a shit about this actuary in particular."

"Well, a few years ago, my wife died. Cancer. It was a long illness, and we didn't have very much insurance."

"You see the irony there, right?"

He bristled at my comment. "There's no irony at all. She was a healthy woman under forty. Her risk was very low. There's no reason she should die for at least another fifteen years, according to the numbers."

"Yeah, except for the reason that the universe likes to laugh at the numbers," I said. "Sorry for your loss, by the way." I'm not a total dick. Some days.

"Thanks. Anyway, when she died, the medical bills, coupled with me missing work for a month to be with her at the end, bankrupted me. Our daughter was in her second year at UT Knoxville, and tuition was coming due. I was about to lose my house, my car, everything. I didn't have anywhere else to turn."

I didn't like where this was going. "This is about to get bad, isn't it?"

"Yeah. I got drunk at a bar trying to think of something to fix it, or at least forget about it for a little while. On my way, home a guy came up to me. I thought he was going to rob me. I mean, who just walks up to a guy at one in the morning on the sidewalk outside a bar?"

There was a pretty long list, most of whom preyed upon drunk and lonely people. I just stood there waiting for Robbins to tell me which one found him. "He wasn't a mugger, was he?"

He let out a laugh that hitched up like a sob before it got loose. "I would have been better off if he was. But no, he didn't rob me. He offered to get me out of all my money troubles. Said he'd been in the bar and overheard me giving the bartender my sob story. Told me he could get me plenty of money, and all it would cost was something I wasn't using anyway. Something I'd never even miss if it was gone."

Yep. This poor, stupid bastard. I knew what was coming but motioned for him to continue anyway.

"You know what I did, don't you?"

"Yeah, but I'm gonna make you say it anyway. Own your shit, Mark."

"I sold him my soul for a million dollars and a guarantee that my daughter would never get cancer."

"Now he's ready to cash in on the deal, and you aren't done using your soul, is that about it?"

"Yeah. I didn't read the contract all the way through before I signed it. I thought I'd get to live out my normal life, then end up in Hell when I died. But his only promise was that I'd have a million dollars, my daughter wouldn't die of cancer, and I'd have time to enjoy my money."

I've dealt with a lot of Fae, a lot of demons, and a lot of attorneys. They all use the same tactics. They never lie, but they only tell you part of the story and expect you to fill in the holes incorrectly based on your assumptions. That's what happened to this poor moron. "He never told you how much time you'd have to enjoy your money, did he?"

He looked embarrassed that I figured it out that quick, but he nodded. "Yeah. Last week I got a note on my doorstep that just said, 'Time's Up,' and now there are hellhounds on my trail. He's trying to kill me and drag my soul to Hell. You have to help me, Mr. Harker. You're my only hope."

Aw, fuck. He had to go and quote Star Wars *at me.*

4

I looked at the skinny little guy sweating in the men's room of Zeek's bar. He looked like exactly what he was—an insurance guy in over his head who was shit-scared of the consequences of his bad decision. A big part of me wanted to help him, but the bigger part of me, the part that wanted nothing to do with Hell or its minions ever again, won out.

"Sorry, pal. You're on your own."

His buggy eyes got even bigger, until I was worried they were going to roll out at me like a Tex Avery cartoon. "What? You're not going to help me?"

"Yeah, you're fucked. You got the wrong guy, and it sure sounds like you got yourself into a really shitty situation. If I were you, I'd look into emigrating to Vatican City. I hear that place is pretty holy."

"But...but..."

I didn't plan to listen to any more of his sob story. I couldn't help him, so I might as well go back to my drink. I stepped past him and put my hand on the door handle.

His grip on my shoulder was surprisingly strong, given his slight frame. "You can't just walk out of here and leave me to this shit, man!

You're fucking Quincy Harker. You're the one guy who can deal with this shit. You can't just walk away!"

I turned back to look down at him, scowling. "Fuck you, Mark. Fuck you for getting yourself into this mess. Fuck you for trusting your tables to tell you when to buy life insurance. Fuck you for getting drunk and not reading the contract, and fuck you sideways with a rusty chainsaw for coming into my workplace and accusing me of being some famous demon slayer. I'm not that guy. I'm just a bouncer at a blues joint with a little bit of magic. All I want out of life is to be left alone. I'm nobody's hero, least of all yours." With that little bit of truth hitting home a lot closer than I intended, I whirled around and stalked out of the bathroom. I made a beeline for the bar and downed my second vodka cranberry of the hour. It had no effect, of course, but I liked the burn as it went down.

A couple minutes later, Mark came out of the bathroom with water stains on the collar of his shirt. I guess he washed his face to help get his shit together before returning to the main room. He didn't look at me, just walked up to the opposite side of the bar and leaned over. I didn't hear what he asked Zeek, mostly because I didn't give a fuck, but after a few seconds, he looked around the room and walked over to the Welch Brothers, a trio of twentysomethings that were just about to move out of being hipsters and start contributing to society. But not quite yet. For now, they were still worthless layabouts and smartasses, drinking away whatever money they got from their day jobs and running a paranormal investigation business out of Zeek's on the side.

"Aw shit," I muttered when I saw him pull out a chair and sit down with the Grape Juice Boys, as I had termed the Welches in my head. I waved Zeek over. "Dude. Did you tell the dork to go talk to Bart and his two idiot brothers?"

"He was looking for someone to solve a metaphysical problem for him."

I raised an eyebrow at Zeek's choice of words.

"That's exactly how he phrased it. A 'metaphysical problem.' Bart's the only one with even a shred of talent that will do stupid shit for money, at least for the amount of money that idiot looks to have."

Zeek wasn't wrong. There were several discreet solution providers that frequented the bar, but most of them only took on projects they found interesting, morally compelling, or *exceptionally* profitable. I was trying very hard to stay out of the game. Neil the Templar only dove in when the cause was truly righteous, and welshing on a deal, even with a demon, was a long way from righteous. Sandra was a vampire with a lust for action as much as blood, but she was seriously old and not interested in much anymore. It would take more than hellhounds acting as collection agents to pique her interest. The Kaba twins had a reputation as being seriously capable, so much so that no one seemed to really even know what they were, but they also had a reputation for being pricey. Last I heard, their services started at seven digits and went up based on complexity.

That left the Welches, the bottom feeders of Zeek's clientele. Bart, Waylon, and Charlie Welch were the hosts of *Paranormal Blues*, a ghost-hunting show on YouTube that boasted somewhere in the high tens of subscribers on any given day. They wandered around Memphis alleys, cemeteries, and old houses with GoPros strapped to their heads and EMF detector apps on their iPhones, talking about feeling cold spots and jumping any time a cat came out from behind a dumpster. Bart had a little magical ability, just enough to know where not to go, and usually enough sense of self-preservation to keep him from getting in over his head.

Of course, he didn't usually have a shit-scared actuary waving a roll of Franklins under his nose, so of course, he pocketed the cash and shook Mark's hand after a whopping thirty seconds of conversation. I sighed a little at the stupidity of it all and offered up a little prayer to anyone who might be listening to look after the good-natured and stupid, if a little greedy, Welch brothers. They were going to need all the help they could get.

I felt a need to be moving, to at least smell clean air. Watching people dive right into a pile of shit always makes me twitchy. I pushed off the wall where I leaned and turned back to the bar. "Zeek, I'm taking off. It's pretty quiet tonight. Henry should be able to handle anything that comes up."

Zeek just nodded, and I grabbed my coat off the rack by the front door as I headed out to clear my head. I felt bad about leaving Mark to the protection of the Welches, or maybe I felt bad about getting the Welches mixed up in Mark's bullshit. Either way, I felt like an asshole and wanted to take a walk to see if I could get away from myself for a little while. Or at least find a mugger to beat the shit out of.

My guardian angel gave me a block before she stepped out of an alley and fell into step beside me. "You need to help him." That's Glory. No preamble, no niceties, no "thanks for getting me my wings back" or "sorry I haven't spoken to you in six months while you've been tearing your life apart." Just right to the point.

"Fuck that guy," I said. "He made a bad deal, but it was a deal. He's gonna have to live with it."

"Most of the time I'd agree with you. Except it's not just him who has to live with it. Or not live it, rather."

"Yeah, I feel bad for the kid, too. She lost her mom, now her dad's going to kick off. But look on the bright side—at least this time I bet there's insurance."

"Too bad she won't be around to spend it," Glory said.

I stopped cold on the sidewalk and turned to look at her for the first time. She was wearing her old familiar form, that of the tall blond hottie in torn jeans and an obscure band t-shirt. This time it was a vintage Nash Ramblers 1992 tour shirt under a leather biker jacket. She looked good. It felt good to see her again, especially since she just popped in out of nowhere. She had her powers back, and it seemed like she was willing and able to use them just like the old days. The days before she got her wings cut off saving my life, sending me on a two-year quest to collect all the missing Archangels to restore her divinity. Before I pissed off the King of Hell so bad I could never see anyone I loved again without putting them at incredible risk.

23

"What are you talking about, Glory?"

"He's not the only one the hounds are after, Q. They're coming for the girl, too."

"What? Why? How? Why the fuck wouldn't he tell me that?"

"I don't think he knows. Not for sure. I'm fairly certain he would have used that tidbit if he knew without a doubt she was in danger. He's an idiot, but even an idiot would recognize that the girl is a more compelling reason for someone to help him."

"How, though? He can't sign away her soul, that's not allowed. And she has to at least be given a chance to read the contract, whether she takes the opportunity or not."

"She's kinda the one that started the whole thing, not him."

I froze, then slowly turned to look at Glory, who had nothing on her face that screamed, "I'm joking."

"You're joking," I said, knowing full well she wasn't.

"Nope."

"Why would she do that? *How* would she do that?"

"She wanted her dad to feel better. She knew he was all torn up over losing her mother, and that they were about to lose the house, and she was afraid he was going to do something rash."

"So she did something even rasher?"

"More rash. But yeah. She went to the crossroads and performed the ritual, and then when a demon showed up to make a deal, she negotiated for someone to give her dad what he wanted. She made her end of the deal pretty solid, but she left it too open-ended on Dad's end. She just told the demon to give him what he wanted; she didn't specify that she was paying the tab."

"So the demon got Daddy Dumbass to sell his soul for something she'd already paid for. Fuck me, that's evil," I said.

"Demons, remember? Evil is kinda their whole thing. Anyway, I was at the Robbins's house earlier tonight, and there are half a dozen hellhounds circling the exterior just waiting for her to cross the threshold."

"They can't get in?"

"No. The threshold is intact, and there's a little of the mother's protection still on her."

"Like Harry Potter?" I asked.

"More like a dying wish and a low-level guardian," Glory replied. "That's how I knew about the girl's part in this. Her mother's last thoughts were asking God to take care of her baby girl."

"But he's still on walkabout," I said, not even trying to hide the bitterness in my voice. Finding out that the Big Boss of the universe was on permanent vacation since right after the Big Bang still rankled me.

"He is, but the Host isn't. The cherubim deal with things like prayers of the dying, and if they aren't too big of a deal, they usually just take care of it. As long as Elizabeth Robbins was an ordinary college kid, her guardian could handle anything that came at her. When the hounds showed up, they needed a little more muscle."

"And that muscle is you?"

"No, shithead. That muscle is you. You went into *Hell*, remember? That got the attention of every one of those winged assholes. You've been on every radar on the other side of the Pearly Gates since the second you came back to Earth."

"Well that's comforting. If I'd known I was on a cosmic episode of *Big Brother*, I'd have walked around naked more. Really given them a show."

"You walk around naked plenty. Not that I'm watching you naked," she said quickly, with a hint of a blush creeping up her cheeks. Maybe the time she spent trapped as a human did her some good.

"Whatever. Angels are Peeping Toms. Not exactly a news flash. So now I'm supposed to drop everything and haul ass across town to dive right into the metaphysical fire because there's a kid involved?"

"You going to say no? She's a kid, Harker. You know you're going to do it, so why not just quit fucking around and call a Lyft?"

I let out a long sigh, but she was right. Too many kids have died on my watch. Too many innocents of all types. If it was just her idiot father, I'd let him roast in the Pits for the rest of eternity. But not a kid. Never a kid. I pulled out my phone and summoned a ride.

"You back with me?" I asked the angel.

"Never left you," she replied. I gave her a skeptical look, and she said, "You might not have seen me, Harker, but I never left you. I never will, no matter how big a dumbass you are."

"Well, I guess that's some comfort. Break out the wings and the angel mojo, kiddo. We've got hellhounds to kill."

5

Yep, those are hellhounds," I said, looking at the exterior of the Robbins's home in my Sight. We stood under a big oak tree across the quiet street from Idiot Mark's nice little bungalow. Half a dozen pissed-off pooches circled the building, eyes glowing red and smoke billowing from their mouths. This was my first encounter with the demon dogs, but it didn't take a rocket scientist to figure out what they were.

The hounds were about the size of full-grown Dobermans, with all the fierce appearance and without the sunny disposition. I figured half a dozen of them would have no problem dragging a full-grown human wherever they wanted. I turned to Glory. "What can you tell me about these critters? I'm guessing rabies isn't so much a concern?"

"Not exactly. They will bite if you get close enough, but the real danger is in their breath. They can breathe fire for a pretty good distance. I'd guess at least twenty or thirty feet. And it's hellfire, not normal flame, so you can't just stop, drop, and roll. You get hit with a blast of that stuff and you're going to have a bad night."

"I'm already having a bad night," I said. "What else?"

"They're smart," she said. "Like demon-level smart. You're not going to be able to treat them like a pack of wild dogs. You've got to approach it like fighting humans."

"Humans that breathe fire, are invisible to the naked eye, and would be happy to drag me back to Hell to be their chew toy."

"Yeah, pretty much."

"How do they do that, anyway?"

"Do what?" Glory asked.

"Take people to Hell. Can they just open portals whenever they feel like it, or is it a specific thing?"

"I don't really understand the whole process. There's not a lot of information up top about demonic pets. But apparently, they can open a gate only for their designated prey, although they may be able to transport anyone that Hell's leadership has a particular interest in."

"So you're saying I need to watch out because I might be on the list of people they want to drag home for dinner?"

"Nailed it, Q. Now what's the plan?"

"I thought I'd make it up as I went," I said, stepping out from behind the tree and calling power. It felt good to draw on the native magic of the city. Memphis has a lot of mojo running around it, what with the blues and all the racial turmoil stirring up strong emotions. All that emotion soaks into the stones of a city after a while, and the bedrock of this chunk of Western Tennessee fairly oozed anger, injustice, heartache, triumph, and soul. I called to that power as I walked across the street, wrapping myself in a shield of pure energy.

Glory muttered a string of profanities and followed me, summoning a gleaming white sword out of thin air. I went the more direct route, throwing sizzling purple balls of energy at the nearest hounds. My first shot went wide, but the second caught a demon dog right behind the shoulder and turned it into reddish vapor on the wind.

"Holy shit, it blew up!" I said. "That was kinda cool."

"They're demons, Harker. They act just like demons when you kill them," Glory said, catching up to me and taking my left side as the remaining five hounds converged on us.

We stood back to back in the middle of the street, keeping our line of sight clear and ensuring that any stray blasts didn't hurt the walls, and therefore threshold, of the Robbins's house. I was there to save the girl, not make it easier for the dogs to get at her.

Glory booted one hound in the face while her sword cleaved another one's head in twain. I blasted one in the face with an energy bolt, but another one clamped its teeth into my leg before I could dodge. I turned my attention to it and felt something slam into my back. I pitched forward, my knee hyperextending as it bent in a way that knees aren't intended to bend. I wrenched my leg free of the dog's jaws and held up my fist to its face.

"*Infiernus!*" I shouted, unleashing a blast of fire right into the dog's slavering face. It just stood there grinning at me as I poured power into it.

"Hellhounds, remember?" Glory said, her sword taking another dog's head and turning it to red dust. "Fire kinda tickles."

"Shit," I muttered, letting the fire go and wrapping my fists in a nimbus of pure energy. I punched a dog in the face, then jammed my left fist right into a hound's mouth as it dove for my face. Its teeth locked on my hand, but the energy field protected me. It also kept me from doing anything useful with that hand, so I just stood up, dragging the hound with me, and proceeded to beat the remaining hellhound with its friend until they both disappeared in a cloud of red dust and the stench of brimstone.

I dropped my Sight and looked around in the mundane spectrum. The tree-lined street was dark, the only sign of life coming from the Robbins's house, which was lit up like a Christmas tree. I saw a curtain twitch in one of the front windows and hoped young Miss Robbins had some idea that a fight had happened, even if it was invisible to the mundane spectrum.

Glory walked over and looked at the large pile of demon dust in the street. "That was...unique."

I rubbed my sore knee and grinned at her. "I had to improvise."

"Not the stupidest thing I've ever seen you do."

"I can't imagine it even makes the Top Ten."

"Unfortunately, no. Now how do you plan to deal with the girl?

Because the demon that sent those hounds is going to know that it's dealing with someone with some power, and it's going to be pissed."

"Well, I guess the first thing to do is knock on the door and make introductions," I said, walking the rest of the way across the street and up the three steps onto the narrow stoop. I raised my hand to knock but froze when I heard an unmistakable sound from the other side of the door.

"Get the hell away from here," a trembling female voice called. "I've got a gun and I'm not afraid to use it."

"You've got a shotgun, by the sound of it," I said, raising my voice just enough to carry through the door, but hopefully not enough that the whole neighborhood overheard me. It didn't look like the kind of street where people routinely opened fire on door-to-door salesmen. Too many Priuses for that kind of scene.

"Yep," the voice replied. "The barrel is pressed right up against the door, and it'll turn you into Swiss cheese if I so much as twitch."

"Let's not do that, Elizabeth," I said. "It is Elizabeth, right? Elizabeth Robbins?"

"How do you know my name?"

"Your dad sent me. He hired me to…help you deal with your problem. The problem like the dogs that were sniffing around here a few minutes ago."

"You could see them?" The relief in her voice was palpable, even through the door.

I cocked an eyebrow back at Glory. She leaned forward and whispered, "The ones the hounds are set upon can see them. No one else can, unless they have some extraordinary abilities."

I turned back to the door. "Not only could I see them, I killed them. With a little help," I added after Glory cleared her throat behind me.

"They're gone? All eight of them?" I smiled a little at the hope in her voice, then paused for a second.

"Eight? There were only—" My words were cut off as an invisible form slammed into my shoulder, knocking me off the stoop and into the sparse grass of the front yard. I felt a couple of rocks dig into my back, but that wasn't the biggest concern, since I was buried under nearly a hundred pounds of slavering hellhound. I quickly slipped into my Second Sight, stared up into a steaming dog's mouth that looked like it was ready to turn me into a fricassee. I got my arms up to block the creature's breath just as it belched forth a stream of hell-fire at my face.

With my magically-reinforced coat protecting me, the hellfire made it hot, and seriously uncomfortable, but the leather didn't catch fire, and neither did my face. I rolled to my right, shaking free of the dog and punching it in the ribs as I scrambled to my feet. Once upright again, I spun a shield in my left hand and blasted the hound to dust, then turned around to look for Glory.

She had a lot less trouble with the other dog than I did, what with being able to fly and all. She was back out in the street, hovering a couple feet off the ground while the last beast snapped at her. After a few seconds of this, the dog planted its feet and aimed its head at her, readying a blast of flame that would burn off the wings we'd just spent two years getting back. Glory wasn't having *any* of that shit. She called up her sword, swooped down, and with an almost negligent slice of her arm, separated the hound's head from its shoulders and turned it into just another pile of crimson dust.

I limped back up the steps, my wrenched knee feeling no better from having been slammed into the turf at full speed, and sat down on the stoop. "Yeah, we killed all eight of them," I said to the door. "You wanna let us in, and maybe get me an ice pack?"

The door opened, and a tiny redhead appeared, the twelve-gauge shotgun looking almost comical against her tiny frame. "Come in, come in. I'm sorry, I should have let you in sooner."

"No, you shouldn't," Glory said, hauling me to my feet. I'm not a small man, but angels are strong, so she just yanked me to my feet without so much as a grunt of effort. "You didn't know who we were. Still don't, if we're being honest, but this time it's okay. We're the good guys. My name is Glory, and this is—"

"Eddie," I said, cutting Glory off in case she was about to let my real name slip. She was smart, but angels are not known for their duplicity. "Eddie Nolen. Your dad told me a little about your predicament, but let's head inside so you can give us the full scoop."

"Yeah, Eddie." A new voice came from the street. "Why don't we *all* go inside and talk about the case?"

My heart sank. I hadn't heard them come up because the damn Nissan Leaf they drive is so frigging quiet, despite the loud paint job. I turned around, and my worst fears were realized. Hanging out of the open window of his custom-painted electric car was Bart Welch, in his full Ghostbusters regalia. They even had the Leaf painted white with a bunch of geegaws welded onto it to look like an eco-friendly version of Ecto One from the movies.

I could see Charlie in the driver's seat and Waylon crunched up in the back seat amidst all their "paranormal detective gear," which is a fancy name for a bunch of electronic shit with blinking lights that made beeps at random intervals and had a big screen that changed colors whenever the temperature of the room changed, or the barometric pressure changed, or the wind blew, or there was a loud noise, or the holder pushed a button.

"Hey, aren't those the guys from that YouTube show? I think I saw them one night when I was looking for cat videos," Elizabeth said from the doorway.

"Yep," I said. "We're all saved. The Welches are here to protect us. It's all going to be fine now."

Spoiler alert. It totally wasn't going to be fine.

6

Why are you here, Eddie? I thought you told Mark you weren't interested in helping him." Bart paced the living room like a general, a pudgy little Napoleon of a man in khaki coveralls. Even if I was the type to be intimidated by humans, a fat guy who tops out at five-six walking around in a shit-brown jumpsuit carrying a prop backpack with a bunch of LEDs blinking on it wouldn't be the thing to put me in my place.

"I'm here because the girl actually needs help, Bart. And I was afraid if I didn't provide that help, that you'd end up getting a lot of people killed, starting with yourself." I sat on the Robbins's couch, with Glory perched on the arm of the sofa next to me. Elizabeth shared the couch with me, while her dad sat in what was obviously "his" chair across the oval rug from us. Charlie sat in the other arm chair in the room, with Waylon perched on the ottoman, his knees up almost parallel to his ears.

"Oh?" Bart stopped his pacing and turned to me, a haughty look on his face that immediately made me want to punch him. "And what exactly has your long career in breaking noses and tossing drunks taught you about dealing with threats from Beyond the Veil?" I swear I could actually hear the capitalization.

I didn't want to be anywhere in the same time zone as this conversation. I didn't want to be anywhere in the same time zone as Bart and his idiot brothers, if I'm being honest, but it seemed that ship had sailed. I sure wasn't going to tell Bart the truth. I opened my mouth to lie, but Elizabeth cut me off.

"He destroyed the hellhounds that were after me tonight. They both did. Just came right in with magic lightning bolts and swords and turned them into piles of evil doggy dust! You should have seen it, Dad. It was like something out a Harry Potter movie."

"You're totally a Slytherin," Glory muttered to me.

"Not arguing," I said under my breath. "Gryffindors are pansies."

"I don't know what you saw, Miss Robbins," Bart said. "But I assure you, Mr. Nolen no more threw magical bolts around in the street than I did. We're trained paranormal investigators, and we've been around Eddie for months now in our base of operations—"

I snorted, and Bart glared at me. "What?" I asked. "I'm not the one claiming my office is in a dive bar. And I actually *work* at the bar."

"Nonetheless," Bart continued. "We certainly would have had some hint from our equipment if Mr. Nolen was anything more than a moderately competent bouncer. And none of our instruments detected any hint of vestigial supernatural residue, so there certainly were not any hellhounds present near your house tonight."

"Oh, that's good to know," I said, standing. "Since you guys have everything so well in hand, I'll just go back to the bar. Elizabeth, if you need me, call Zeek's Bar. Mark, if you need me, fuck you. Bart...fuck you, too." I took one step and found myself looking at Waylon's chin. I stepped back and looked up at the tallest Welch brother.

"You want something, Waylon?" I asked, dropping my voice down into the "don't fuck with me, I'm the goddamn bouncer" register.

Waylon, never the sharpest knife in the drawer, said, "Apologize to my brother."

I didn't break eye contact with Waylon. "Bart, I'm sorry you're a fucking idiot."

Waylon's frown deepened. "That's not what I—"

His words cut off as I grabbed him by the throat and yanked him down to my eye level. "Waylon, you have two choices right now. You can get the fuck out of my way, or I can start breaking off parts of your body that you're really fond of. Now what's it going to be?" I let go of his neck, and he stepped aside, rubbing his throat.

I made it as far as the foyer before Elizabeth caught up to me. "Where are you going?"

"You heard Bart. There's no danger. Never was. So I'm leaving."

"Please stay." She lowered her voice. "These guys look like total morons. If we count on them to protect us, we won't see the sunrise."

She wasn't wrong. I looked over to Glory, who still sat on the arm of the couch. She leaned over and patted the cushion. "Okay," I said. "I'll stay, but I'm not responsible if I decide to punch Bart. A lot."

"You have my permission. And feel free to beat the shit out of the other brother. He keeps trying to look up my skirt."

"You're wearing jeans."

"That's the creepiest part of it."

If Bart was the brains of the Welch brothers, and Waylon was the brawn, then Charlie was indeed the creep factor. Out of the three of them, he was the one who did his job the best, because between the greasy, unwashed shoulder-length hair and the permanent leer on his face, Charlie made me want a shower after about five minutes in his presence. I shook my head a little and walked back into the den.

"You going to stick around, Eddie?" Bart asked. "Good. You sit there on the couch and let us show you how the pros do it. Come on guys, let's haul in the gear." He actually snapped his fingers, and his brothers got up and started moving toward the door.

I walked to the foyer and watched as the trio of try-hards trooped down the steps and over to the Leaf. Bart pulled out a key fob and pressed a button, raising the hatchback as they got to the car. Waylon dragged out two huge neon green plastic bins and hauled them back into the house. Then Charlie grabbed a huge duffel bag and slung it over his shoulder. Then he leaned back into the car and dragged out two smaller green plastic cases. While he hauled those into the house,

Bart grabbed one last military-grade plastic case with wheels on one end, closed up the car, and dragged the case up the steps and into the house.

I watched in awe at the sheer mass of shit the trio pulled from those boxes. It was a well-oiled machine. I just wasn't sure that the machine was meant to actually *do* anything. Every box was lined with foam, and every item in the case had its own slot specially carved out of the foam. In a matter of seconds, Charlie had one of the biggest cases open and a pair of flat-screen monitors set up on the Robbins's dining room table. He pulled a laptop out of a mil-spec case that I hadn't even noticed in the parade of tech toys and plugged the monitors into a USB hub that went into the laptop. Within a minute, he had a display stretched across all three screens.

Meanwhile, Bart had a medium-sized case open and was attaching suction cups to GoPro cameras and sticking them all over the windows in the house. He must have had a dozen little video cameras, and when he was done slapping them on every piece of glass he could find, he settled down to rig up a trio of chest harnesses with cameras.

Waylon was sitting cross-legged on the floor of the den with another pair of monitors and laptop perched on the narrow coffee table, and a power strip with a long extension cord running across the floor to the wall. He then started pulling various handheld sensors and meters out of a case and syncing them with the laptop. As each device came online, a new display popped up on the monitors, each with a different label under the image, like "IR," "EMF," "EVP," and "NV."

They fiddled with their equipment and plugged in and tested gear for a solid half an hour before Bart looked around the first floor and gave it a satisfied nod. "Okay. That all looks good. Waylon, you monitor the readouts while Charlie and I begin the investigation. We'll start outside where Miss Robbins thinks she saw a supernatural phenomenon." He turned to Elizabeth and Mark, who vacillated between looking impressed at the stunning amount of technical shit the trio of brothers had dragged into his home, and dubious that they had any idea what the fuck was going on. "You three stay here. We'll take Eddie along, and he can show us where he thought he encountered the...what was it you called them?"

"Hellhounds," Elizabeth said without even a hint of a smile.

"Right," Bart said, the condescension dripping from his tongue. "We'll check out the spots where Eddie thinks he saw these ethereal canines and try to determine what really happened."

I didn't say anything, just made a "don't waste your time" gesture to Elizabeth. Bart was really moving into the "too stupid to live" category, so I just hoped that he didn't totally live up to that potential before the night was through.

Bart started for the front door, Charlie so close behind him I thought their belts were looped together. I followed, shaking my head a little, and Glory fell in step behind me.

We got to the door, and Bart turned around. "I'm sorry, miss, you should really stay inside. Even though I'm sure Eddie just thought he saw something, on the off chance that there is something out there, I'd hate for you to get hurt."

It took me a second to realize that Elizabeth hadn't come along, and that Bart was talking to *Glory* like she was a helpless woman. *Wow,* I thought. *He's either braver than I thought, or stupider.* I kept my mouth shut, though, just looking from Bart to the angel in the foyer and back.

Glory didn't even slow down, just opened the door and walked out into the street. "Come on, dipshits. Let's get this farce over with so we can get back to the saving of the mostly innocent humans."

Apparently all that time spent with me as a human left Glory seriously deficient in the fucks department, because she wasn't sparing any for the Welches. While Bart and Charlie stood looking after her with their mouths hanging open, I walked outside and joined her on the sidewalk.

"Anything around?" I asked. I didn't want to drop into my Sight, because it makes it harder to focus on the mundane world, and if anything came near us, I was in at least as much danger from the Grape Juice Boys as I was from a hellhound.

"Coast seems clear," Glory said. "But there's enough ambient mojo coming off those piles of demon dust that anyone or anything with even the slightest ability to pick up on magic should go nuts."

"Okay, Eddie, where were these hellhounds?" Bart asked, holding something in front of him that looked suspiciously like an old iPod with a handle stuck to it and an antenna jammed into the headphone port.

"Well, you're standing in what's left of one of them," I said, pointing to the dust under his left foot. "And there were two here in the street, but your car blew away most of that residue. Then there were another couple beside the porch. What are you picking up on your scanner?" I asked.

"There's nothing here," Charlie said. "I've got a completely clear screen."

"What do you see when you point it at me?" I asked. I was honestly curious to see if their devices were real or just props.

"Just another normal guy, just like me and Bart."

"God forbid," I muttered.

"What about over there?" I waved a hand over at the shrubs that got coated with devil dog dust when Glory sliced one in half on its way to the door.

"That's an azalea. They're pretty, but not magical," Charlie said. I was impressed. I didn't think it was possible for me to want to punch him any more than I already did, but he managed.

"Let's see what I can find with the big daddy," Bart said, coming out the front door with a huge rifle-looking contraption with a viewfinder and a swiveling radar dish mounted on the end of the barrel. "This thing can detect EMF from half a mile away."

But was apparently incapable of finding demonic residue three feet from its holder. I looked at the thing again, then my brow knit as I saw a long orange drop cord running from the butt of the detect-rifle all the way back into the house. The front door stood wide open, and the cable passed right into the foyer, effectively breaching the one thing that gave us any sort of edge—the home's threshold magic.

I saw Glory start to move the same time I did, both of us realizing that Bart's idiot move had wrecked the integrity of the home's inherent magical defense and sprinting for the front door. I made it as far as the porch before the screaming started.

D ammit," I muttered as I burst into the den and surveyed the scene in front of me through my Sight, dropping a layer of hazy purple over the mundane world and displaying the hellhounds in all their demonic glory. Waylon Welch was hiding behind the flipped-over coffee table, trying to make his lanky frame compress behind the tiny surface. Elizabeth had her back to the darkened fireplace and a poker in one hand, warding off a hellhound, while her father stood on the sofa kicking at two others.

The hounds were playing. There was a full half a dozen of them, and they knew the humans couldn't stop them. Hell, Waylon couldn't even *see* them most of the time, just when they took a bite out of him or belched little jets of flame at his exposed appendages. Unless they were attacking, the hounds were invisible to all but their prey and those of us "blessed" with Second Sight.

"What is it?" Bart called from the foyer.

I tossed a glance over my shoulder and saw Glory holding back the other two Welch brothers. Good. It was going to take every bit of finesse I had to save the people already in this mess without the other two idiots blundering into the middle of it.

"*Animatus!*" I shouted, waving a hand at the scattered gear lying on the rug. Electronic gadgets flew into the air and whirled around the room, striking hounds and giving the Robbinses a few seconds to breathe. "Get out of there!" I shouted.

Elizabeth bolted for me, and I stepped aside to let her pass, lashing out with a kick to the jaw of the dog following her. I felt the burn all the way up to my thigh as the eldritch flame of the hellhound wrapped around my leg, but the pyro-pooch rolled back into the den, and Elizabeth put her back to the far wall where Glory could keep an eye on her.

That left four pissed off pups circling the couch while two kept Waylon pinned behind his makeshift barricade. I wasn't too worried about him. Unless he came down with a case of terminal bravery, the hounds would be content to leave him trapped behind the furniture and out of the fight. They were there for Mark and Elizabeth, and they would pursue their prey with a dogged determination, pun completely intended.

One hound peeled away from the couch and came at me, barring the door with a snarl and a fireball the size of a cantaloupe. It wasn't trying to kill me, not yet. It just wanted me to leave it alone and let it do its job. I could relate. I really wanted to be back at Zeek's thumping drunks on the head and telling lust demons to keep their hands to themselves. But no, here I was, back in the middle of another little hell on earth, cleaning up some other asshole's mess.

I postponed my pity party and squared my shoulders. "Okay, Lassie. You've got two choices. You can get out of this house, or I can send you back to Hell with your littermates. Your call."

The hound sat back on its haunches and cocked its head at me, then a deep, rumbling voice like two hunks of obsidian rubbing against each other came from its mouth. "We cannot abandon our prey. We hunt. We kill. We return prey to the Master. We cannot leave prey. You leave. You leave, we do not kill. You stay, we kill."

Well, that was new. My dealings with hellhounds were pretty limited to this point, but that was certainly the first time I'd ever heard anything about them *talking*. I hazarded a glance back to where Glory stood, but she looked as surprised as I was. Okay, demon dogs are smarter than I thought. Just another piece of shit news in a shit night.

"Fair enough," I said. "Okay, Rin Tin Tin, time to go home." I raised both hands and stepped over the threshold into the room. "*Glacio consto praestingo*," I chanted, calling up power and spinning it in a circle around me. I felt the air temperature drop dramatically, then even more as I repeated the chant for the third time. I said the incantation again, holding my arms high over my head and summoned even more energy into the room, then slammed my hands toward the floor and released the stored power in a wave of frost.

A wall of ice formed around the den, sealing off the doors and windows with a thick sheet of frozen water vapor. The air in the room plunged into the arctic, and a fine misty snow began to fall, covering everything in a haze of white. The hellhounds steamed in the cold, outlining their shapes against the ice and snow.

"Waylon!" I shouted. "Get your lanky ass up and beat the shit out of a dog!"

"With what? I ain't touching that thing!" the skinny ghostbuster called back, pointing at a steaming dog-shaped spot of air.

"Use some of those overpriced Tinker Toys you've got laying in the floor!" I yelled back. I dropped my Sight, since I could see the hounds easily against the cold environment and needed all my energy to hold the freeze spell and fight.

The cold slowed the dogs and made their fire breath far less effective, but it didn't do the humans in the room any favors, either. I saw Elizabeth's teeth chattering as she swatted at a hound with her poker, and I knew I had to end this quick.

"This is gonna suck," I grumbled, drawing the Glock from the back waistband of my jeans and taking aim at the nearest hound. The flat *crack* of the pistol was deafening in the small ice cave of a living room, and the cold made my hands far from steady, but at ten feet, even I can hit the broad side of a hellhound. The demon pooch yelped and whirled at me, then sprang for my face, its jaws open wider than really should have been possible. I put two more rounds into its face, and the only thing that hit me was a shower of crimson demon dust.

I sneezed, then recovered and shot two more devil dogs before my gun clicked empty. I had another magazine, but the other three hounds had turned their full attention on me by that point, so bullets weren't going to get me there.

The dogs fanned out to attack from as wide an arc as possible, and for the first time, I was happy to be having this fight in the living room of a three-story townhome because there was only so much room for them to outmaneuver me. I caught Elizabeth's eye and gave her a nod, then did the same with Waylon, who now stood tall behind the overturned coffee table with a laptop held in his hands like a club. I dropped my cold spell and called up pure energy, shrouding my arms in it, and the second my hands flashed purple, the dogs sprang in unison.

I knew they were coming, and I really hoped my backup caught the meaning in my eye contact and head nods. It meant a lot more "cover me" than "run while the bad guys are distracted," but without ever being in a fight with these folks, I had no idea how they would react. It wasn't the first time that night I wished I had Luke and Becks by my side instead of two of the demons' targets and an amateur paranormal investigator with more YouTube followers than sense.

Well, one out of two ain't bad, I guess. I dove to the side, throwing one energy-wrapped arm into the mouth of the center dog and ramming a powered fist through the chest of the other, turning it to dust. I hit the ground hard and rolled over onto my back, grappling with the hellhound to keep its jaws clamped around my magically encased forearm and not my unprotected throat. The third hound hit the wall behind me head-first, then dropped to the floor and pivoted to come after me.

That's when Elizabeth Robbins turned from prey to predator and buried the fireplace poker in the hound's skull. The iron rod pierced the demon's head, and eldritch power flowed up the shaft and turned the entire poker red-hot in an instant. Elizabeth screamed and dropped her weapon, but the dog was down and melting away into red motes of disembodied asshole.

Waylon either read my nod as something completely different, or

43

he was just a chicken shit, because as soon as I went down and the snow stopped inside the building, he went right out the nearest window with a huge crash and a shriek of pain as he landed in a holly bush. Serves the cowardly bastard right.

I lay on my back wrestling with the demon dog for a few seconds until Glory stepped into the room, her gleaming soul sword held down by her side, and ran the angelic blade through the hound's side. It exploded into dust, which mixed with the melting ice into a nice crimson slurry all over Mark Robbins's carpet. I didn't feel even the least bit sorry for ruining his floor.

"Thanks," I said, holding up a hand to Glory.

"Kinda the job, Q," she said, pulling me up without even the least bit of effort.

I released my hold on the power, letting the glow fade around my arms as the room slowly warmed. I looked around at the Welches and the Robbinses and said, "Why don't we all have a seat around the dining room table, and we can talk about what just happened?"

Bart and Charlie looked around for a second, seemingly in shock at everything they'd just seen, then Charlie went to the door. "Waylon! Get your ass in here!" he yelled.

"I'm in a sticker bush! Come help me!" came the plaintive cry from outside.

"No problem," I called back. "I'll just burn the bush away with you still inside it. How's that sound?"

"I'll be there in a second," Waylon replied.

Sure enough, half a minute later, the lankiest Welch brother appeared, bleeding from a dozen tiny cuts all over his face, arms, and neck.

"Damn, Waylon," I said. "You probably would have been better off to let the hellhounds get you. All they would have done is kill you. That shit looks like it *hurts*."

"Are they coming back?" Elizabeth asked. I looked at her, and for the first time realized how damn *young* she was. If this kid had seen her twentieth birthday, I'd eat my hat. She still had a little bit of that gangly adolescent in the way she stood, but her eyes were shadowed. This was some dark shit, and she knew it.

"Not a chance," Bart said, and suddenly the officious prick was right back to pontificating. "Supernatural beings cannot abide the touch of sunlight. We are less than an hour from dawn, the time when the Veil becomes strong again, and we are safe from those that move Beyond."

Elizabeth looked at me. "Mr. Nolen, will they be back?" She didn't even give Bart a glance, which I had to respect. This kid was no dummy.

"Yes," I said, then held up a finger as Bart drew in a breath. "But not tonight. Bart's an idiot, but he's right about one thing. Demons don't like the dawn. They aren't real fond of operating in daylight usually, but hounds don't give a shit. Since they're invisible except to their prey and those of us that can see in the supernatural spectrum, they can move around pretty much whenever and wherever they like. But sunrise is a holy time, a time of cleansing, and demons try to stay inside until it's over. So we've got a couple hours. But make no mistake, they will be back. Unless whoever you morons cut a deal with decides to send in the real muscle."

"What do we do then?" Mark asked.

"That's what we're going to figure out," I said. "You got any bacon? I find planning for war against the denizens of Hell goes better on a full stomach."

"No, but there's a diner just three blocks away," he said.

"Good. You and Glory go pick up some grub while Bart and his brothers put all their toys away, then by the time you get back, I'll have your window repaired, and we can have breakfast and figure out what to do about your demon. How does that sound?"

Everyone nodded except Bart, who folded his arms across his chest and scowled at me. "That sounds stupid," he said. "My brothers and I are professional paranormal investigators, and we will be taking the lead on this operation. You and your girlfriend can provide support and logistical assistance, but we will handle the planning and the protection details. Is that clear?"

I cocked my head to the side and looked Bart up and down. Then I took a deep breath and counted to ten. I was still pissed, so I tried it in Latin. That didn't help, so I cycled through every Earthly language I knew, plus Enochian. Nope. Still pissed.

I figured if I still wanted to break his face after that much counting, I was probably justified. So I walked over to Bart, picked him up by his belt with my left hand, and wreathed my right in crackling blue power. "No problem, Bart. You can be in charge. Just as soon as you can demonstrate even the slightest shred of understanding of exactly what is going on here, I'll consider listening to you. When I have any faith that you can go toe to toe with a demon and survive, I'll take your tactical advice. When you finally fucking realize that lives are at stake here, then I'll stop thinking you're three of the stupidest people I've ever met, and I might trust you to get me coffee! Until then, pack up your shit, shut your mouth, and try not to get in the way while the grownups lay out a plan to keep us all alive for another couple of days. Can you do that?"

I let a little tongue of power lick out from my fist to his nose, running just enough current into him to make his hair stand up, then I dropped him.

Bart immediately stepped forward, bumping his chest into mine like we were gorillas challenging for a mate or some such bullshit. "Who the hell do you think you are, Eddie Nolen? Do you—"

I slapped him. I slapped him once across the cheek, and it rang out like the crack of a twenty-two and dropped Bart to his knees. "I think I'm not your average bouncer, and my name isn't Eddie Nolen," I said. "I'm Quincy Fucking Harker, and I'm here to save the day. Again."

8

An hour later and the smell of bacon filled the room, the gizmos were loaded in the hipster-mobile, and I'd magicked up a replacement window. Not really. What I was able to do was to cast a spell to reassemble the pieces that were close enough to come when I called them, and then I thinned out the glass so that it stretched enough to make a solid pane again. There's a lot of benefits to working with a liquid medium, not the least of which being that if you know how to do it, glasswork is really stretchy. I know how to do it.

With the window repaired, I spent a few minutes reinforcing the threshold around the house, then set Charlie and Waylon to running a thin line of salt all the way around the house. It took every salt shaker in the place, plus a bag of rock salt the Robbinses kept in the tool shed out back for snowy sidewalks, but they made a continuous line. I placed a drop of my blood at the cardinal points of the circle and bound the barrier to myself, adding a little piece of my power to it, as well as making sure I'd notice if anything breached the perimeter.

We all sat down, and I dug into a plate full of eggs and greasy pork goodness, washing it down with about half a gallon of coffee. I used to be able to stay up all night fighting monsters and feel none the worse for wear, but after the first century, that shit starts to wear on a body. My stomach full and the tiniest bit of my energy reserves restored, I leaned back in my chair and looked around the table.

"Okay. Does anyone think that we faced anything other than hell-hounds last night?" I asked, nailing Bart in place with a stare.

Glory, Mark, and Elizabeth shook their heads, and after about half a second, so did Waylon. Charlie looked from me to his brother and back again, clearly torn about where he was supposed to align himself, but finally nodded.

Bart leaned forward and put his elbows on the table. "I'm willing to concede that there was some paranormal activity in the area last night. I'm even good to give you that it might have been abyssal in nature. But we don't know what it was. It didn't show up on our scans, and it was invisible to the naked eye. Without some grounding of our experiences in hard science, how are we supposed to explain any of this?"

I shook my head. "How's this for an explanation, Bart? IFM. It's. Fucking. Magic. There isn't any science behind it because this shit predates the scientific method. We're dealing with some cave paint-ing-level old shit here, so any technology past grinding up ochre and peeing in it to make pigment is probably too new to deal with it."

Complete bullshit, of course. I'd seen some shit when I was working with the Department of Homeland Security that could track demons, ghosts, and most other supernatural creatures on a cell phone. But Bart was so far from being cleared for that info it wasn't even funny.

The pudgy man just sat there, arms folded across his chest and bottom lip stuck out far enough that it could be a diving board, but he shut up. That's really all I was looking for—a little quiet out of him so I could get this show on the road.

"Okay, then. There was some bad shit here. We're going to call them hellhounds, mostly because that's what they are. Glory, you wanna fill in the Muggles on what you know about Satan's own Bloodhounds?"

She stood up, and I somehow refrained from slapping Creepy

CARL PERKINS' CADILLAC

Charlie, as he was coming to be known in my internal monologues, as he slowly ran his eyes up and down every inch of Glory's form. I understood the temptation. She was a good-looking woman, but even without knowing she was divinity personified and had the mojo to rip his head clean off his shoulders, the asshole could have at least *tried* to be a little subtle.

"Hellhounds are more like Retrievers than Bloodhounds, if we're going to use dog metaphors," Glory said. "They can track, but mainly they're set upon someone who is bound for Hell, but not willing to go easily when their time is up. Most often, these are spirits with a tie to a specific place, or some unfinished business, and the hound just pops in, clamps their teeth around the soul, and drags them off to their eternal torment."

"But I'm not dead," Elizabeth said.

"Yet," Glory added. Elizabeth paled, and my blunt angel continued. "In some cases, living people make deals with demonic entities, and the hounds are sent out as collection agents. In those cases, there's normally an escalating pattern of their appearances. One hound shows up at first, and if the person they're after is ready to go, a portal is opened to Hell and they go through. No muss, no fuss."

"I'm guessing that doesn't happen often?" I asked.

"About as often as a stripper passes up a twenty. Usually, the hound appears, then things escalate. This is where the old legend of the black dog comes from. People who at first saw one hound, knew their time was running out, but they didn't want to own up to selling their soul, so they made up a story about seeing a black dog that's come for them. Once the first dog shows up, more and more hounds appear until they overwhelm the person's ability to fight or run, and they're dragged to Hell."

"But how can we get dragged to Hell if we're still alive?" Mark asked.

"You can't," Glory said. It took a second, then the realization crept across his face.

"So you're saying that we battled some mysterious demonic bloodhounds that came to collect the Robbins's souls because they made some deal with the devil? That's got to be the most ridiculous thing I've ever heard!" Bart said, sputtering a little in his, I don't know, outrage? Disbelief? Whatever, he spit all over his chin, whatever caused it.

"Yep. That's exactly what we're saying." I leaned forward, elbows on the table. "Elizabeth, being noble but stupid, sold her soul to make her grieving father's life better. Mark here is a dumb fuck who took a demon up on his offer to make his life better, so he sold his soul too for a little bit of fun and cash. But he didn't check the dates on his contract, and instead of buying himself three years of happiness, he bought himself a few weeks. Now it's time to collect, and the dogs are at the gate, as it were."

"This is some biblical shit. I'm out." Waylon pushed his chair back from the table, stood up, and pulled out his phone. "I'm calling a Lyft. You guys want to stay and fight demon dogs with the magician, go for it. I just got into this ghost-hunting thing to pick up chicks, not deal with any inter-dimensional badasses. I'll tell Mom you guys will be home later. Try not to die." Then he walked to the door, picked up a backpack, and stepped out onto the porch. I watched him light a cigarette and sit down on the front steps as the door swung closed.

"What about you two?" I asked, looking at Bart and Charlie. "You in, or you out? If you're in, I'm going to expect you to do what I say, when I say it, no questions asked. It might be the only way we can keep you alive. If you're out, leave now so we can figure out our next move."

"As long as you're in, Legs, I'm in." Charlie leaned back in his chair and leered at Glory. Images of her summoning that big white sword and cutting him from neck to navel ran through my mind, and I wasn't all that upset by any of them.

"I'm in. I'm in, and I'll record all of this for our show so we can debunk you once and for all, Mr. Quincy Harker, Demon Hunter." Bart pressed a button on the camera strapped to his chest. The GoPro flashed a red light and beeped a couple times, then the red light stayed steady. Looked like I was on Candid Asshole.

"So what's the plan?" Mark asked. "You ran off the hounds, but something tells me that's not the end of our problems."

"Not even close," Glory said. "Now that the hounds have all been sent back to Hell, the demons in question will likely escalate the collections process to a supervisor."

"You make this sound like a bill collector," Elizabeth said.

"Who do you think developed the human collections process?" Glory asked. "That's one hundred percent a hell-spawned concept. Shit, Lucifer *invented* the middle manager. Now that the hounds are back in Hell, the next step is Retrieval Demons. They're bigger, stronger, and harder to kill, but they're not much smarter than the hounds."

"So they've still got more brains than Bart," I said. The ghostbuster gave me a one-finger salute to show how highly he regarded my opinion.

"Any*way*," Glory said, wrangling us back on track before I completely derailed the briefing. "These Retrieval Demons will likely show up tonight, and they usually hunt in five-demon teams. We should strive to be somewhere else when they get here."

"Can we shake them?" I asked.

"Not for long. The problem we're always going to come back to is the blood."

"What blood?" Bart asked, going a little pale. Apparently our brave ghost hunter didn't like dealing with corporeal injuries. That might be good to keep in mind in case I had to bloody his nose later.

"When Elizabeth and Mark signed their contracts, I'm guessing they had to provide a drop of blood, right?" Glory looked at the Robbinses, who both nodded. "That gives the demons with a binding contract on their souls a way to always find them. They can't hide, and they can only run for a day or two at best before the demons track them down. So even though we want to be somewhere else tonight, it's more about being somewhere we can defend than it is about hiding."

"We want someplace with limited access, defensible entry points, and maybe some inherent magical defenses," I said. My eyes went a little wide, and Glory caught my look.

"No."

"It might be the ideal place."

"He'll kill you."

"Better than him have tried."

"You two want to fill in the rest of the team?" Mark asked. "Where should we go?"

"Harker wants to go to Zeek's," Glory said. "I think it's a terrible idea."

"How bad could it be?" I asked. "There's only one way to get to the bar, down the pier. There's only one entrance, and it's easily defended. Magic doesn't work there, so we'll be on mostly even footing, and we'll even have a little backup if they come at us during business hours. It's the perfect place for a fight!"

"It's a terrible place for a fight," Glory shot back. "There are likely going to be civilians there. Magic doesn't work, so your biggest element of surprise is blown. And yes, there will be some creatures there that might lend a hand, or be bought to lend a hand, but there are at least that many more that will want to *help* the demons, or just want to watch the world burn."

"But you're forgetting our secret weapon," I said.

"What's that?"

"Zeek. Anybody violates the rules of Sanctuary in his joint, he's going to go medieval on their ass."

"Harker, we don't even know what Zeek *is*, much less what he can do in a fight against demons. This is a terrible idea."

"And we're *still* not on the Top Ten list of my worst ideas. Come on, we'll make the demons pick a fight with us in the middle of a monster Sanctuary where we have home-field advantage. How bad could it go?"

There I go, tempting fate again. Of course, the answer is very, very bad indeed.

9

W hat the literal fuck are you talking about, Eddie?" Zeek stood behind the bar, arms folded, with a look on his face hard enough to crack a pane of glass.

"We need a defensible place to throw a big fight, and the more we can take magic out of the equation, the better we are. You have the best place for that." I was standing in front of the bar, my own arms spread wide in supplication. Glory, the Robbinses, and the two braver of the Welch brothers were arrayed behind me. Henry was behind the bar with Zeek, looking back and forth between us like we were the best action movie he'd ever seen. Or maybe cartoon.

Bart and Charlie had a pair of cameras apiece strapped to them, one to their chest and one mounted on the modified bike helmets they wore. The plastic helmets had little straps that came down over their ears and buckled under their chins, and Bart had slapped stickers all over them with their show's logo and website prominently displayed. They also had dug some scraps of athletic gear out of the back of their Prius and strapped it on as body armor, so they looked like the world's fattest extreme sports videographers.

"Can you not read? Any of the languages on that sign?" He pointed to the sign over the bar, which read, "Sanctuary - Start No Quarrel

Within These Walls, Under Penalty of Death." It started off in English, then went down the long sign in Latin, German, Mandarin, Japanese, Hindi, Ge'ez, Enochian, Summer and Winter Fae, and about four other languages I *couldn't* read.

"Yeah, I can read. About two-thirds of the sign, actually. But that doesn't mean this still isn't the best place for me to lure a demonic retrieval team into a bottleneck so I can kill them."

"Retrieval team?" Zeek's eyebrows climbed so high it almost looked like he had hair again. "Just one team?"

"Maybe two," Glory chimed in.

I gave her a sharp look, and she shrugged her shoulders. "You couldn't lie? Just a little?"

"Harker. I don't lie. It kinda comes with the outfit." When she said "outfit," Glory spread her wings. And when Glory spread her wings, it made an impression. Since she got her groove back, as it were, her wings were bigger and more majestic than ever, stretching over eight feet from wingtip to wingtip, and so white they almost glowed. I'm not going to say the Hallelujah chorus rang out whenever she cut loose, but I will say that I could see where Handel drew his inspiration.

"Holy. Shit." Zeek took an unconscious step back from the bar and bumped into a shelf with his ass. Bottles rattled behind him, and he held out a hand to his left to catch a tumbling bottle of Wild Turkey without ever taking his gaze off Glory. "I've...um...welcome to my establishment. Eat, drink, and rest knowing that you are under my protection as long as you remain within these walls."

A knowing look crossed Glory's face, and she looked at Zeek. "Thank you for your offer of hospitality. It is accepted, with gratitude." She gave him a slow nod, which he returned, then she looked at me.

"Okay, now that's settled, where are we setting up the fight, and where are we hiding the Robbins family until it's over?" she asked.

"Wait a minute," I said. "What's settled? What did I miss?" I felt a lot like the kid who knew the grownups were saying something important but didn't understand anything being said around him.

54

"Zeek has agreed to lend us his aid, and I have agreed not to divulge his identity." I looked at the angel and the barman, and they nodded.

"His identity? You know what Zeek is?" Bart asked.

"Of course," Glory replied. "He told us in his offer of hospitality. By accepting, I agreed not to divulge anything about him that he didn't want made public. He has offered us the protection of his hearth, and I have offered my protection in return. Although perhaps discretion would be the better word."

I knew there was something oddly formal about his offer, something that should be familiar, but I wasn't getting it. I filed it under "Things to Work on If We Don't Die" and started making preparations for a fight. "Okay, here's the plan. Humans, go hide in my room. Bart, Charlie, this means you, too."

"But what about our footage?" Bart asked, pointing to his chest cam.

"You can have fifteen minutes to mount cameras around the room, but after that, you have to guard the door into my place in case something gets past us."

"You're not coming with us?" Elizabeth asked.

"I'm staying out here to fight. There's no back way into my room, so the only way anything gets to you is by going through me. And I promise you, tougher demons than these have tried."

"He's not exaggerating, for once," Glory said. "Harker can hold his own against some supernatural heavyweights. I've seen it."

"So we're doing the real name thing now?" Zeek asked.

"Yeah," I said. "If you need to yell at me in the middle of a fight, let's not take a chance on me not remembering to answer to 'Eddie.'"

"How long do you think we have before they get here?" Zeek asked. His words were answered by the sound of heavy footsteps on the boards outside. Sounded like a lot more than five demons, but maybe they had extra legs or something. That's what I tried to convince myself, anyway. Maybe setting up this fight in a place where I couldn't throw magic around wasn't my best move.

"Sounds like about thirty seconds," I said.

"Harker," Zeek called.

I turned, and he tossed a necklace at me. "What's this?" I asked.

"Put it on. It'll counteract the wards and allow you to cast spells."

I looked at the necklace, just a simple silver disk with four stones in a ring around a larger center stone. Lapis, jade, garnet, and milky quartz surrounded a sparkling black opal with every color imaginable glittering in its depths. There were runes etched around the center stone, but they were in no language I had ever seen. I put the silver chain around my neck and tucked the medallion inside my shirt. The second it touched my skin, I felt my connection to the earth restored. I could spin my magic again, as strong as if there were no wards at all.

I looked up at Zeek, my eyes wide, and they grew wider still when I looked at him. He didn't look anything like the slim bald man of around forty that he had been a few seconds before. Now he was a towering behemoth with dusky skin, a topknot of jet-black hair cascading down his back, and tree trunk arms ringed with golden bracelets and bands. His eyes glowed a deep green the color of richest emeralds, and it seemed like a haze of smoke emanated from all around him.

"Holy shit," I said. "Okay, then." I've been a lot of places and seen a lot of things, but Zeek was the first djinn I ever met, at least to my knowledge. Creatures of legendary power, djinn were renowned not just for their spellcraft, but also for their combat expertise and for their impatience with foolish humans. I briefly wondered how he hadn't murdered Bart, then realized that I was just as stupid as the Welch brothers most nights, so I should count my blessings, too.

I looked him in those glowing green eyes and nodded, trying to convey that his secret was safe with me. He nodded back, which I took to mean "I understand," but could have just as easily meant "if it isn't, I'll feed you your spleen." And he could do it. Djinn are among the rarest of supernatural beings, but they swing in a whole different weight class than most of the stuff I fight. My beer-slinging boss had mojo to rival an Archduke of Hell.

"We've got company, gang. Let's get to battle stations!" I called, motioning for Bart and the rest of the humans to get into my room. I looked to my left, where Glory stood, wings out and mystical blade glowing in the dim light of the bar. A glance to my right showed me Henry had half-shifted, replacing the skinny barback whose beard grew in patchy with a seven-foot tallest with claws that would carve through flesh like warm butter. I didn't see Zeek in my peripheral vision, but now that my magic was unfettered by the wards around the bar, I could *feel* him.

I called power around my fists and stood in the middle of the room facing the door. I didn't have to wait long, because a few seconds after I heard the door close to my room, the one leading out blew apart into a cloud of splinters. Five demons walked in, every one doing their best Hellboy impersonation. They were tall, at least as tall as Henry, and they all wore long coats with the tips of their tails just poking out from beneath them. Their skin was crimson, and short horns protruded from their foreheads. Other than that, and the orange eyes, they looked pretty much human. Really big human, but human.

"Give us our due, mortal," the one in front said, his words slurred as his tongue tried to wrap around his fangs. Demon fangs aren't retractable like Luke's, so they're always in the way. That and the amount of smoke that scars their throats in the Pits makes it almost impossible to understand what demons are saying when they're in their true form. It's okay because usually they aren't saying anything worth listening to. Just threatening to show you your own heart as it stops beating while you die, that sort of thing.

"Give the devil his due?" I asked, smiling. "That's too old to even get partial credit for creativity. Why don't you boys just piss off back to old Lucifer and tell him his old buddy Quincy Harker says go fuck himself?"

I decided valor was the better part of valor, and charged right in, fireballs flying from my fingers. Demons aren't really afraid of fire, but any creature that stores its brains above the neck tends to duck when something comes at its head, and that's what I was counting on. The lead demon ducked, and I put on a burst of speed to slam a knee into its face. The big red asshole dropped like a big red rock, and I called lightning on the two behind him.

Lightning does bother demons, and these two certainly didn't enjoy me playing Thor all over their asses. They twitched, they danced, they dropped to their knees screaming. I poured on the power, ducking and weaving as the last pair of demons both swung at my head with a pair of giant hammers they pulled from under their coats.

They never got a second swing, though, because Glory lopped off all four of their hands at the wrists, then spun through the mass of assembled demons like a Tasmanian Devil in the cartoons, leaving a mass of disassembled demon parts in her wake.

I let go of my stream of electricity and looked around as the *thump* of demon heads hitting the floor sounded again and again through the bar. "Well, shit, Glory," I said. "If they were going to be that easy to take out, what was I so worried about?"

"You were probably worried about the reinforcements their master almost certainly sent along, Reaper," came a voice from the doorway. It was a sultry female voice, a horrifying combo of the sound of fingernails on a chalkboard and a lover's purr, and when I looked to the door, the woman standing there looked like either a lethal amount of trouble, or a featured entertainer at a fetish party, or both.

She pulled a pair of short swords from her back, and as she took her first step toward me, purple-black flame sprang to life, wreathing each sword in a glittering sheen that had death written all over it. She was a Bathory, one of a cadre of female demons dedicated to sex, death, and the intersection of the two. They were among Hell's most lethal assassins, and their reputation for completing an assignment was without peer. They took the name after a human woman condemned in the fifteenth century who rose through the ranks of Hell faster than anyone in history, in large part because of her incredible ferocity in the Pits.

"Well," I said, calling up a blade of power of my own. "I was wondering when the varsity was going to get here. Let's dance."

58

About half a second after the fight started, I realized exactly how bad an idea jumping into single combat with a Bathory was. That's how long it took for the indigo-skinned demoness to cross the twenty feet of floor between us and bring her swords around in a whirl of purple flame and death. I caught one on my soulblade, and the other on a shield of power I coalesced around my left forearm.

Both of these sucked. The force of the impact nearly tore my sword from my right hand, and when I caught the other blade on my left, my vision whited out for an instant from the pain. I managed to rotate my right wrist and make a futile slash at her left leg, but she batted it away with a sneer.

I let the shield go from my left arm and threw raw energy into her face instead. That at least made her back up a step. Of course, then all she did was shake her head and bare her fangs at me before leaping forward again, burying her shoulder in my chest and sending me sprawling. Her swords clattered across the floor and we fell, and I let my sword blink out of existence as I tried to keep her dagger-like claws from my throat.

"I will bathe in your blood, wizard," she hissed at me, and I jerked my head to the side to prevent her barbed tail from taking out my right eye. The spike *thunked* into the wood floor and buried itself half an inch into the wood. The Bathory's eyes widened as she tried to pull herself free, but her tail was stuck fast.

"Oops," I said, grinning. Then I cut loose with another blast of raw energy, this one into her jaw from both hands. She flew backward off me, got to the end of her tail, and slammed back into the floor with a resounding *THUD*. I rolled to the left and scrambled to my feet as the demon assassin stood on shaky legs. But she stood, and as she reached down to scoop up one of those flaming swords, I realized that even knocked loopy and down a blade, she was still one of the deadliest things in Tennessee.

But not *the* deadliest. That honor may well have belonged to the ebon-skinned man who stepped up to my side with a blood-red glow in his eyes and a gleaming golden scimitar held in both hands. "Go find whoever is sending them, Quincy. I will handle the Bathory."

"You will, sandworm?" the demoness hissed, her words a seductive sibilance that put a stutter in my step.

"I will," Zeek replied. "Go, Harker. The Bathory is not a demon you can rule from afar. Whoever summoned her must be nearby." Then he pulled back his lips in a snarl and charged. When the Bathory and the djinn clashed, the impact shook the very pilings that held up Zeek's Bar. I looked at Glory, who was busy dispatching the last remnants of demonic essence from the Retrievers. She gave a nod, and I pushed through the door and up the stairs.

I came through the upper door and looked around. Zeek's was the only building on the pier, with a good hundred feet between it and the parking lot. There were no visible threats, but that didn't necessarily mean anything. I called up power and murmured *"Reperio,"* breathing a little of my essence into the word and spinning a trickle of magic into a sphere of yellow light. The globe hovered in front of me until I wiped off a drop of Retriever blood from my jeans and stuck my finger in the aura.

The will-o'-the-wisp vibrated in the air for a second, then floated away from me, heading along the pier toward the parking lot at an easy walk. I activate my Sight, scanning my surroundings in the supernatural spectrum. There was a ton of trace magic all over the place, which was to be expected since Zeek ran the most popular joint in town with the magic-wielding set. But nothing aside from that. No active spells at all that I could see, except for my own.

I followed the bouncing ball along the pier to the parking lot until it came to a hover right outside of a dark blue van that looked like exactly the kind of vehicle middle school parents warned their kids to stay away from. Hell, I didn't really want to know anything about what went on in that van, and I was a lot older than a middle schooler.

The van glowed like white phosphorous in my Sight, so it had to be the base for whoever summoned up the Bathory and her hunting dogs. I scanned the area for traps but saw nothing in the magical spectrum. I dropped my Sight, just to make sure I wasn't about to fall for the old "tin cans on a string" trap, and seeing nothing, I walked up to the side door of the van, grabbed the handle, and gave it a yank.

The door slid open with the rumble of metal on metal, and I caught just a glimpse of someone sitting on the floor cross-legged before a huge force slammed into my chest, kicking me back into the side of a Camry parked a few feet away. I heard glass shatter behind me and something crack inside me, then I was rolling to get away from a set of razor-sharp claws and snapping fangs. Another friggin' hellhound? What was this, magical *Cujo*? I was getting really tired of playing demon dogcatcher.

I wedged my left forearm into the slavering mouth of the hound, feeling the fiery breath scorch my arm through my jacket and thanking whatever tiny bit of common sense inspired me to weave some fire protection into the garment. Oh yeah, that wasn't common sense. That was Becks after the last time I got set on fire.

I shoved aside my regrets about Flynn and vented my frustration on the demon dog trying to rip my arm off. It latched onto my leather-wrapped arm and worried it back and forth like I was a chew toy. There are very few things that can make a grown man feel small more than being shaken to and fro by a magical Rottweiler. I tried to call power, but the beast was shaking me too much to concentrate.

"Fuck it," I muttered, and balled up a fist. I reared back and punched the dog right on the hinge of its jaw. My leverage sucked, and the angle was crap, but I managed to hit it hard enough and in the right spot to pop the mutt's jaw out of the socket, and my arm sprang free. I still couldn't move much, on account of the hundred-plus pounds of hellhound on my chest, but at least I had both hands and the dog couldn't really bite for a second.

Unfortunately, teeth and claws weren't the only weapons the dog had. Eyes blazing red, it decided to remind me that it wasn't an animal at all, not even a real asshole dog soul that got sent to Hell. Nope, hellhounds are just low-level demons forced into the shape of dogs and used to track down errant souls. That meant that not only was it made from infernal magic, it also had access to some limited demonic abilities. Like summoning hellfire. Which it proceeded to do. Right in my face.

The hound cut loose a Smaug-worthy stream of hellfire, and the only thing that kept me from getting turned into a fritter was the wards on my coat. Even so, I felt the heat through the leather and smelled a little bit of burning hair.

The dog let up to take in another breath, and the instant I was no longer being flambéed, I moved, channeling all the rage and pain I felt and sending it straight into the demon dog's chest. The hound's body lifted off me, suspended six feet off the pavement and shrouded in purple energy for a couple of seconds, then the corporeal form of the infernal pooch gave way under the assault of energy, and the damned thing exploded, spreading red doggie dust over a ten-foot radius.

"Ow. Fuck." I let my head sag back to the asphalt for a second, taking just a moment to recover, and pat out any lingering flames on my scalp, before struggling to my feet and glaring over at the van, with its sliding door standing wide open. "I swear to God if you send another fucking hound after me, I'm going to feed it your genitals."

I wanted to leave myself an out in case the asshole in the van wasn't male. It was, though. Of course it was. It was pretty much exactly the kind of guy you would expect to have a conversion van with an airbrushed wolf howling at a full moon on the side of it. As I wobbled on my feet, I watched a fat, forty-something guy with long, greasy hair and a patch of what looked like gray pubes sprouting from his chin roll out of the side of the van and close the sliding door. Then he walked around to the driver's door, opened it, and got behind the wheel. I heard the engine turn over and rolled my eyes.

"You've got to be fucking kidding me," I muttered as I drew the little Ruger from its holster on my right ankle. I squeezed the trigger twice, and the passenger side front and rear tires deflated, giving the van a marked lean. The nebbishy little shit was undeterred, backing the van out of its parking space on flopping flats. I holstered the pistol, stood up, smoke ringing my head, and held up both hands.

"*Prohibere!*" With my shout, I sent a stream of force out to the van, and glowing blue chains sprouted from the ground, arcing over the roof of the fleeing cliché and slamming it to a halt. I stomped over to the driver's door and knocked on the window.

It rolled down in that jerky motion that all cars had before automatic windows, and I was face to many-chinned face with the guy that I assumed to be the source of all my night's problems. "H-h-hello? Can I help you?" His voice was high, querulous, like a nervous starling.

"I sure hope so," I said, giving him my best friendly neighbor voice. "I've heard a nasty rumor that a prick driving a van just like this has been summoning demons and sending them after some friends of mine. I was really hoping that you and I could have a little chat about that. If that's okay with you, of course." The solicitude of my voice was perhaps belied by the fact that my face was a smoking ruin of smoke-stained flesh and my hair was burned off to the skull. I was pretty sure there were second-degree burns all over my scalp, and I didn't know if I had both ears, but I still had both eyes, and they were trained on Captain Douchepants here, just hoping he'd give me an excuse to break his nose.

"Um...what happens if I say no?" Tears welled up in his eyes, and I think I smelled a little bit of pee. This was not a dude who was accustomed to having a smoking shell of a wizard leaning on his driver's side door.

"Then I haul you out of this window and pound you into paste against the side of the van, because I'll have to assume that anyone who doesn't want to have a little chat with me *must* be a bad guy. And I don't like bad guys." I put a little red glow in my eyes and a wicked smile on my face, and now I *definitely* smelled pee. "So why don't we go inside, and if my friends haven't destroyed your Bathory by now, you can send her back to Hell and we can have a little chat. How does that sound?"

"G-great?" he asked more than said, as if he wanted me to tell him what I wanted him to say. What I wanted him to say was how the hell a schmuck like him got enough juice to cut deals for souls in the first place, but that conversation was probably best handled somewhere other than a public parking lot.

"Good. Let's go." I opened the door and jerked the schmuck in question out of the van. I put a hand on the back of his neck and walked him down the pier to where a group of supernatural beings and adventurous humans were crowded around the locked door to Zeek's joint.

"We're gonna be closed tonight, guys. Emergency cleanup. We had a little infestation earlier, but we've got it under control," I said as I pushed through to the door and fished my keys out of my pocket.

"Infestation? Infestation of what?" asked a cute vampire chick who looked to be about twenty-five.

"Assholes," I said, sliding through the door and pulling it closed.

"Looks like they missed one," she muttered as I dragged my fat quarry down the stairs to see how Zeek and Glory were doing with the psychotic demon assassin. I was expecting a lot of things, but none of them were the sight that greeted me when I opened the door into the bar.

11

I don't mean to pick the most obvious metaphor, but what the hell is going on in here?" I asked as I looked around the bar. There were still chunks of Retriever scattered all over the floor, but where I expected to see carnage and a shit-ton of destroyed furniture, instead I saw a dark blue-skinned woman doing tequila shots with my guardian angel and my boss. Assuming, of course, that Zeek hadn't fired me after tonight.

"We had a contest before our battle to determine weapons. Beth lost. Zeek picked alcohol. Now we're a little drunky," my soused divine protector said.

"I didn't think you could get drunk," I said to Glory.

"Yeah, me neither. But I guess between spending two years as a human, and Zeek's wards cutting off most of my contact with the Host, I can get the teensiest bit of a buzz." She held her hand up, thumb and forefinger about a quarter inch apart, proving without a doubt that she had more than a bit of a buzz. As if I couldn't tell that by the fact that she leaned heavily on one elbow on the table, and her hair was a disheveled mess.

I looked from Zeek to the Bathory, to Glory, and back again. "So... we're not going to fight? Because I'm good with that. We can throw down if you've got your heart set on it, and let's be honest, you getting shithouse drunk is about the only way I'd stand a chance, but I don't mind if we never test that theory."

"Don't worry," the demoness said, one corner of her mouth twitching up just the tiniest bit. "There isn't enough booze in Tennessee to give you a fighting chance."

"Fair enough. But that's okay, because this idiot is here to cancel the job." I pulled the schmuck around in front of me and shoved him toward the table where the angel, the demon, and the djinn were having a drinking contest. "Tell her the hit's off," I growled.

"Um...you can go. You don't have to collect the souls for me. I won't be needing them anymore." The schmuck wasn't any braver now that I could see him in full light, and the view from behind wasn't great, since there was a solid four inches of ass crack peeking out above his sagging belt line to say hello.

The Bathory stood up and walked over to Schmuck, moving like a panther, all sinewy grace and lethal sexiness. She was incredibly hot when she wasn't trying to kill me. She sidled up to Schmuck, laid a finger across his chin, and locked eyes with the trembling mass of bipedal jelly. "Just because you don't want the souls doesn't mean I don't want to kill something."

She looked around the room, a thoughtful look on her face. "Who could I kill? Oh, I know!" A big grin split her features, and almost before I saw her reach over her shoulders, that pair of flaming swords appeared in her hands. "I'll kill you, you human slug!" She swung both blades at Schmuck's neck, but fortunately for him and any hope of me finding out what the hell was going on, I was prepared for something like that.

"*Ferrus!*" I shouted, flinging power at the back of the terrified human's neck. He froze in place as a cast of iron wrapped around his entire body, leaving just his face open. The demon's swords *clanged* off the metal-clad idiot, and she turned to me with a hiss.

"How dare you? You would interfere with me collecting my due? I was summoned, I must draw blood before I return to Hell." She was in front of me in a blink, both blades at my throat. "Or would you rather I take my payment from you?"

"Go for it," I said, looking her straight in the eye and trying hard not to blink.

She stepped back, surprise warping her face. "What?"

"You need to draw blood? Draw mine. One drop. I promise you, return to Hell with Quincy Harker's blood on your blade, and you'll be the baddest bitch in the Pits from the second you arrive." I leaned forward. "I don't know if you heard, but your boss kinda hates me."

A calculating look crossed her face. "Two drops. One for each blade."

"Fine," I said. "But no more than that." I held out my arms, palms down. She laid the edge of each blade across my forearms, not moving. I felt a tiny burn, then watched as a drop of blood welled up from each arm. The demoness rolled the blade back and forth, sliding it along my arm to coat the steel as much as one drop of blood can. Then she sheathed her blades, bowed her head to me, and vanished in a puff of brimstone.

"Nice exit," Zeek said.

"I'm betting you can do something similar," I replied.

"Oh, much better. But that was pretty good. For a demon. Now that you aren't going to destroy my bar, you want to tell the Welches they can bring our guests out of hiding? I need to open the doors and see if I still have customers, or if they all decided to drink somewhere else." Zeek waved a hand at the empty bottle and overturned shot glasses littering the table, and they were all whisked away in an instant.

"I wouldn't worry too much, Zeek. Most of your customers have been banned from everywhere else that serves alcohol. Now what are we going to do about him?" I pointed at the sleeping form of Henry, who was curled up on the floor like a comfy puppy.

"Leave him," Zeek said. "I just won't use that table tonight. Now you all go get tucked away in your room and try to keep it down. If I hear screams over the sound of the house band, I'm going to come back there and kick all your asses."

Glory gave him a sloppy salute, and I led Schmuck through the bar. I caught glimpses of Zeek throwing magic around while I went. With a flick of his hand, he straightened chairs, rebuilt broken tables, scrubbed demon guts off the ceiling, made chunks of Retriever vanish. You name it, Zeek cleaned it, all without touching any of the crap himself.

"Now I know why people dream of genies," I muttered.

"I heard that!" Zeek called. "And don't ever call me Jeannie!"

"Do you wiggle your nose when you make magic?" I asked as I reached the door to my room. I pulled the door open and slipped inside before whatever bolt of magic he flung at me landed.

Bart spun around and faced the door with his hands up in what I would have thought was a parody of a karate pose, if he hadn't had such a completely sincere look on his face. I swallowed the laughter that bubbled up inside me and said, "Good job, guys. The situation is averted, and we can resume our normal drinking activities. I need to interrogate Mr...." I turned to Schmuck. "What was your name again?"

"Jerome. Jerome Clarence Thomas Rietenback." He held out a hand, and I reflexively took it. Then instantly regretted my lapse into good manners. His handshake felt like I was holding a warm fish, all damp and wriggly.

"Did your parents name you after a Supreme Court Justice?" I asked. He looked to be in his mid to late twenties, which made the math work.

He beamed at me. "Yep! My parents said that naming me after a successful man would inspire me to be the same kind of success that Justice Thomas became."

Glory and I shared a look, but I said nothing. There wasn't enough time in even my life to unpack all the weird this dude's parents had saddled him with. I felt a little sorry for him, honestly. My folks just gave me demon-laced vampire DNA.

I turned to the Robbinses. "Is this the guy you sold your soul to? Either of you?"

They both looked confused, but Elizabeth spoke first. "No. I've never seen this guy before in my life, unless it was on www.creep-ers.com."

"Hey!" Jerome protested. "I'm not a creeper!"

"Dude, you were raising demons from a conversion van in a parking lot, literally down by the river. That ranks pretty high on the Creeper Meter," I said.

"But that's because I needed the souls," he said, his jowls wobbling a little as he tried to hold himself together.

"For what?" Glory asked.

"To store in the ring. The guy at the magic shop told me if I locked five souls into the ring, it would grant me three wishes. But it wouldn't do anything before I got all five." He held up his fish-white left arm and showed me a gaudy ring on his index finger. It was huge, like a championship ring on steroids, with a dark red gem in the middle, Enochian script around the stone, and glyphs from several ancient languages scribed into the sides.

I opened my Sight, and the thing was magical, all right. It glowed in the supernatural spectrum with a golden hue streaked through with oily black, like the gold was being corrupted by whatever it was touching. There wasn't another hint of magic on the guy; he just had a ring with some significant horsepower to it.

"What magic shop?" I asked. "Did somebody *sell* you that thing?" Glory and I exchanged a look. If somebody was selling trinkets with this kind of power to the mundane citizenry, we had either a psychopath with a ton of magical talent on our hands, or somebody who just wanted to watch the world burn. I wouldn't want that ring around *me*, much less somebody with no training or shielding.

"Yeah," Jerome/Schmuck said. "It looked kinda like one of those pop-up costume store places you see at Halloween, just a storefront that was there for a couple of days and abandoned the next week. I know, because I tried to go back and get more magic items a few days later, but the place was gone."

"And the man who sold you this ring, he said if you collected five souls in it, the ring would grant you wishes?" Glory asked. She had her eyes locked on the ring, and there was a look on her face I'd only seen there a couple of times before. She was scared. Maybe this thing was more powerful than even I thought.

"Yeah." Jerome nodded, his chins waggling and his lanky hair falling in front of his face. "Hey, can I get a grape soda? Summoning demons is thirsty work, you know." He winked at Elizabeth, who showed him her appreciation by raising her middle finger in his direction.

"Sure," Zeek said. "And I owe these fine gentlemen a couple of beers on the house for their help tonight." He clapped one hand on the back of each Welch brother's neck and gave them a push to the door, which he closed after him.

Now my bedroom could almost accommodate the number of people it held, if there wasn't sufficient seating for everyone. The Robbinses sat on my bed, Jerome took the chair by my desk, and Glory perched on my dresser, trying very hard to look casual as she thumbed through the paperback of *A Fall in Autumn*, a sci-fi novel I picked up online a few days before.

I leaned on the door. Zeek wasn't coming back with a grape soda. I knew this because Zeek's Bar didn't have grape soda. But he got the Welch boys out of the room, and now it was time for Jerome to tell us a story about how a fat creeper from Tennessee came to be stealing souls with a ring powerful enough to scare an angel.

"So, Jerome," I said, fixing him with my very best "you lie to me and I will fuck you up intensely" stare. "Where did you get this ring and how were you impersonating a demon to get people to sell you their souls?"

Somehow Jerome found a spine between Zeek leaving the room and me asking the question because he gave me a smarmy little smile and said, "What's in it for me? The other guy promised me three wishes. What have you got?"

I took two steps across the small room and held my hand up in front of his face, index and middle finger held pointing toward the sky. I channeled a little energy into them and said, "*Infernus.*"

I didn't shout. I didn't raise my voice even in the slightest. I just held my hand in front of his eyes, two jets of flame shooting six inches off my fingers and said, "If you tell me everything I want to know and swear to never dabble in magic again, I promise not to melt your eyeballs in their sockets. How's that sound?"

Beads of sweat popped out all across Jerome's forehead, and I was pretty sure they weren't from the heat. He nodded and said, "That would be great."

"Good." I straightened up and extinguished my fingers. I'd need some aloe for that later, but Jerome didn't need to know I wasn't fire-proof. I walked back over to the door, leaned against it again, and glared at the wannabe wizard. "Talk."

Jerome talked. And the more he talked, the worse the sick feeling in my stomach got.

12

I t was just this guy, you know? He didn't look like much, just a skinny little dude who looked like he should be home watching *Wheel of Fortune* instead of at an IRL meetup of former Silk Road travelers."

I looked at Schmuck like he was speaking a different language, which as far as I was concerned, he was. "What the fuck are you talking about?"

"Which part?" Jerome looked at me. "The IRL part or the Silk Road part? I assume you know what *Wheel of Fortune* is."

"Both, and keep the smartass comments to a minimum if you don't want me to flash-fry your nose hairs."

Jerome's pudgy face took on a rapturous glow and the kind of gleam came into his eyes like I've only seen in snake-handling churches in Appalachia. Or Packers fans. "IRL means In Real Life. The Silk Road was...think of it like a flea market on the Dark Web. It was the kind of place where you could buy anything, no matter the rules against it. A totally free market, unfettered by societal rules or someone else's social mores. If you had money, and you wanted to buy something, chances are there was someone on the Silk Road selling it. No matter what it was. The original Silk Road shut down a few years ago, but there are still places, if you know where to look."

"Horrible places, Harker. Be glad you don't know much about them," Glory said.

"How do you know about it?" I asked. "Given your origins, you're the last person I'd expect to have knowledge of something called the Dark Web."

"Dennis and I were tight. He helped me shut down quite a few of the more disgusting vendors on the Silk Road. But people like that are like cockroaches. Whenever you squash one, it seems like two more pop up to take their place."

"Dennis?" Jerome asked. "Dennis *Bolton*? You knew the Boltron? Wow. That guy was a hacker legend. They had to invent a whole new term for him—rainbow hat, for the avatar he used. He could get into *anything*. Everybody on the Road knew that if Boltron found out about you, and he didn't like what you were doing...you were done. That dude made Anonymous look like Innocuous."

I smiled to hear him talk about my little buddy in such reverential terms. Seemed like Dennis had done more good as a disembodied soul trapped in the internet than I even knew about. Maybe he deserved to get transformed into an Archangel. But that wasn't getting me any closer to the person who gave Jerome this soul-stealing ring. I snapped my fingers. "Back to the matter at hand, Jerome. Who gave you the ring, and how did you make these folks think you were a demon?"

"Well, the second part was really easy. I hired an actor."

"What?" the rest of us said in unison.

Jerome looked inordinately pleased with himself. "Yeah, I hired an actor off Craigslist. Paid him a hundred bucks to play a demon and contract for a soul. He was a good-looking dude. Tall, stubble, British accent, skinny. You know, he looked like he oughta be on *Supernatural* or something. I bought him a pair of red contact lenses, coached him on what to say, and had him make sure to get a drop of blood on the contract. Then almost a month later, I send a copy of the contract to the person who signed it, except this copy didn't say they had three

73

years of prosperity, this contract said they had three *weeks* of prosperity. Then they were to report back to our meeting place for the harvest."

"What happened when they came back?" Glory asked, suspicion heavy in her voice.

Jerome looked down, a slight flush creeping up his cheeks. "I...I don't know. Nobody ever came back. These two were my first clients, and they reneged on our deal." He glared at Mark and Elizabeth, and I shook my head. There was no point explaining to Schmuck that you can't breach a fake contract, not even in Hell.

"So you sent hellhounds after them," I said.

"Yeah. When I started this project, I just wanted to get a little skinnier. You know, get fit, move out of my mom's attic, get a girlfriend, that kind of thing. But when I saw that these people were willing to sell their souls for a little bit of money...well, that's when I started thinking bigger."

"Bigger?" I asked. There was no way I was going to like where this was going.

"Yeah, bigger. I figured if this wizard was willing to grant me three wishes for five souls, how much would somebody give me for ten? Twenty? And then what if I just bought and sold souls for a profit? I mean, that's all I ever did on the Silk Road. I bought images from people, then I sold those images to other people."

"What kind of images?" Glory asked, her voice dark.

Jerome held up his hands. "Nothing bad, like kiddie stuff, or snuff films. That's gross. I never dealt with anybody that bought or sold anything with kids. I've got standards, you know."

"Obviously," Elizabeth muttered. "Only someone of the highest moral fiber would fake being a demon to con people into signing away their souls on a fake contract."

Jerome went on justifying his illegal and immoral business as though she never spoke. "Nah, I just hacked people's phones and personal computers and put some of their personal photos online. For a price. I mean, if you don't want the world to see you naked, why would you take pictures of yourself naked?"

"So you didn't do kiddie porn; you just invaded people's privacy and exposed their secret personal photos for the world to see?" I'd seen that look on Glory's face before, and it usually came around right before she ripped a demon's head off its shoulders. I needed her to not do that with Jerome until we got all the relevant information from him, so I put a hand on her shoulder. She glared at me and shrugged me off, but she didn't put a magical sword through the schmuck's oversized gut, so I took the win.

"Well, it sounds bad when you say it like that." Jerome kinda withdrew into himself, like a turtle sucking back into his shell.

"How did you summon the hellhounds and the Bathory?" I asked. This guy seemed to have about the magical talent of a turnip, so I still didn't really understand how he was calling up demons to do his bidding.

"Oh, that? Same as the contracts. If it's for sale, or if someone will do it for money, you can find it on the new Silk Road. So I paid a guy. I mean, I *hired* a guy. I technically haven't paid him, since the hounds didn't deliver, so I don't feel like I owe him anything. That makes sense, right?"

"You hired someone to summon demons to enforce a fake contract you swindled people into signing while you pretended to be a demon. And now you're asking me if it's okay not to pay the guy who summoned demons for you because his demons didn't deliver the people who didn't actually owe you anything?" I asked. My head spun a little at the dizzying logic this idiot employed to keep himself on the moral high ground.

"Well...it sounds bad—"

"When I say it that way," I finished. "Yeah, I get it. Look. I don't give a flying shit if you stiff the demon-summoning asshat that called up the hounds. I don't give a shit that you duped these people into signing away their souls for nothing. I don't even care that you invaded innocent people's privacy for money."

"I do," Glory interjected. "I care about that one."

I looked over at her. She had storm clouds all over her face, and I decided that it wouldn't be the right time to ask her if she was sensitive because some rogue angel posted nude selfies of her on the heavennet. She didn't look like this was something she had a sense of humor about. So I just went on. "Noted." I turned back to Jerome. "But I do care about you having a ring that harvests souls, and that you were going to sell those souls to the highest bidder. So this is how the rest of your night is going to play, Jerome. Are you listening?" I put a lot of growl into that last bit and was gratified when his attention zeroed back in on my eyes.

"Good," I went on. "You're going to give me that ring. You're not going to argue about that, you're not going to try to run, and you're sure as fuck not going to try to fight me over it. We clear?"

Jerome nodded.

"Then you're going to tell me everything you remember about the guy who sold you this ring, his shop, and anything he told you about how you were going to get in touch with him to deliver the souls once you stole them. Still with me?"

Jerome nodded again.

"Then you're going to walk out the door to this room, walk across the bar and out *that* door, then you're going to forget you ever learned the minuscule amount of crap you've learned about magic and the world beneath the world you live in, because the fact that you're still alive to sit here in my bedroom and snivel makes you the luckiest bastard in Memphis tonight. You got all that?"

"But...what about my wishes?"

That was it. I was completely full up on dumbass, and that was the last straw. I backhanded Jerome so hard his head spun around and he fell to his knees on the floor beside the chair. I grabbed a handful of greasy hair and yanked him up to his feet, then spun him around and laid an open-handed slap across his other cheek that sat him right back down in the chair. His eyes watered, but he didn't cry. He sat there staring up at me with his bottom lip quivering, but he held it together as I leaned back down into his face.

"Jerome, every wish you've got right now is being granted. Because the only fucking thing you're wishing for is me not ripping your heart out of your chest and shoving it up your ass. You have stepped in real

CARL PERKINS' CADILLAC

shit, Jerome. Real, world-class, demons and angels kind of shit. The kind of shit that doesn't just roll downhill, it fucking *cascades* downhill like molten lava, turning houses into kindling and destroying everything in its path. And do you know what's standing at the bottom of that hill watching all this metaphysical, interdimensional, *way* above-your-pay-grade shit pouring down upon him? You, Jerome, you worthless fucking schmuck. You're at the bottom of the hill with the kind of shit pouring down toward you that would make cherubs shit their little angel diapers.

"Here's your first fucking wish, Jerome. You wish that you could walk out of this room and go hide in Mommy's basement for a month and only come out to nuke Hot Pockets and order more Mountain Dew from the grocery store down the street that delivers."

"Attic," Jerome corrected. "I don't live in a basement. I live in the attic."

I slapped him again. Not as hard this time, but hard enough that he hopefully learned the error of his ways and didn't interrupt me again while I was on a roll. "Your second wish is that you can avoid the magician that really *could* summon demons and hellhounds, and pray to every saint you can think of to protect you from that dude, because if he'll summon monsters like that for the promise of cash, what the *fuck* do you think he'll do to collect that money?

"And your third wish? Your final fucking wish, Jerome? That's you wishing that you could pretend like this shit never happened. That's you going back to whatever pitiful fucking existence you led before you decided to step to the goddamn dark side and try very hard not to ever set foot in it again. So there's your fucking wishes, Jerome. Now give me the fucking address of the store where you got that ring so we can try to make sure that asshole doesn't have any more artifacts that really shouldn't see the light of day."

Jerome's mouth opened and closed a few times like a trout on a dock, but after almost a full minute of sitting there gasping in terror, he told me what I needed to know so I could go after whatever son of a bitch was selling super-powerful magical artifacts to morons in my city.

77

13

The sun came up slow over Zeek's bar, turning the Mississippi from black to purple to reflected gold as the light bounced off the water. I watched the shadows recede over the river and into the distance as I sat there on the narrow strip of pier that ran around behind the bar, feeling the grain of the wood press into my back as the dawn's light chased the dark away. It didn't do anything to send any of my shadows scurrying for cover, though. Every time I looked inside myself, all those dark spots still lingered, just waiting to envelop me like they were doing right then.

"Penny for your thoughts," Glory said, sliding down the wall to stretch her long legs out alongside mine.

"You always overpay," I said. I laid the bottle of Gentleman Jack across my lips and frowned as nothing came out. I tossed the bottle into the water and watched it sink.

"That's littering."

"It'll biodegrade."

"No, Harker. It really won't."

"Oh well. The world will probably end before anybody gives a shit, then."

"Wow, aren't we a ray of sunshine this morning?"

I still hadn't looked at her, other than the tips of her plaid Chuck Taylor high tops pointing straight up. "What do I have to be all sunny about, Glory? I'm stuck in Tennessee, working a crap job ten hours away from the woman I love because I don't want my personal shit-storm to find her, and I find myself nuts-deep in somebody else's shit-storm! Tell me what about that feels sunny to you?"

Glory didn't answer. She didn't say a word. She just reached over, put her arm across my shoulders, grabbed the back of my collar, and flipped me into the river like I was an unruly kitten.

I came up spluttering and looked at her for the first time that morning. "What the fuck was that for?"

"You sober now?"

"I was sober before!"

"Oh. Sorry. I assumed if you were being a maudlin pussy, it was because you were drunk. If you were being a maudlin pussy sober, then...nah, dumping you in the river was still the right play."

"You going to help me out of here?" I scowled up from the water. Zeek had several ways to get into the river from the bar, with varying degrees of stealth, but no routes *in* from the water.

"Nope. Swim around and meet me in your room. That'll give you a chance to look around the bottom of the river."

"What exactly am I supposed to be looking for in the Mississippi?" I asked, starting toward the shore.

"Your balls, Q. Your balls. This is some major league bad shit we've got to deal with, and I can't help you if I have to babysit a whiny little bitch the whole way." I gave one more look up and watched her pop to her feet and walk back into the bar. I muttered nasty things about smartassed angels my whole swim around the bar.

A short swim, a quick incantation to steam the water from my clothes, and a grumpy walk through a closed bar and I was sitting at my desk looking at the angel perched cross-legged on my bed. Blond hair cascaded over a vintage Debbie Gibson t-shirt and her jeans were artfully split at one knee. "What's this look? Eighties chic?"

"Comfy," Glory replied. "Now what are we going to do about that?"

79

She pointed to a small box beside me, a warded container that I kept around for just this kind of discovery, but usually held my car keys.

"The ring? I haven't figured that out yet," I said. "We have to figure out some way to destroy it, and we probably have to find the asshole that sold it to Jerome before he sells anything else with enough power to totally fuck with the rules of reality. I mean, catching and storing souls like Pokémon? That's the kind of thing that could do a lot of damage."

"Yeah, if souls become something that can be transported, that can live outside a human body without any kind of wards, or circle, or anything, then I can see a whole black market in Hell for buying and selling souls. With the right temptation, or the right persuasion, demons that don't have the power to get to Earth could amass an army of souls. They could tip the balance between Heaven and Hell."

"Yeah, there's that," I said. "I was thinking more about how bad mortals are going to fuck it up if this dick is selling things that have even more power than this ring."

"And if he has the ring, does he have the other pieces?" Glory asked.

I stared at her. "Other pieces? Like…the ring is part of a set?"

Glory met my eyes, and the fear was back in hers. "Yeah. They are. And there's nothing good about them."

"That sounds like there's a story."

"Not one I really know much of. I just know that there are four pieces of jewelry: a ring, an amulet, a bracelet, and a clasp that's, at different times, gone on a robe, cloak, or belt."

"Alright, so they're magical bling. What is it about them that makes them so powerful? That ring was practically humming when Jerome handed it to me." I pointed to the box where the ring rested. The lid was closed, but I still thought I could feel the thing in there, pulsing, almost like it called to me. It wasn't a very impressive piece in the mundane spectrum, just a twisted metal circle that looked almost as if someone took a vine, bent it around their finger to size it, and then dipped it in molten silver to make a ring. It lost its shine years ago, and now it sat in a warded lead box on my desk, a hunk of blackened metal with an ominous aura.

"These are artifacts from some of mankind's darkest moments. That ring? What did it look like to you?"

"Not much," I said. "Just twisted metal, kinda viney or like it was molded around wood. It wasn't so much about what it looked like as what it *felt* like. It was hungry, somehow, like it had a taste of power and wanted more."

"Power," Glory said. "Or blood. One man's blood, specifically. That ring was made in Jerusalem almost two thousand years ago, when a greedy merchant took a bloodied ring of vines off the head of a convicted criminal, cut it into pieces, made rings from it, and dipped them in silver. Then he sold the rings as trinkets. Souvenirs."

"You've gotta be kidding me," I said, looking back at the box. "You're telling me that ring…"

"Was made from the crown of thorns placed on Christ's head when he was crucified. That's exactly what I'm saying."

"Your boss, wherever he is, has a helluva sense of humor," I grumbled.

"What do you mean?" Glory asked, puzzled.

"It's not enough I can't get away from magic, I can't even get away from Golgotha! Last year I had to hunt down the Spear of Destiny, and now I've got a chunk of the crown of thorns cast in silver sitting in my bedroom! What's next, Glory? You gonna tell me that one of the other things we're looking for is Pontius Pilate's cock ring?"

The angel blushed at that one. Since spending all those months as a human, my guardian angel hadn't quite managed to shake the last vestiges of her mortality, and the ability to blush seemed like it was sticking around. I kinda liked knowing I could mortify even an angel.

"No, but they are equally dark. The bracelet is fashioned after the serpent that Eve met in the Garden of Eden, and the gem that makes up the serpent's eye is amber."

"Okay, other than being a missing kid alert, what's the big deal about amber?" I asked.

"This was made from the sap of the Tree of Knowledge of Good and Evil," Glory said.

"You're telling me all that shit really existed? The Garden, the Tree, the serpent? Gimme a break, Glory."

"Harker, you've been to Hell. Literal Hell, with fires and devils and the whole deal. Why is this so hard to believe, but passing between worlds is perfectly reasonable?"

"Because..." I didn't have a reason. It wasn't any more unreasonable than anything in my life. It made as much sense as my uncle, who happened to be a centuries-old Eastern European noble, having a sliver of demon soul buried inside him that made him immortal and forced him to drink human blood to survive. It was no more unreasonable than drinking in a bar with a guy created from chunks of corpses sewn together and shocked back to life. And yeah, it was no more unreasonable than going to Hell and coming back alive.

"Okay," I said after a long moment to consider the implications of everything in the Old Testament being way more literal than I'd ever allowed for. "We've got a ring made of the Crown of Thorns, a bracelet from the Garden of Eden. What are the other two? Saint Peter's key ring? Cain and Abel's matched set of baby rattles?"

"No, but we'll get back to those guys. The clasp has been used for all kinds of things down through the ages: a cloak clasp, a brooch, a belt buckle. So who knows what it's being used for now. But like all the artifacts, it's what it was made from that matters."

"What is it made of?" I asked when she paused. If she was willing to play the dramatic card, I was willing to give her the cues when she asked for them.

"Gold."

I waited, but she didn't go on. *Okay, so we're really milking this one.* "What's so special about the gold, Glory?"

"It was once cast into an effigy of a calf and worshipped by the Israelites as they fled Egypt."

"This thing was made from the calf that Moses smashed the Ten Commandments on?" I might have been to Hell and back and spent a year with Archangels sleeping on my couch, but talking about

Moses and the Garden of Eden was still enough to boggle me a little.

"Yep. Most of the gold was melted down and mixed with base metals to make coins or lost to the sands of time. But this one piece of jewelry has been at a lot of truly awful events throughout man's history and has been close by for some legendary murders."

"Like what?" I couldn't help myself. She had me hooked, and she knew it.

"It served as a centerpiece to the necklace Julius Caesar wore when he was assassinated, for one."

"Yeah, I'd say that has some historical significance."

"It was affixed to a ribbon and awarded to Franz Ferdinand as a medal, and he was wearing it when he was shot. Lincoln was rumored to have made it into a pocket watch and carried it to the theatre. It was never found with his body."

"So it's a murder magnet, is what you're telling me."

"I'm telling you that all of these objects have a bloody history, but none more so than the amulet."

"What's the deal with the amulet?"

"Like the rest of the artifacts, if you look at it, it's not impressive. It's a silver medallion with a polished disk of agate set in the middle of it. But if you know where that agate originated, it's the most notorious murder weapon in history."

I wracked my brain but couldn't come up with it. I knew it wasn't anything having to do with the Crucifixion because we had already talked about the Crown of Thorns, and I knew where the Spear of Destiny was. No other murders even came close as far as notoriety. "I give up. Where did the agate come from?"

"It was in a field in the Middle East thousands of years ago. It was a rock, just lying there minding its own business, as rocks do. When suddenly it was snatched up by an angry man, who smashed the rock into his brother's temple, splashing blood across the face of the stone and killing the brother. And thereby becoming the first murder weapon."

I felt myself go pale. "Are you saying..."

"Yeah, I'm saying. The amulet's blood-red agate was brilliant white until the afternoon Cain snatched it up from where it lay in the field and slammed it into his brother's head, killing him and streaking the ground, and the stone, with blood. This was the stone that slew Abel. This was the first weapon man ever used on man."

"And now some asshole with a Harry Potter complex might have sold it at a flea market in Western Tennessee," I said, mentally calculating how much alcohol it was going to take to get me to sleep tonight. It was a big number.

"Yeah," Glory said. "Q, these aren't trinkets. These aren't even like the Implements, which were useless unless in Divine hands. These are soul-stealing artifacts from the dawn of man's history, and if they're all in play at the same time, that means there is some serious power at work. Whoever sold these pieces of jewelry has a lot of power, a huge plan, and absolutely no moral compass."

"So you're saying it's time to save the world," I said.

"Yeah, that's exactly what I'm saying."

"Okay." I stood up and reached for the doorknob.

"Wait," Glory said. "Where are you going? We need a plan."

"I have a plan, Glory. I'm going to drink four and a half bottles of tequila, pass out on the floor of my room, and deal with this shit after I've processed everything you just told me. If the world ends before I sober up, put in a good word upstairs for me."

"You're going to go get drunk? At ten o'clock in the morning?"

"If that's what time it is, yes," I replied. Then I walked out into Zeek's bar, with the sunlight streaming through the closed blinds and making pretty little dancing motes of gold all throughout the air, and I proceeded to deal with my Biblical artifact problem by getting biblically drunk.

14

That was not my best idea," I said seven hours later when I woke up. The blessing and curse of my part-vampire metabolism was my difficulty in getting drunk and relative impossibility of staying drunk. *Good thing I work in a bar, or this morning's bender would have bankrupted me*, I thought as I rolled out of my bed to *thump* flat on the floor.

"Not your worst, either," Glory said from the chair by the desk. "At least this one didn't involve interdimensional travel, and you managed to avoid setting anything on fire this time."

"We'll call it a win, then," I said, getting to my feet with a groan. "I'm going to grab a shower, then we'll go look for this magic shop. I don't expect our artifact vendor to still be anywhere in the vicinity, but maybe he left a trace." I started peeling off clothes and tossing them toward the hamper.

—"Good grief, Q," Glory said. "Have you no shame?"

I turned around in my boxer briefs to find the angel blushing. "What the hell, Glory? The sight of my manliness affects you all of a sudden? I didn't think angels had those kinds of feelings. Or the appropriate equipment."

"My equipment is none of your business, Harker. And just because

I don't want to see your bare ass doesn't mean that you have any kind of effect on me. Now go get cleaned up. You smell like a distillery." But I noticed she never stopped blushing.

A hot shower did wonders for my head, and my room was empty when I came back. I dried my hair, threw on a Ray Wylie Hubbard t-shirt, jeans, and my Doc Martens, and stepped out into the bar. Glory sat at a table with Mark and Elizabeth Robbins, Zeek, and of all people, Bart Welch. I motioned for Henry to hand me a bottle of whiskey.

"Sorry, Eddie. Harker. Quincy. Shit, man. What am I supposed to call you now?" the skinny werewolf stuttered.

"Call me whatever you want, just fork over that bottle of Wild Turkey," I said, putting a little snarl into it so Henry would remember who was the Alpha dog.

"No way, dude. Zeek and your scary girlfriend both told me not to give you any booze, so I'm not giving you any booze. No offense, dude, but that chick looks like she could break me in half."

I looked over at Glory, who looked more like a fitness model than anything, but when I took in Henry's narrow shoulders and twig arms, I tended to agree with him. The angel sat with one arm thrown over the back of her chair and her body twisted to look at me, and the look she gave me was one full of warnings to behave. A lock of her blond curls sprang loose from the ponytail she wore it in and covered her left eye, and no man in his right mind would argue with her. I wasn't often considered to be in my right mind, but I still just went along with her orders and walked my sober ass over to the table.

"I thought you guys were out of the supernatural business?" I asked the Robbinses as I pulled out a chair and spun it around, resting my arms on the ladder back.

"We are," Mark said. "At least, we really want to be."

"After," his daughter chimed in.

"Yeah, after," Mark agreed, but it was that kind of father agreeing with his daughter where he makes it apparent that he doesn't agree at all and is just going along in the hopes that someone else can talk sense into her. I guess he missed the memo: talking sense into people isn't exactly my thing.

When it became obvious they weren't going to go on, I took the bait. "After what?"

"After we know the guy sending demons to murder us is taken care of," Elizabeth said. "Or did you forget about that?"

I kinda had. Once my attention ratcheted up to the world-saving stuff, I completely forgot that there was a dude running around Tennessee calling up the soldiers of Hell for money. Shit. I looked at Glory, who shrugged. Then over at Zeek, who spread his hands.

"Sorry, Harker. I know most folks in the supernatural community around here, but I don't really mess with demon summoners for hire. Those folks don't usually abide by the rules of sanctuary, or anything else."

I looked at Bart. "And what do you want? Is somebody after you, too?"

"No," he said. Then he reached over to his chest and pressed a button on the camera strapped around himself. It beeped three times, and Bart said, "I'm volunteering my services in your quest. Welch Brothers Investigations, LLC will be happy to assist with your paranormal needs." He held out a hand, looking down to make sure it would be in frame.

I just stared at his hand until he let it drop like a dead fish. I'd made the mistake of shaking Bart's hand once and didn't need to repeat the unpleasant experience. "No."

"No, what?"

"No, I don't want your help." I scotched down a little to put my face directly in front of the camera. "Quincy Harker, SOB, does not want any assistance from Grape Juice Boys, LLC. He does not want them in the bar. He does not want them in the car. He does not want them on a boat. He does not want them on a float. He does not want them, Sam I am." I straightened back up. "Now fuck off, Bart. I don't have time to worry about keeping you alive, keeping the demons off these nice people, and keeping the rest of the artifacts that go with Jerome's ring out of the hands of idiots. I can handle maybe two of those things, so the least important one has to go. Guess where you fall?"

Bart looked like I'd just kicked his dog. No, he looked like I just kicked his puppy out into the road where it got run over by a cement mixer. "But, this could be our big break. This could get us off public access and YouTube. This could get us the blue check mark by our names on Twitter, man!"

I had no idea what that meant. I spent a little time on Twitter close to a decade ago, but quickly saw it as a wretched hive of scum and villainy and ran for the hills. "Bart." I reached out and put a hand on his shoulder. With the other one, I poked the power button on his GoPro until it beeped off. I put on my best sincere face and tried to soften my voice so I didn't sound like someone who would rather strangle Bart than look at him. "It's not that I don't like you. I mean, I don't. But that's not why you can't be a part of this. You can't be a part of this because you have no magic, you have no real tech that will be worth a damn against any of the stuff I'm likely to run into, and you're in peak physical condition. For a turnip. You come with me, you'll die. Not the kind of die where you respawn in the same spot and shoot the guy that killed you, the kind of die where there's a coffin and a deep hole involved. If there's enough left of you to bury. So I'm sorry, but you've got to sit this one out. If I come across any haunted houses, I promise to call you guys in. But as long as I'm chasing demons, I gotta keep you on the bench. Okay?"

His bottom lip quivered, and I swear I saw moisture well up in one eye, but he held it together long enough to nod. "Okay. But if you need us, you know who to call." Then he reached into his shirt pocket and put his business card down on the table. I glanced at it, and was pretty sure the little green monster image in a red circle was trademark infringement, but it wasn't my place to tell him. "My personal cell number is on there. You can call me anytime, night or day." Then he patted my hand and stood up, leaving me with a lingering glance and the impression that Bart might have taken my moment of kindness for more than it was. I'm as hetero-flexible as the next guy who lived through the seventies in Studio 54, but Bart wasn't my type. I really prefer my partners, male or female, to bathe regularly.

I turned to the next problem at hand, the Tennessee Family Robbins. "Now what are we going to do about you guys?" I asked.

"I don't think you do anything about them, Quincy," came a cultured voice from a far corner of the bar. I looked to my right, and there was a well-dressed slender man sitting with his face completely hidden in shadow. Then he leaned forward, and it did absolutely nothing to lighten his complexion, although now I could see his midnight-black skin clearly.

The demon Faustus uncrossed his long legs and stood up, bringing his tumbler of amber liquid over to our table and lounging in the chair formerly occupied by the eldest Welch brother. He nodded to Zeek and me, then extended a hand to Glory. "So lovely to see you again, my dear. I can't say how thrilled I am to make your acquaintance once more."

"Fuck off, Pit-lizard." I whipped my head over to Glory and was stunned to find her staring daggers at the demon. "I may have sent for you, but I don't have to let you paw all over me."

I swung my face back and forth between the angel and the demon until I finally spat out a confused "Whu?"

"I called him," Glory said. "He's the only number I had that wasn't divine or someone you wouldn't let within ten miles of you, so I called the demon. Thanks for putting me in that position, by the way. *Please* let me know as soon as you're over your martyr complex so we can go home and I can deal with normal assholes like Watson and Gabby."

"But what is he going to do?" I asked. Glory jerked her head at Mark and Elizabeth, who sat there looking at least as puzzled as I felt.

"What? You want to ask a demon to babysit them and protect them from...demons?" This was turning into the weirdest thing that had happened to me in days, and I just got hit on by a low-rent Venkman cosplayer.

"I don't want him to babysit. I want him to find whoever is sending hounds after these two and take care of it."

"Him?" I asked.

89

"He's kinda famous for making deals and finding loopholes in them."

She had a point. Every tale of Faustus, going back centuries, was all about a deal, and screwing somebody out of something. Now we had a bounty hunter that Jerome was trying to screw out of cash, so who better to negotiate for the Robbins's safety?

Glory saw me wavering and went for the kill. "He's our best option, unless you think they can hide out in your bedroom while we go deal with the threat to the world?"

"Not happening," Zeek said. "And you're moving out, Harker. Sorry, but I could only let you stay as long as your shit didn't end up on my doorstep. Now I've got Reaper shit all over my floors, and I just mopped yesterday. Metaphorically, of course."

"That's cool. I understand. Can I leave my stuff here for a few days while I deal with this potentially catastrophic set of jewelry running around the world?" I was bitter. I'll own it. I liked the gig, I liked the music, hell, I even liked Henry. I was going to miss masquerading as a normal human(ish) bouncer. But Zeek's Place had a reputation as a safe haven, no matter who or what you were, and having somebody known all over two or three dimensions for killing demons wouldn't be good for that. It worked as long as I was Eddie Nolen, but Quincy Harker couldn't live in the back room of a Sanctuary.

"Yeah, that's fine. I'll even ward your room when you're gone. But once you've got the rest of the artifacts, you're out of here." Zeek's tone brooked no argument, and I had no faith I could fight a djinn with any hope of winning, so I just nodded.

"Fine," I said. "Faustus will take care of the demons coming after the Robbins family while we hunt down the rest of your matched set of magical murder bling. Anything else?"

"Don't I get a vote in any of this?" Robbins the elder asked.

"No," I said. "Fuck you, Mark. If you hadn't gotten greedy and tried to sell your soul for a fucking mystic payday loan, you wouldn't be in this mess. Faustus will find Jerome's bounty hunter, pay him off or kill him, and Glory and I will take care of the less important problems, like saving the world. Again. Is that okay with you, Mark? Or do you need me to mow your fucking lawn while I'm at it?"

Nobody said anything, so I reached out, knocked back the dregs of Faustus's drink, and stormed off into my room to gear up. Looked like it was time to go be a fucking hero again.

15

I had the address of the magic shop from Jerome. Hell, the place even had a website that listed its hours and displayed merchandise for sale online. It was all your typical mail-order bullshit, of course: love potions to slip in your spouse's drink that was probably nothing more than a lot of ginseng and maybe some horny goat weed, amulets that would protect you from evil spirits but would turn your neck green wherever the cheap silver touched it, and special Himalayan Warding Salt to sprinkle on all your windowsills to keep out malevolent presences. I swear, *Supernatural* has done more for domestic rock salt sales than any other show on television.

The place wasn't much to look at from the outside, just a narrow storefront in a row of run-down and mostly closed businesses in what once was a busy main street of the neighborhood but now was home to the businesses that couldn't afford the rent downtown or catered to a more working-class population, like a Family Dollar store and a NAPA auto parts shop. Wedged in between a shuttered Mom & Pop drugstore and a seasonal income tax return office was a little purple awning with faded gold letters. If you walked by the place on the sidewalk, odds are you'd think the place had been deserted for twenty years, but there was a new sign in the front window with the hours on display, and a fresh set of gold letters on the door in an arc that read "Dr. Mephisto's Curios and Antiquities."

I looked at the name on the door, then over at Glory. "I don't think it's ever a good sign when the name on the door is basically 'Satan.' Do you?"

The angel shuddered. "Not really, no. I mean, we just went through the devil's front door once. Do we really want to walk right up and ring the doorbell?"

She had a point. If the artifacts in this joint had the kind of power she was worried about, my typical method of entry, which included applying my foot to the front door, probably wasn't our best plan. I let my Sight slip over my vision and checked the door for wards, traps, or any other potentially unpleasant surprises.

"We're gonna want to find a back door," I said to Glory. The glow that met my eyes in the supernatural spectrum was enough to make my soul want sunglasses, there were so many spells laid on that front door. I saw alarms, immobilization spells, repulsion spells, fire spells, and a couple of charms that I didn't know what they did, but they pulsed in my Sight with angry red and purple light, so I was pretty sure they didn't blow noisemakers and throw confetti when a wizard walked through the door.

"This place is warded all to hell, and I think they're attuned to alert the owner if someone comes in with real magic," I said.

"That makes sense," Glory replied. "If I was running a business built mostly on hoaxes and gimmicks, but I had a few pieces of real power lying around, I'd want to know if somebody with significant power came in, so I could defend myself."

Nothing about those wards looked all that defensive to me, but I kept my mouth shut for once. Just because someone puts spells on their threshold to immolate the first magician that walks through the door doesn't necessarily mean they're a bad person. It's a clue, though.

"Well, according to the sign, we've got about ten hours before they open up in the morning, so that should give us plenty of time. Let's see if there's a back door." I also wanted to get us out of sight because the clerk at the 24-hour convenience store across the street was looking our way more than I was comfortable with. I didn't expect her to have some hotline to the store's owner, or worse, whoever cast those wards, but I also didn't want to spend the rest of the night explaining myself to the Memphis PD. My Homeland Security credentials were expired, and I was trying hard to go at least a few months without beating the shit out of any cops.

So we skulked. Glory and I walked down the sidewalk holding hands like teenagers on a date, then when we came to a convenient alley that looked like it was built for lovers' trysts and muggers' wet dreams, we ducked down it and slipped around to the back of the row of connected buildings. The back parking lot, too, the story of exactly how far down this neighborhood had fallen, with its cracked asphalt, dented dumpsters, and heaps of garbage piled against the back of one store. The upside to all that was it provided cover to a pair of decidedly unstealthy burglars, one of whom was trying to sneak around in a light gray Wynona Earp t-shirt and her blond hair flying in the breeze.

"You couldn't have decided to look less conspicuous?" I asked, motioning at my dark jeans, black shirt, and black shoes.

"I like this shirt, and my hair looks like crap after I tuck it all up in a hoodie. Anyway, it's not like you planned that wardrobe. Everything you own in Tennessee is black shirts, jeans, and your Docs."

She had a point. I left all my decent clothes in the closet in Charlotte when I walked out on Becks and the rest of the good parts of my life. I didn't miss the clothes. "Glory, you can change your appearance at will. You literally never have to have a bad hair day. Why not just magic up something less glow in the dark?"

She didn't say anything for a minute, and when I stopped walking and looked at her, there was a weird expression on her face. I didn't say anything, just held my tongue until she was able to say what she wanted to.

"Something's different, Harker. With me. Since I spent all that time as a mortal, I'm not the same as I was."

"Well, that's normal," I said. "Anyone—"

She cut me off. "Don't try to mansplain this shit, Q. You don't get

94

it. I've been around for *eons*. I *saw* what went down in the Garden. I *watched* the Crucifixion. I was here before there were humans, but then...I was one. And now I'm not. But I'm not...completely divine, either. It's not that my magic doesn't work. It does, obviously." As if to prove her point, she manifested a pair of eight-foot stark-white wings in the middle of the parking lot behind a shuttered H&R Block office at two in the morning. Because we were being subtle.

Her wings blinked out of existence. "But it's different. When I use my abilities, when I change form, when I shift between Earth and Heaven, something doesn't feel the same. It's like I don't belong. Like I'm this halfway thing, and I don't belong anywhere. Not here, not in Heaven...nowhere. So I don't use my powers much. Or at least I try not to. And that's why I didn't just turn myself into a brunette for the evening. Because my head is all fucked up, Harker, and I don't know how to un-fuck it."

Then Glory did something I didn't know she could do. She cried. My guardian angel stood in the parking lot behind a shitty row of mostly abandoned businesses in Tennessee, between a pile of discarded mattresses and a dumpster that really needed to be emptied, and she broke down sobbing. I stepped up to her and wrapped my arms around her, pulling her close, and I held her as she wept against my chest. Her shoulders shook and her whole body felt frail, and I mentally kicked my own ass for not seeing how this whole mess would affect her, too. I'd been so focused on my own shit that I couldn't help Glory deal with hers. Not that I was qualified to play therapist to a millennia-old angel, but I could at least be a friend. And I'd been a pretty shitty friend.

So I held her. I held her, and gave her a shoulder the cry on, and for about two minutes in the middle of a summer night, with the sound of traffic rolling over the buildings in front of us, I did the guarding.

Then she sniffled once, blew her nose on my sleeve, and we were back to skulking. The back door was warded, too, but it depended more on mundane security measures. The rear entrance looked like it was mainly for deliveries, with a small ramp of concrete leading up beside the few steps to the landing. The door was a featureless gray slab of metal, and I could see the wire running from a contact sensor for the alarm. My Sight revealed a couple of simple spells binding the door closed, and one trap designed to basically electrocute a trespasser, but nothing like the cornucopia of badness wrapping the front door.

I called up power and overloaded the alarm, then dispelled the wards, at least all the ones I could see. I reached out, put my hand on the knob, and paused. Nothing happened, so I smiled at Glory and pulled.

With absolutely no effect. The alarm was cooked, and the spells on the door were dissolved, but I still hadn't unlocked the damn thing. I ran a tendril of magic into the doorknob, tripped the tumblers, and opened the back door. We slipped in, closing the door but leaving it unlocked behind us. If I had to make a quick getaway, I'd rather not blow a hole in the wall to do it.

We passed through a short hallway with a lone fluorescent tube flickering over the door. I guess the evil wizard hadn't gotten the memo about LEDs yet. A simple wooden door opened up into a tiny storeroom with a couple of shelves loaded down with imported Buddha statues, lucky cats, boxes of different colored quartz crystals on silk cords, more incense than a Grateful Dead concert, and a few boxes of New Age-y self-help books with half an inch of dust on them. It didn't look like anything more than a hippie "magic" shop on its way to bankruptcy court, even in the supernatural spectrum. There were traces of magic here and there, but nothing with the kind of horsepower we were looking for. Mostly traces where a mid-level artifact may have sat on a shelf for a while.

I pushed through the swinging door into the shop and stepped into something out of a movie. It looked like a parody of a magic store more than anywhere an actual practitioner would shop. There was a spinning rack of different Tarot decks, a shelf full of multiple sizes of crystal balls, two long glass cases filled with cheap sterling silver jewelry on black pseudo-velvet fabric, and one entire bookshelf dedicated to the collected published works of Anton Lavey. I'm talking hardbacks, paperbacks, CDs, *cassette tapes*, and several framed and "autographed" photos. It was like a shrine to the little Satanist, which was much creepier than most shrines to Satan that I'd seen in my days.

But what we were looking for was in the front case, right by the battered old cash register. I saw the glow as soon as I looked around using my Sight. The light coming from that case had the same streaky yellow-black aura as the ring Jerome had, only this time the yellow mixed with a sickly green, a blood red, and a cold blue that made goosebumps run up my spine. Four different auras, for four artifacts. We had one. If the other three were here, we could destroy them and call it a day. I walked to the front counter, letting go of my Sight and looking into the case with my mundane eyes.

"Well, shit," I said as I took in the empty expanse of velvet.

"They're gone?" Glory asked.

"Oh yeah." They hadn't been gone long, judging by how much aura still permeated the cloth and the case. If Jerome bought his ring three weeks ago, the other items were all here longer. Maybe they were still in the case as recently as a few days ago.

"Well, what now?" my guardian angel asked, walking over to me.

I slipped around behind the counter and slid the back panel open so I could reach in. Maybe I could come up with some psychometric radar off the cloth these things laid on. But of course, the second I opened the case, the one ward I didn't see, cleverly hidden behind the latch of the case, went off, and the entire fucking shop exploded into flames. I was thrown backward a good ten feet and had just enough time to think *"Goddammit, not again"* before I slammed into a glass shelf full of trinkets and my world went dark.

16

I came to sitting with my back against a dumpster, smoldering, and covered in broken glass. The first thing I saw was my shoes. There was a tendril of smoke drifting up from my right foot, and I cocked my head to the side, wondering why my foot was smoking. That was enough to set my whole world to spinning, and I fell over onto my side, nausea rolling over me in waves. I got up onto my elbows and vomited up a truly phenomenal pile of whiskey, bacon, and stomach acid. Then I shoved myself to my feet and looked around, moving my head very slowly as to keep a tenuous hold on my balance.

More smoke poured out of the back entrance to the magic shop, and I heard the small popping sounds that told the tale of glass trinkets exploding in the extreme heat. Glory was nowhere to be seen, and I took a step toward the conflagration before I realized two very important things. First, Glory was an angel, therefore immortal, only corporeal when she wanted to be, and thus immune to being burned by mundane fire. Second, I was probably concussed, and there was very little chance that I could get into the fire and back out safely without going up like a Roman Candle. I am not an angel, and as I have learned through many painful experiences, I am most decidedly *not* immune to fire.

So I staggered over to a nearby garbage heap, grabbed a slightly bent metal folding chair, straightened the legs, and sat down to wait for her to reappear. I muttered a camouflaging incantation so I could hopefully avoid any uncomfortable questions with the local fire department, and waited for my head to stop spinning.

"You okay, Q?"

My head snapped up, and I gave it a second or two for my eyes to come into focus, then I turned my head to look at Glory. She looked immaculate, of course. The ability to magic up new clothes at any moment was one I envied some days. Like those days when I had to do laundry. "Yeah, I'm good. Mostly, anyway."

"Concussion?"

"Yeah."

"Anything broken?"

I took an internal inventory, testing all my appendages. Everything felt okay, and I'd managed to get up off the ground and into the chair all right, so I shook my head. "I'm pretty sure I'll feel like one big bruise tomorrow, but a few hours sleep oughta heal my head up right."

"Good. Because we should go. The firemen are done, and the cops are starting to poke around. Your little hidey spell is decent, but I'd rather be somewhere that's not here in case the guy who set that trap comes back to see what he caught."

I let her help me up and picked up an almost empty beer bottle from the ground. I didn't think whatever was in it was still beer, but I just wanted something to explain my shitty balance to the police, not anything to actually drink. We meandered around to the front of the store, and I slid behind the wheel of my battered pickup. The truck fit right in among the beaters on the street in front of the smoldering magic shop, and apparently no one had caught enough sight of me weaving along the sidewalk to think they should stop me for driving drunk, although in Western Tennessee that's a spectator sport.

"Where do we go from here, Glory?" I asked, leaning forward and putting my forehead on the steering wheel. The pressure made the world spin a little less, so I kept it there and closed my eyes for a few seconds.

"You're not going to like my suggestion," she said, and I knew she was right.

"Then how about we skip the part where you suggest we call Luke and Flynn for help. They can't know where I am, Glory. It's too dangerous. Lucifer said he would destroy everyone I care about. The only way to keep them safe is to stay as far away from them as possible."

"Do you really think that's going to work? Lucifer is the King of Hell, Harker. I'm pretty sure he knows who's important to you."

"Yeah, but it's the best chance I have of keeping them safe until I can make some kind of arrangement with Lucifer."

I still had my head down on the steering wheel, so I couldn't see Glory's face, but all hint of motion from the other seat stopped, so I knew she was stuck in place, just staring at me with that "are you nuts?" look on her face.

"Are you nuts?" she asked.

"Probably."

"You want to make a deal with the literal devil. The Father of Lies. The Serpent in the Garden. Lucifer fucking Morningstar. Jesus Christ, you've got to be the biggest idiot in the history of the world."

"That's a pretty high bar," I said. I was pretty proud of myself for that one. Cut me some slack; when in the middle of completely shit situations, you've gotta take the small victories wherever they come. "So you're saying I probably shouldn't try to outwit Satan, I guess?"

"A lot smarter and more devious men than you have tried. It never ends well. Just give it up, Q. Go home, or at least call Flynn. Get her and Luke up here. Hell, you can even bring that annoying Homeland Security agent if you want. But we need backup on this one. These artifacts are a big deal. The kind of big deal that can make a low-level demon into an Archduke."

I sat up, blinking to clear the sparkles out of my vision. "That's it. Glory, you're a genius!"

"Well, yes, compared to humans. But why specifically are you realizing that now?"

I cranked the truck and put it in gear, digging around in the console for a pair of sunglasses as I pulled away from the curb. The blare of a horn and subsequent spinning that put into my head told me in no uncertain terms I was not fit to drive. But I'd ridden with Glory. Immortality does something to a person's fear of crashing. Like eradicates it completely. I'd take my chances with the concussion.

I pulled into the light morning traffic and headed west, toward the river. The ritual we were looking for needed quiet and isolation to cast, and I knew exactly where to find that in spades.

I t took forty-five minutes of navigating Memphis traffic, and another fifteen minutes of meandering around looking for the right place, but finally I found a dead-end street down near a park overlooking a little tendril of the Mississippi River and parked the truck. My headache was almost gone, and I could see straight again, and I'd managed to get us from Point A to Point B without crashing, so I decided my amped-up healing had taken care of my concussion. Then I took my sunglasses off, and the Tennessee sun proved that I wasn't as over it as I thought. Wincing, I put the cheap black plastic frames back on my face and turned to Glory, who stood with her arms folded across her chest giving me a seriously dubious look.

"What the hell are we doing down here, Q?"

"Hunting, G," I replied. "There are only a few places in town, especially a town with as much supernatural activity as Memphis, where you can summon demons, serious demons, without attracting notice." I pointed across the harbor to a stretch of woods with a ten-foot high chain-link fence surrounding it. "And one of those places is right over there."

"If the place we want to be is over there, why are we over here?"

"Because the place over there isn't very welcoming to random people just popping by to say hello and ask about someone summoning demons in their hundred-acre wood. The government frowns on that shit. Most days."

She looked across the water, then back at me. "No."

"Come on, Glory." I heard the whine creep into my voice and wasn't even ashamed of it. If whining is what it took to get me across and onto the chunk of floating mystery Memphis called Treasure Island, so be it.

"I am not a supernatural taxi service, or air freight carrier, or carrier pigeon, or any of those things."

"Nobody said you were." I held out both hands. "Look, we can row if you want. But that's going to take a lot longer, and we're going to be a lot more exposed."

"It's broad daylight, Harker. I can't just go flying around a major city in the morning sun!"

"It's Memphis," I replied. "Half the town will think you're a seagull and the other half will think you're a hallucination." I looked at her, but she wasn't budging. "What's going to be less conspicuous, Glory? You flying us across the water hidden by my camouflage spell, or me walking across the water in broad daylight?"

She sighed but unfurled her wings and held out her hands. I turned my back to her, and murmured a brief incantation, then released a bubble of my will around us. Now anyone who happened to be looking would see a big seagull, not a gorgeous blonde with a giant pair of white fluffy wings carrying a scruffy-looking wizard across the river at ten in the morning.

Thirty seconds later, she set me down on the far shore, a foot or so away from the razor wire-topped fence I'd spied from across the water. She looked at me, curiosity wrinkling her face. "Why didn't you just mask yourself from view while you walked across? Would it be too much for you to carry two spells at once?"

"Nah," I said. "I just wanted to get a better look at the island's layout and having you carry me across killed two birds with one stone."

"And you got to feel like you got one over on the angel by conning me into it."

"The thought never crossed my mind." I didn't look at her when I said it. Years of experience taught me that if I am to have any hope of deceiving Glory, and usually I do not, I absolutely cannot look her in the eye while I lie to her.

"You are such an asshole," she said, but I could hear the smile in her voice as she said it.

"Does that mean you won't manifest that big glowing sword of yours and slice through the fence?"

"It does mean that I won't manifest my big glowing sword and slice through the fence," she confirmed.

"Okay, fine," I said. "We'll do it the hard way." I looked at the height of the fence again, then the amount of space I had to get a running start, which was practically none. I gathered my will, forced it out behind me in a kind of magical jetpack, shouted, "*Wingardium Levitato!*" and flew over the fence in one big jump.

Glory, of course, just blinked out of existence then popped back into view right next to me in the small cleared strip of land ahead of the large wooded plot the U.S. Government kept deserted on the banks of the Mississippi River.

"I'm pretty sure you got the spell wrong," Glory said as we started to push through the underbrush.

"I'm pretty sure mine actually worked, so we have empirical evidence that it was Rowling, not me, who got the spell wrong."

"Now you're just being difficult. You know as well as I do that it's the intent, not the words, that make the magic."

"Yeah, but my intent was not to get sued for copyright infringement."

"We're in the woods of Tennessee, at least a mile away from the nearest anything, Harker. Who in the world is going to sue you here?"

"Lawyers are sneaky, Glory. You can't trust those little bastards. Look at Watson. He's a lawyer, and he's like three of the least trust-worthy people I know."

"Three?"

"I really don't like lawyers." We fell quiet then, as I broke through the initial thick brush and found some scrap of a trail. We followed it for a few hundred yards until the trees thinned more, and I called up my masking spell again. "Well, that isn't exactly what I expected to find," I said.

"Yeah, no shit," Glory replied. We were really going to have to have a talk about her language. Since coming back from Hell, she sounded downright un-angelic.

But I couldn't disagree with her. Because in front of us was a small concrete building with a metal door set into it and a sign on it that said, "NO ADMITTANCE. TRESPASSERS WILL BE PROSECUTED TO THE FULLEST EXTENT OF THE LAW." Some enterprising soul had added in Sharpie underneath the warning "and then shot." There were two soldiers in full camo guarding the door, pistols on their hips and rifles on their shoulder. On top of the little outbuilding was another soldier, this one in a chair with an impressive-looking machine gun mounted to the roof.

Above the door was another sign, this one a pentacle with a convoluted name scribed into the arc. "Department of ExtraDimensional, Mystical, & Occult Nuisances."

"Shit," I said. "You know what this place is?"

"Yep," Glory said. "Cryptid Gitmo."

She wasn't wrong. In looking for pieces of haunted bling, I'd just stumbled into one of the government's most closely-held secrets: the location of DEMON headquarters, and the holding facility for the baddest monsters still in this dimension.

I heard a twig snap behind me and turned to see four grim-faced young men pointing impressive rifles at my face. I raised my hands and smiled at them. "Hi fellas," I said. "Take me to your leader?"

17

Around an hour later, or seventeen days if you judge by how bored I was, a black woman in a tailored pantsuit, the jacket cut to hide her shoulder holster, walked into the room with a manila file folder two inches thick in her hand.

"My name is Special Agent Melissa Walston, and you, Mr. Harker, are in some serious trouble." She dropped the folder onto the table with a *thud* and sat down across the featureless metal table from me. Her brows knit as she sat, and I gave her my best irritating grin.

"I figured since you guys went to all the trouble to remove one of the feet on this chair so it wouldn't sit evenly, I'd do you the same favor." I reached into my pocket and flipped a small plastic disk onto the table. I'd spent enough time in interrogation rooms to know that's where I was, and I knew all the tricks. The perp chair is always missing a foot, so they'll be off-balance and can't get comfortable. The interrogator chair is always rigged to be a little taller than the perp chair so they look like they've got more authority.

This chick had seen way too much *SVU*, or maybe *NCIS*. She had all the moves down, even the casual toss of the folder onto the table so that I could see my name on the tab and be curious what was in it. She missed one important thing, though. I didn't give a shit.

105

"So are you gonna lure me in to thinking you're Good Cop with the nice expensive suit that doesn't scream Fed at all, then spin into Bad Cop so I'll crack? Well, I'll never crack, copper. I'm not going back to the big house, see? You'll never take me alive!" I put on my best Jimmy Cagney voice, but it was obviously lost on her. Of course, she looked like he was born about the time Jimmy Cagney died, so that shouldn't have come as a surprise.

"Why are you here, Mr. Harker?" she said, and the cultured voice went perfectly with the suit. Everything about her might as well have come straight from Central Casting.

"Well, your guys outside? The ones with all the bullets? They were pretty insistent that I come with them. And since I'm working really hard on the whole 'don't kill humans' thing, I decided to give compliance a shot. You know, just for a change of pace."

She leaned back in her chair and pinched the bridge of her nose, like she was fighting to stave off a headache. I was pretty sure that headache was the better part of a century and a half old and sitting right in front of her, but I let her exercise her futility for a few seconds.

She took a deep breath, then another. Then she looked at me and said, "The file was right. You're an asshole."

"And you're an officious prick," I said, leaning forward and holding out my hand. "Now that we've gotten that shit out of the way, you want to let me go?"

"Not until you tell me why you were on President's Island," the prick said, scowling.

"Would you believe me if I told you a took a wrong turn at Albuquerque?"

"No."

"Worth a shot. How about if I told you I dropped my pencil?"

"Nope."

"What about if I said I'm hunting down artifacts with the potential to rupture the fabric of space and time, and I have a deadline to find them, but nobody has bothered to tell me what the artifacts look like, where they might be other than a general 'in Memphis,' or exactly when the deadline is?"

"Not a...wait a minute. That one sounded like..."

"The game is called Two Lies and a Truth for a reason, lady."

"I think it's called Two Truths and a Lie, actually."

"I had a unique upbringing."

She sat there staring at me for a minute, then picked up the folder and started leafing through it.

"Don't bother," I said.

Her eyebrows went up over the sheet of paper she was pretending to read. "Oh? What shouldn't I bother doing?"

"Trying to convince me you have something in that folder that I'm going to give a shit about. You don't. I know you guys. You're the *other* supernatural division, the one with the lame acronym. You've got maybe two dozen field agents, tops, and not even that many office types. You've got a shit budget, you have to cadge troops from nearby National Guard units whenever you need something protected, and last year you laid off your most effective employee. You guys are like magical Keystone Kops, only without the fun soundtrack."

"And you are a foul-mouthed, magic slinging miscreant that hates authority and has killed more people than influenza."

I grinned at her. "Stop it. You're going to make me blush."

I didn't blush, but a little bit of color darkened her cheeks. She stood up and leaned on the table, her knuckles whitening with the strain of not reaching across and throttling me. I was a little gratified to see I hadn't lost my touch. Her voice dropped half an octave, like she was trying to be intimidating or her testicles unexpectedly descended. "You were caught trespassing on federal property, at a facility that requires Top Secret or better clearance even to hear a rumor about. Give me one good reason I don't lock you up and throw away the key."

"Because you couldn't hold me of you tried," I said, leaning my chair back on two legs and lacing my fingers behind my head. "I don't know what you've got on me in that fake file over there, but I'm kind of a big deal."

"You're nothing without your uncle and your pet detective," she snapped.

I dropped my chair down onto all four feet and let the momentum carry me to a standing position. Then I reached out and grabbed the snotty woman by her lapels and pulled her in very close to my face. I called up just enough power to make my eyes glow red, and I said, my voice very low and my words very slow so she wouldn't miss any of them, "If you ever so much as think about letting mention of Detective Flynn cross your lips again, it had better be with the utmost respect, you pissant mid-level bureaucratic cockwaffle. Because if I even think you've *thought* about disrespecting her, I will knit a sweater out of your intestines and wear it to the office Christmas party. You got that?"

I expected her to quail before my threat, or escalate our little war of words, but she didn't. Instead she reached down with one hand and slowly pried each of my fingers off her jacket, then took one step back and backhanded me across the face. I was too surprised to avoid the shot, and even more surprised at how much mustard she put on it.

"That actually hurt," I said, wiping away a drop of blood from the corner of my mouth.

"It wasn't meant to tickle, Mr. Harker. I will ask you one more time: why are you on President's Island?"

I thought about it for a second before I answered. My instinct was to mouth off, cause a ruckus, knock this chick out cold, then punch and magic missile my way out of this place, leaving a string of unconscious and bleeding, but hopefully alive, soldiers in my wake. But after taking a second to review the situation, I decided that for once, I'd err on the side of cooperating with an authority figure. Who says you can't teach an old dog new tricks?

I looked her in the eye, this time without any magic tricks, and said, "I'm looking for a quiet place that someone may have been raising demons, or working with some powerful artifacts. There are a few items running around Memphis right now that need to be disposed of somewhere safe, like the bottom of the ocean, or the moon."

"Are these anything like the trinkets you were collecting last year?"

I sat down. "Are you asking me if these are Implements of Archangels? No, they aren't. They...lean toward the opposite end of the spectrum. That's why I don't want them just bouncing merrily along out where anyone can get hold of them. Bad things tend to happen."

"Like what?"

"Like a dozen hellhounds running through the city chasing down a father and daughter who sold their souls to the wrong guy."

"That does sound like the kind of thing we should put a stop to."

"Yeah, I agree. That's why I'm here. Someone has been throwing serious magic around, and this is the most secluded spot for twenty miles. Hell, my cell phone barely works out here."

"That's my fault. We have a jammer."

"And I don't suppose you want to give me your Wi-Fi password so I can update my Facebook, huh?"

"Not likely, no. What exactly are you looking for?"

"You see, that's how I know you're new at this, and not a vampire who just looks like a kid. Because I don't know *exactly* what I'm looking for. I might be looking for a circle where somebody summoned an Archduke of Hell. I might be looking for a clearing in the woods where someone performed a major working to find these artifacts. I might be looking for nothing at all, because there might not be anything here. I just don't know. I basically have to go to the hottest of magical hot spots until I find something that smells like the —" I snapped my mouth shut, cursing my own stupidity.

Special Agent Melissa Asshole Walston didn't let the slip go. "Like what, Mr. Harker? Do you already have one of these artifacts? Is it on your person now? No, you wouldn't carry something like that around, not if it's as powerful as you say. You must have left it somewhere secure."

I didn't bother to correct her. She didn't need to know I wandered around the tunnels under New York City with the Archangel Gabriel's book last year. "Of course it's secure."

It was, mostly. I mean, Zeek's bar was pretty secure, with a werewolf on guard duty and a djinn running the place. It would be pretty hard for anyone to get through Henry and Zeek. Now, the fact that I left the ring in a warded box on my dresser, right out where any idiot who got into my room could just pick it up...well, that was more troubling. I just had to count on Zeek being as powerful as I thought djinn were.

"Well, that's good," Walston said. "If it's as dangerous as you say, we definitely don't want it falling into the wrong hands." The look she gave me told me that mine were without a doubt some of the wrongest hands she could think of, but she wasn't going to say that while I was this close. "But unfortunately, your time here has been wasted. There have been no unusual paranormal surges or activities on the island for the past six months. Our instruments constantly monitor EMF, Infrared, UV, Infrasound, and radio and micro-waves. I assure you, the second anything larger than a squirrel sets foot on this island, I know about it."

She seemed really sure of herself, but I'd known a lot of idiots that were really confident right up until the moment they got themselves and everyone around them killed. "Yeah, but you won't mind if I just take a little peek for myself, will you? I do have certain...skills that tech just can't duplicate."

"I'm afraid I can't allow that. We have some...permanent guests here that would not benefit from interaction with humans. Nor would the humans. I'm sorry, Mr. Harker. I must insist. But I don't want to send you away completely empty-handed. Have you spoken to Raxho yet?"

"Ummm...no," I replied. "What's a Wax Ho?"

"*Raxho*," she corrected. "Raxho is one of the most powerful demon crime bosses on the Mississippi. He has a floating card game on *The Pearl*."

"What's the Pearl?"

"*The Pearl of Dixie* is an abandoned riverboat casino docked about five miles south of here, just on the Arkansas side of the river. I think. Raxho moves his boat from shore to shore, depending on which local sheriff is trying to score points with the voters by cracking down on vice. If there's something shady going on around Memphis, and it didn't happen at Zeek's, Raxho will know about it. He might not want to tell you about it, but he'll know."

I thought for a second, then nodded. "That makes sense. Whoever this guy is I'm looking for, he's going to need a lot of demonic contacts. Sounds like my next stop is a poker game."

"Then I'll have some of my men escort you out and return you to your truck."

I stood up and held out my hand. "Thanks, Agent Walston. I suppose I'm sorry for being a dick earlier."

"From everything I've heard, Mr. Harker, that's like a leopard apologizing for having spots. Don't bother, just don't ever set foot on my fucking island again, or I'll have you bound with cold iron and tossed in a lead box at the bottom of the Mississippi River."

We shook hands tentatively, and she knocked on the wall by the door. It opened, and a soldier in camo that looked barely old enough to shave stepped in. "Sanders, escort Mr. Harker back to his vehicle. No detours. If he so much as looks like he's going to try to give you the slip, shoot him in the back of the head." She motioned for me to go with the kid.

I walked to the door. "Goodbye, Special Agent Walston," I said. "I honestly hope I never see you again." Then I stepped out into the hall and pulled the door closed behind me.

As it swung shut, I was almost certain I heard her mutter, "I should be so lucky."

18

Glory lay stretched out on the hood of my truck, leaning back against the windshield with her shoes off and toes wiggling in the late morning sun. I thanked the Junior Woodchuck who brought me out of Redneck Gitmo, hopped out of the little motorized raft he'd used to get us to the riverbank, barely managing to clear the edge of the water. I probably should have tried to dive off in the deep end and get a little of the smoke, soot, sweat, and splinters washed off. After being blown up, breaking into a secure government facility, and sitting in an interrogation room for half the day, I was betting I didn't smell the freshest. Of course, that was outweighed by not knowing just what lurked beneath the surface of the mighty Mississippi near the Memphis shoreline, so I opted to stay dry and smelly as opposed to wet and smelly.

I tromped up the slight gravel incline and walked around to the driver's door. "Nice of you to come to my rescue," I grumbled, yanking open the door with a rusty screech and sliding behind the wheel.

Glory appeared in the passenger seat, her seatbelt already fastened. "You were in no danger. I was watching the whole time."

"Seriously? You were?"

"Harker, I'm your freaking *guardian* angel. I'm not your take-out angel, your porn angel, or your Victoria's Secret angel. I look out for you. It's kinda my thing. In fact, it's literally the only reason I'm on this plane of existence. So don't get all mopey because you can't see me. I'm there. I'm always there. It's like that old devotional poster old people put up in their nursing home rooms. The one about Jesus and the footsteps? You can't always see the proof of it, but I'm always with you. Even when you're an obtuse jerk and don't deserve me."

I cranked the truck, not looking at her. That was a little more than I'd ever really considered. I mean, I knew she was my guardian angel. I just didn't know she was *only my* guardian angel. I assumed she had a few clients, and someday I'd end up in a bucket of shit and she would be off dealing with somebody else's bucket of shit, and that would be all she wrote for me. *Huh. I guess I really do have backup*, I mused as I backed the truck out of the parking spot and called up a navigation program on my phone.

"According to this, we're about forty-five minutes from this casino. I need new clothes, unless you want to magic me up some clean pants?"

"Not a chance, Q. That's so not what you get a guardian angel for. Your fashion catastrophes are all your own."

I nodded and dialed in a local jazz station on the radio, then started looking for a thrift shop so I could pick up at least some jeans and a shirt with a collar. Maybe a jacket to hide my shoulder holster wouldn't be a bad idea. I assumed any security worth their salt would frisk me before I got to talk to Big Tony, or whoever the Mississippi mobster wannabe that owned the casino was called, but there was no point in advertising my bad intentions.

It was an hour and half later when I pulled my pickup into a shipyard parking lot between a Lincoln Town Car and a Porsche Cayenne. I was pretty sure my battered Ford Ranger lowered the resale value of those cars just by being in the same lot, and I found that oddly comforting. I like having nice things, but cars have always been more about transportation than status for me. I guess it comes from being raised in an era before they were really common. I still remembered people moving around by literal horsepower when I was small, which gave me a little perspective on how fleeting technology can be.

"How will we find this place?" Glory asked, looking around.

It wasn't so much an issue of finding a dilapidated and apparently abandoned riverboat casino docked at the salvage yard. It was more an issue of figuring out *which* dilapidated and apparently abandoned riverboat casino we were looking for. There were four different monstrous offerings to the gods of greed and lust bobbing merrily in the river, tethered to the Tennessee shoreline with huge chains.

I opened my Sight and looked at the boats with a magical filter over my eyes. I pointed to the farthest one from where I parked and said, "That one."

"You sure?"

"It's the only one with even a hint of magic on it, so I'd say yes."

"Anything interesting on the others?"

"Not that I can see, but there are about half a dozen people moving around on the boat next door. I can't tell if they're security, scrap thieves, or ghost hunters, but they're not giving off anything supernatural."

"Okay, then let's go get our gamble on. What's the plan? Craps? Roulette? Poker? I love poker. Humans are so bad at bluffing."

"I thought I'd hang out for a few minutes, throw a little mojo on the roulette wheel, get caught, and use that to get me hauled in front of the boss."

"Not bad," Glory said with a nod. "You're going to use your ineptitude at lying and cheating to your advantage. Way to turn your negatives into a positive, Harker."

I wasn't sure how I felt about the level of enthusiasm she was showing for my "ineptitude" at cheating, but it still felt like the quickest way to get in front of WaxOn, WaxOff, or whatever this demon's name was.

Unless I could just walk up the gangplank onto the boat and have a gorilla in a double-breasted suit walk up and say, "Mr. Harker, welcome to *The Pearl*. Please accept this voucher for some complimentary gaming chips, courtesy of the house. We do ask that you surrender any firearms at this point, and please observe our strict no magic policy while in our game rooms."

Glory and I exchanged a look, and I took the small stack of black chips from the giant security guy. I passed them over to the angel and reached beneath my coat for my pistol. It was a testament to the confidence of the security goons that none of them so much as flinched, even knowing I was about to pull out a weapon. Confidence, or stupidity. I wasn't sure which. I passed over my Glock, and a goon standing against the ship's railing off to my left spoke into a lapel mic.

"Stand down. He's complying."

Okay, so it was confidence. Made sense. I was pretty confident anytime I had a sniper backing me up, too. I dropped to one knee and handed over my Ruger backup piece, too.

"Anything else to declare, Mr. Harker?"

"Just my hands and my date," I said, putting an arm around Glory's waist and giving her a squeeze. "You don't need to search her, do you?"

"That won't be necessary, sir. Our briefing was that she was unlikely to carry mundane weapons, and anything she had, we couldn't touch." My eyes widened a little at this, and I looked more closely at the goon. Sure enough, he was a demon. His meat suit was *good*. It must have cost him, or more likely his boss, a pretty penny in currency, favors, or magic. I started to think maybe this Wax Ho was a serious dude after all, regardless of his poor choice of names.

"Now, when you say no magic, what exactly do you mean by *no* magic?" I asked.

He smiled, one of those creepy demon smiles that doesn't even come close to the eyes and lets you know that he's thinking of how much he'd like to floss his teeth with your soul. "We mean do not, under any circumstances, use magic to affect the outcome of a game. No speeding up or slowing down the roulette wheel, no tweaking the deck in blackjack, no manipulating the dice at the craps table, no using clairvoyance to read someone's hole cards at the poker table, nothing. You may, of course, use your Sight to determine if someone has active magic on themselves. You may cast any glamours you like to conceal your tells or disguise yourself from the rest of our guests. You may use any means you desire to purge alcohol from your system, or to enhance the effects of alcohol or other substances. In short, Mr. Harker, don't fucking cheat." The mild smile slipped on that last sentence, and I could tell he'd had folks ignore that last order before.

"We don't have any authorities locally that can deal with magical offenders, so any supernatural cheating must be dealt with in house. I'm sure you understand that we will not be handing anyone over to the authorities."

In other words, we won't call the cops if you cheat in our illegal casino, we'll just kill you. I thought for a brief moment about telling him that there was a whole building full of people less than an hour away who did nothing *but* deal with supernatural offenders, but as much as I would enjoy seeing Director Shaw interrogate a demon, it didn't seem like it would get me any closer to finding the artifacts, so I let it slide. For now.

I nodded to the goon squad, and they parted to let us walk across the deck and into the casino proper. The place was modeled after one of the old paddleboats that cruised up and down the Mississippi in Mark Twain's heyday. It had three large decks stacked one on top of the other.

When we stepped into the casino, we saw that the first and second deck were combined to make one massive gaming hall. The place had to be at least the size of a football field, and a good twenty feet high inside. When we stepped over the threshold, the noise hit me in the face like a hammer. From the deck, I could hear just the slightest hint of bells, pop music, and computerized coins jangling as slots hit digital jackpots. But once we were inside, the sound dampening spells no longer applied, and it was a sensory onslaught of Phish-sized proportions.

Everywhere I turned there was neon, and LEDs of all colors, and strobes, and spinning colored lights, and patterns projected on every flat surface. The lighting was brightest around the center gaming tables, and dimmer at the edges, where the slot machine junkies sat, their eyes glazed over as they pushed buttons again and again and again for hours on end, chasing the jackpot, or the free play, or whatever passed for comps in underground casinos.

I stood in the doorway for a long moment, just taking it all in and trying to keep my post-concussion symptoms from roaring back with a vengeance. I thought I was all healed up until I stepped into the digital funhouse. As I became accustomed to the din, I looked around the room, trying to determine the best place to get noticed by management.

"Roulette," Glory said in my ear.

"I can't rig the game there," I said. "I'm thinking poker. I'll have to play it clean, but I have a century of reading people to draw on. I should be able to make it pretty big pretty fast."

"Trust me, you want roulette. We won't use any magic to manipulate the game, I promise." The gleam in her eye promised mischief and quite possibly mayhem.

"What are you planning, Glory?" I asked. I started walking toward the roulette table, but I wanted to know exactly how much trouble I was about to land in.

"How do you think being a guardian angel works, Harker?" she asked, that too-sweet smile still plastered across her face.

"I have no idea. To be honest, I don't know anything about how angels work. You guys haven't exactly been my primary subject of study, you know?"

"We have very limited precognition. That's how we can see exactly how much trouble our charges are about to get into." I noticed that she didn't say "if our charges are about to get into trouble," but rather "how much trouble." Of course, if you aren't the type to get in shitloads of trouble, you probably don't need your very own heavenly babysitter.

"So you're saying…" It was dawning in my head, but I wanted to be completely sure we were on the same page before I started flinging hundred-dollar chips around.

"I'll know which numbers the wheel is going to stop on," she said, and her grin went from mischievous to downright devious. "Come on, Harker, let's go bankrupt a demon!" She took my elbow, and we walked off to cheat the demon out of his due. There's no way this didn't end up in a right donnybrook, as a leprechaun I used to drink with in Dublin always said.

19

It only took about an hour and a half before I felt the familiar tap on my shoulder. It felt more like somebody hitting me with one of those little rubber mallets the doctors use to test reflexes than a finger, and when I turned around, the reason was apparent. The owner of the finger was a solid seven feet tall and had to be on the north side of four hundred pounds, with at least three hundred of them being muscle. He was one of the biggest humans I'd ever seen, and a quick blink with my Sight told me that he was, in fact, entirely human. Just disproportionately large.

"Would you come with me, sir?" he asked. His tone was exceedingly polite, but he was taking no arguments. I didn't have to notice the bulge under his left arm to know the gun was there, but his size alone was enough to make me go with him. If I had to fight this guy, I would, and I'd win, but I wanted to make sure I had room to maneuver.

"No problem," I said, turning back to the table and sliding stack after stack of black chips across the felt to the croupier. "Color me up, please." The dealer, a friendly woman in her fifties with sandy hair and a bemused expression on her face, changed each stack of blacks into a thousand-dollar yellow chip, then exchanged the fifteen yellows into three ceramic plaques representing five grand each. I slid three black chips across the felt at her with a nod of thanks and turned around to face my escort.

"I'll cash your chips in for you, sir," the giant said as we stopped outside a door marked "EMPLOYEES ONLY." I handed over the plaques, never expecting to see that fifteen grand again. Oh well, it's not like it was my money to begin with. My escort opened the door, and Glory and I stepped into a very well-appointed office decorated in early Hieronymous Bosch.

"I'll never understand why demons spend so much time trying to get out of Hell, and the first place they get when they leave the nest, they decorate it just like their old bedroom," I mused, looking at a sculpture of contorted nude forms writhing in agony on a bed of hot coals. The office was a study in red leather and dark brown paneling, with thick carpet in muted tones of black and mottled gray. Or maybe that was just spots where the owner hadn't been able to get all the blood out.

A modest desk held pride of place, with a padded leather chair behind it. The chair was turned around to face a video wall partitioned into multiple monitors, which displayed all areas of the casino in multiple video feeds. "Welcome to *The Pearl*, Mr. Harker. I hope you have enjoyed yourself so far."

The voice was smooth, like silk on skin. Dark and rich, its tones held the promise of pleasure and power and all things men want rolled up into one package. Good thing I don't want what most men want, or I might have fallen under its spell right then. "That's a nice one," I said. "I don't think I've seen that before. Siren, maybe?"

The chair spun around, and I got my first look at the demon Raxho, in his human suit, but no less a demon for that. His grin was as predatory as it was perfectly shaped, and stretched from ear to ear, just a little too far for human comfort. "I spent some time with those ladies, yes." Raxho exuded power and control, and I could tell by the way his eyes tracked everything in the room that this was a guy who didn't miss anything that happened in his world. I resolved to stop making fun of his name, even to myself, and take him more seriously. I had a feeling if I didn't, it could get me killed.

He waved us over to the chairs in front of his desk, nice ones, not even wobbly, or lower than normal, or any of the typical power plays insecure guys do with their guest chairs. Either this guy didn't read any sleazy management books, or he was pretty confident in his abilities and his place in the world.

"Now," he said, leaning forward and unfolding his long arms from across his chest. "What brings the most famous demon hunter in the world to my little establishment? And how in the world were you able to cheat my roulette wheel so effectively?"

I smiled at him, safe in the knowledge that Glory wouldn't reveal her secret to a demon. "Well, I don't like to show my hand until the betting is done, but—"

"That would be me," Glory said from the chair beside me.

Raxho's gaze whipped over to her, and his eyes widened at the realization of exactly what she was. "You're…"

"You can call me Glory. I'm Harker's guardian."

"Angel precognition," he said with a smile. "I hadn't thought of that one. The idea that someone would bring one of The Host into a casino honestly never occurred to my security advisors."

"That happens a lot around Harker," Glory said with a little smile that may have had more smirk to it than smile. "He brings out the unexpected in every situation."

"Well, I suppose I can't be too angry. After all, you did point out a flaw in our security. That has to be worth something. But I get the impression you didn't come here just to make a quick score at my roulette table." That piercing gaze switched back over to me, and his green eyes had a little ring of red around the iris, just enough to give away his heritage.

"We're looking for someone."

"I don't run that kind of boat. I can point you to a nice escort service, but not here."

"Not that kind of someone," I said. "Somebody has been selling magical artifacts out of a little shop across town. Those artifacts are not the kind of thing that humans should have access to. We need to find the items, and the seller, and make sure that it doesn't happen again."

"You want to tell me about these artifacts?"

"Not really, but I can't really ask you for help finding them if I don't, can I?"

"Not so much, no."

"The Amber of the Garden, the Medallion of the Calf, and the Gem of Murder," Glory said before I opened my mouth again. Good thing, since I didn't know these things even had proper names.

Raxho fell back in his chair with a soft *thwump*. "All of those things are in Memphis?"

"We think so, yes," Glory replied.

"Holy shit."

"That pretty much sums it up," the angel said.

A calculating smile crept across the demon's face. "What's in it for me if I help you find these trinkets? It's gotta be worth something, doesn't it?"

I felt the heat rise in my face. That's how it always is with demons. There's always gotta be something in it for them. They can't just do anything because it's the right thing to do. I guess that's what makes them demons. I looked at Glory and said, "You know the worst thing about setting up a criminal enterprise on a boat, G?"

She knew exactly where I was going, and smiled as she said, "No, Q, I don't. What's the worst thing about setting up a criminal enterprise on a boat?"

I stood up and called power to my hands, enveloping them in a brilliant purple glow. "When some dickhead sorcerer comes into your office and tries to play the heavy, saying if you don't help him save the world by reclaiming the dangerous magical artifacts he's looking for, he'll blow a huge hole in the bottom of your boat and sink all your money to the bottom of the Mississippi River."

Glory affected a Shirley Temple-esque surprised face and clapped her hands to her cheeks. "Oh golly, Q! That would be just awful, wouldn't it?"

Raxho stood up, hands outstretched to us, palms out. "Wait, wait, wait. I never said I wouldn't help you. I just said I should be compensated for my time. I think…about fifteen grand seems fair, don't you?"

I remembered the three very attractive ceramic plaques, each worth five thousand dollars, that I handed over to the security goon when I walked in. Oh well, I was playing with house money anyway, so it's not like I really won or lost anything. I let the power dissipate, deciding that Raxho saving a little face was worth me not ripping him off. This time.

"That's fine," I said, and sat back down. "Now, do you know anything about these artifacts?"

He put on the smile that every creep that's ever been interrogated by the police has worn ever since there were police to interrogate creeps and said, "Why would you think I know anything about anything?"

"A little bird told me that you know about every shady thing that happens in this town," I replied.

"That little bird is very flattering, but unless they used their superbling overtly, I wouldn't know about it. You two are the first big cheats we've had in a while that…wait a minute." His brow furrowed as a look of intense concentration came across his face. He leaned forward and pressed a button on his phone. "Send me Terrence."

I opened my mouth to ask what was going on, but Raxho held up a hand. "I had a thought, but I need to speak to one of my employees first. Please be patient."

We waited another minute or so, then the door opened and in walked the most completely bland human I think I've ever seen. He had brown hair of medium length, a little bit of stubble, not thick enough to be called a beard, and not thin enough to be carelessness. He was about five-ten, about one-seventy, perfectly medium in pretty much all things. He was the most taupe person I'd ever laid eyes on.

"Terrence, thank you for joining us," Raxho said. "Please, come closer."

Terrence looked around, didn't see another chair, and stood beside my elbow. I didn't love having him that close and not in my clear line of sight, but I also felt like if I was threatened by Terrence the Taupe Guy, I needed to give up on the demon hunting business.

"Terrence was the dealer for a peculiar poker game a few nights ago at one of our high-limit tables," Raxho said.

"The dealer?" I asked. "I thought you rotated dealers every half hour." Most casinos do this to keep the dealers from colluding with players, and to cut down on players whining about unlucky dealers.

"Not in our biggest no-limit games," the demon said. "When we get a game that big, we have a team of two dealers who alternate as chip runner and dealer for that table, and they don't work any other games. Terrence was one of the dealers that night."

"Who's the other one?" I asked. I didn't know why he thought this game was relevant, but there was no sense in only getting half the story.

"She isn't here today," Raxho replied. "It's her week off. Tell us about the game, Terrence."

"It was weird, you know?" Terrence said, and his voice was anything but bland. He spoke with a nasally rasp that sounded like Jimmy Cagney gargling with razor blades. Ol' Terry might look boring, but he had a voice that sounded like the love child of Leonard Cohen and Tom Waits. He sounded like a guy who had seen some shit in his day.

Terrence went on. "It was a Thursday, which is the night the big game runs, and we had four people. Diamond Dave, Thibodeaux, Lucky Louise, and some LA hillbilly come up the river to show us Yankees how it's done."

"LA stands for Lower Alabama in this context," I said to Glory.

"Yeah," Terrence agreed. "This jack hole made a bunch of money down in Biloxi and wanted to show us Memphis boys how to play some cards. He had balls bigger than his brains, and Louise had done caught him chasing gutshots twice and three-barreling with air one time. She had him read like the damn *New York Times*, man. But that ain't what's weird. We get that every once in a while—some out of towner either takes a run at a big game or hits it big at the little tables and tries to move up. Usually the regulars just take his money, divide it amongst themselves, and go back to moving chips across the table. But that night was different."

"What happened?" I asked.

"About one in the morning, this dude walked in. He didn't look like much, to be honest. He was skinny, dressed like he shopped at Walmart, and his shoes weren't worth a shit. That's how you can tell if somebody's really got money—if they got good shoes. Rich people won't wear shitty shoes, and poor folks spend money everywhere else first. Anyhow. He sat down and dropped the minimum buy-in on the table. Ten grand in cash. That bought him in for one-two No Limit Hold'Em, and I figured we'd see the last of him in about two orbits. Three if he played tight."

"By one-two you mean the blinds were one hundred and two hundred?" I asked.

"Yeah, one-two. It's no-limit, so you don't really want to sit down at that game unless you got twenty grand behind, but if you get lucky, you can buy in short and do okay. I didn't expect this dude to do okay, much less do what he did."

"Let me guess," I asked. "He won?"

"Shit, son," Terrence said. "He didn't just win, he cleaned them other four *out*. He walked in there with ten large; he walked out with over a hundred fifty grand! I been dealing poker for ten years, dealt big rooms all over the East Coast, done the World Series of Poker a couple times, and some of the biggest backroom games you ain't never heard of, but I ain't never seen nobody do what that dude did. He didn't make a bad call not one time all night. He pushed when he had the nuts, he called when the other players had air, and he caught his runners when he had to fill out a flush. I dealt to him for three hours, and by the end of three hours, he had every chip on the table and a stack of hundreds behind that would choke a mule."

"Sounds like he had a little help from somewhere, huh?" I asked, looking around at Raxho and Glory.

"Yeah, but we kept somebody eyeballing him all night. We had witches, demons, vampires, werewolves, everybody we could think of come in and look him over. They smelled him, scanned him, conjured over him, looked at him with their Sight...they done everything except strip him naked and peel the skin off him. Our security director, Mistress Magdalena, she said he had an aura of great power on his right arm, but she couldn't see that it was doing anything directly, so we didn't make him take it off. We figured it was just a lucky charm."

"But it was damned *unlucky* for me," Raxho chimed in. "Ever since that night, none of the high rollers will set foot on my boat. They're saying I'm cursed, and all the whales are playing at the *Blue Bayou*, a casino docked on the other side of the river. I'm losing thousands by not having my highest rollers. I need my gamblers back, and you need to find this artifact. I think our needs might have a big intersection. What do you say, Harker? You want to hunt something *for* a demon for a change?"

20

And that's how I ended up cruising through what passed for a red-light district in West Tennessee with a grainy security camera photo taped to the dash of my pickup.

"How in the world are we going to find this guy in all this debauchery, Harker?" Glory asked, peering through the window at a cornucopia of lewd neon.

"Terrence said the guy who won big spent the whole game talking about strippers, so I guess we have two choices," I said.

"What are those, and why do I have the feeling I'm going to hate both of them?"

"Because you're not just an angel, you're a tiny bit of a prude," I said. "We can either call every strip club in Memphis and ask them if some guy with an antique bracelet is there, which will probably get us hung up on a lot and absolutely no further in our hunt than we are right now, or we can visit every strip club in Memphis looking for the asshole in question. I figure there probably aren't more than two dozen in a city this size."

"Let me guess which one you prefer." Glory's voice was dryer than the Sahara, but she didn't say anything more as I pulled into The Gentleman's EXXXpress, a concrete-block building with nothing cosmetic going for it at all. It was a low-slung stack of cinderblocks with a cheap roof on it, cheaper neon on the roof, and an even cheaper scrolling billboard out front that just said "BOOBIES" in red letters that danced across the dark plastic housing. I guess there's something to be said for managing expectations, and mine were certainly low as I walked up to the front door.

The door was locked, so I pushed the buzzer next to the knob. A small window slid open a little below eye level, and a pair of green eyes (with just enough red to let me know I was looking into the soul of a serious stoner) peered out.

"What's the password?"

I thought for a second, then decided there was only one thing it could possibly be. "Boobies."

The window slammed shut, and I heard four locks disengage from the other side of the door. I looked back at Glory, who stood about ten feet back giving me a dubious look. "I don't think the fire marshal visits very often."

"That wasn't what the look was for."

"I know."

We stepped in, and it was everything you could expect from a speakeasy topless club in the middle of the afternoon. Which is to say, dark, deserted, and more like a place to shoot up and nod off than somewhere to enjoy scintillating conversation with ladies of high moral fiber. A woman who resembled nothing so much as Aunt Bea from *The Andy Griffith Show* took twenty bucks from me in a small anteroom and pressed a button by the cash register. I heard a buzz, then a magnetic lock disengage, and we stepped into one of the most bizarre strip clubs I'd ever seen, and I spent time in Pre-War Europe, where some wild shit went down on the regular.

There was a bar along one of the short walls, a black pleather-wrapped affair with half a dozen padded stools scattered haphazardly in front of it. The surly old man standing behind the three unlabeled taps looked like he last smiled when the bar stools were new. The shelves behind the bar told the story of the place: Wild Turkey was the top shelf, and Aristocrat vodka stood proud right next to it. Even with my constitution and healing powers, I wouldn't be drinking any of the lighter fluid they were likely to serve in this joint.

All the stools but one were deserted, and that one held a thick-waisted stripper, at least I assumed the woman in a sequined thong and Motley Crüe tank top was a stripper. She had rainbow-colored hair falling limply down her back, and as I surveyed the room, she spun around on her stool to survey me right back. I was a little surprised, as much as anything could surprise me at this point, to see her holding a bowl and a spoon, then I noticed the Crock Pot on the bar next to her with a hand-lettered cardboard sign that said "CHILI - $2." I marked strip club chili down as another new experience I wasn't going to try on this trip to Tennessee.

The wall opposite the bar and the chili-eating stripper was taken up by a row of what looked for all the world like bathroom stalls, right down to the metal doors that didn't go all the way to the floor. I raised an eyebrow at this, then raised the other one when I saw the flashing LED sign over the stalls that said "V_P." I could only assume that the missing letter in this game of lecherous hangman was an "I" and that was what passed for a VIP lounge in the cinderblock boobie bazaar.

"This might be the saddest place I've ever set foot in," I murmured to Glory.

"And you were in Hell less than a year ago," she added.

"Yeah. My statement still stands. I'm pretty sure people in Hell were having more fun."

A DJ booth sat on concrete blocks in one corner of the room, and a gaunt girl who lied about her everything if she claimed to be eighteen danced on the stage in a lime-green bikini. I couldn't see a DJ, so it looked for all the world like Surly, Chili, and Bikini Girl were the only people in the place other than me and my angel. Any hope I had of catching a lead went out the window quicker than the hopes and dreams of every other sad sack who ever stepped through the doors of that place.

"May as well talk to the bartender," I said. Glory gaped at me, and I shrugged. "Come on. We paid twenty bucks to get in, we should at least make a token effort."

"Okay, but I am *not* eating that chili."

I couldn't blame her for that one. We walked up to the bar, and Chili Girl gave us a huge smile, complete with a little sliver of onion stuck to her top lip. "Hey sexy, how you doing?" she asked, her eyes firmly locked on Glory's ass.

I waited for a second, then elbowed the angel in her ribs. "Pretty sure she's not talking to me, G."

Glory started, then gave the woman a warm smile. "Oh, sorry. Hi! I'm doing...well, I guess." Suddenly Glory's face crumpled, and if you didn't know her, you'd have thought somebody just ran over her dog. "I'm lying. I'm not doing fine. I'm all messed up. It's...it's Ethan."

Chili shot me a nasty look and said, "What is he doing to you, honey? I know Tae Kwon Do. Just say the word and I'll fuck his skinny ass right up."

Glory glanced over her shoulder, then shook her head. "Not him. He's not Ethan. He's my brother, Quincy. Ethan's my, well he *was* my boyfriend, until the dirty rat took all the money I made dancing in Atlanta last month and ran off to that stupid casino!"

It all clicked into place in an instant. Without ever talking to me, Glory came up with the perfect cover story to get every soul in a ramshackle strip club on our side—the old deserted girlfriend story. Useful because so many men are, in fact, assholes, an truth that hit uncomfortably close to home as I thought about my own deserted fiancée. Glory spun a tale of abandonment and theft as old as time, and within two minutes had Chili, Surly the Bartender, and Bikini Girl all gathered around patting her on the shoulders and asking what they could do to help.

"Well, we went to the casino, and the men there were *so* helpful, but they said he left there with a bunch of money and said something about going to a gentlemen's club. Since this was the closest one to the boat, we thought maybe he came here. I mean, he ain't here now, but maybe one of you saw him? Show 'em the picture, Q." She motioned to me, and I pulled the security camera picture out of a coat pocket and passed it over to Surly.

"Yeah, I seen him. He was in here Thursday night, throwing cash around like it was water. Bought us out of all the good liquor. We usually keep a couple bottles of Makers, but he bought 'em both," Surly said. He looked at the pitiful bar display. "I ain't had time to restock yet."

"Yeah, I danced for him," Chili said. "He was fiddling with this weird bracelet or cuff or something under his sleeve and talking about how there wasn't enough lust in the room for him. Then he asked me where he could find a club with more action. I asked him how much action he was looking for, but he wasn't interested in anything off my 'special menu,' if you get what I mean." She winked at Glory, and I sincerely hoped that my cherubic sidekick did not know what the other woman meant, although given the number of decades she'd been watching out for me before I met her, she probably did. "No, he just wanted a place where there was more people. I dunno, maybe he gets off on watching. I pointed him over to The Panther. They've got three stages, and usually got about two dozen girls dancing. If he was looking for a crowd of horndogs, that'd be the place to go."

All three of the strip club workers' heads were bobbing like dashboard dolls, so it looked like we had our next destination. I dropped six twenties onto the bar and smiled at them. "Thank you all very much. I really appreciate you helping my sister out in her time of need."

"And I appreciate you putting us one step closer to whooping Ethan's sorry ass!" Glory said, turning to go. "Come on, Q. We got us a runaway boyfriend to wrangle!" I followed in the wake of the avenging guardian angel, my mouth still hanging open a little at her floor show.

We burst back into the sunny afternoon, and Glory made it all the way to the passenger seat of the truck before collapsing into peals of laughter. "Oh, sweet Father, that was *fun*! Why didn't you tell me playing these parts was so enjoyable, Harker? I would have helped you more long before now!"

I stared at her. "I...don't think you would have gotten the same enjoyment out of it before you walked a few miles in humanity's shoes, Glory. But I have to admit, that was frighteningly good. And where did you pick up that accent?"

"Harker, you've lived in North Carolina for a long time now. Charlotte might not be a backwoods burg anymore, but there are still plenty of rednecks running around the area. It's not like I had to go far from home to hear a Southern accent."

She had a point. New South or not, there was still plenty of South in North Carolina. "Okay, so I guess we're headed to The Panther?"

Glory had my phone in her hand and was tapping on the screen. She slid it into a cradle on the dash and pressed "START" on the navigation app. "Yep. Our boy is probably long gone from there, but what's the worst that can happen? We end up touring all the strip clubs in West Tennessee until we finally find him."

I had to admit, as plans went, it wasn't the worst one I'd ever heard. And this idea was a lot less likely than most to get me shot, stabbed, or set on fire. Maybe I needed to let Glory make all my plans.

21

R   emind me never to let you make the plan again," I groaned, letting my head drop against the steering wheel. "I never thought I would get tired of seeing naked women, but damn, Glory, I think I'm tired of seeing naked women."

We were sitting in the truck outside Beauregard's Pleasure Palace, the twelfth adult establishment we'd tracked our bracelet-wearing hornball to, and we still came up empty-handed. The sun was long down, my libido had been bludgeoned into insensibility by overexposure to overexposed female flesh, my gas tank was empty, the day was completely wasted, and my stomach was growling. And the day started off so well, too. I actually looked back fondly at getting blown up. At least that was exciting.

"I don't even get it. If the whole point of these artifacts is to collect souls, how does this thing work? I know a lot of guys that have lost relationships, money, even jobs because of strippers, and one guy lost his house, but how do you lose your soul?" I asked. I hadn't managed to open the door yet, a level of existential dread filling my soul with the thought of one more surgically-enhanced gold digger pretending to find me attractive. And I was almost out of cash again and really didn't want to pay strip club ATM fees. That way leads to bankruptcy.

"I don't know, Q. I don't get it, either. He's been to more than half of the clubs we've visited, but didn't linger in any of them for more than an hour or two, and most of them not on the same night. So not only do we not know how he plans to collect the souls, we just know he keeps muttering about there not being enough lust in the room, and leaving."

I sat up, then ran out of energy after that much movement and let my head bang against the back window of the truck. I heard a muffled whooping and blaring horn and opened my eyes to peer into the rearview mirror and figure out what the commotion was all about. A stretch limo was slowly cruising down the road behind us, with a pair of teenage boys hanging out of the sun roof yelling to the heavens. They let out war whoops of the young and testosterone-poisoned as the car rolled past, and I saw the words "PROM 2019" written on the back glass of the limo in big white soapy letters.

"Hey Glory, what's the single horniest place you can think of?" I asked, looking over at the angel.

"I might not be the right person to ask, Q. After all, I may have been around since the dawn of time, but I only spent about two years with working genitals. Horny isn't exactly my area of expertise."

I decided not to spend time wondering about what level of horny my guardian angel experienced when she was human, and instead focused on the matter at hand. "Well, even though I didn't grow up in this country, I've watched enough John Hughes movies to know that there is no place crammed with more lust than a high school dance."

"You think our guy is trolling proms for souls?" Glory asked. "That seems like a reach."

"Really? There are a LOT of similarities between a prom and a strip club." I started ticking them off on my fingers. "Let's start with a preponderance of cheap perfume and push-up bras. Then there's the rampant hormones. Whether there should be or not, there's readily available alcohol, and both places are filled with groups renowned for poor decision-making, namely teenagers and men. One event is just teeming with more frustration than the other."

"Which is that?"

"Oh, the dance," I said. "Most guys who go to strip clubs know they aren't getting laid. The same cannot be said for most boys going to prom."

"You have watched a lot of teen movies," Glory said.

"When you live this long, you find creative ways to keep yourself amused," I replied.

"Tell me about it." Her world-weary sigh reminded me that she'd been watching humanity be stupid for a lot longer than me, and only had mass media for a little over a hundred years. I couldn't touch her level of ennui if I tried.

"So what's the plan? We canvass every prom in Memphis looking for a pervert with a magic bracelet?" she asked.

"Is it really any crazier than going to every topless club in town looking for him?"

"Good point." She pulled a tablet out of her bag and started tapping on the screen. A few seconds later, she looked over at me. "I've got good news, and I've got bad news. Which do you want first?"

"Let's start with the bad news?"

"There are fifteen proms taking place tonight and tomorrow night."

"Ugh. What's the good news?"

"There are only fifteen this weekend. Next weekend there are three dozen within an hour of here."

I let my head hit the steering wheel again. "Okay," I said, my face pointed at my knees. "Let's go to school."

I stepped out of the truck and held out my arm to Glory, who just looked down her nose at me. "You know this is a *formal*, right?" She was magically decked out in a very nice strapless dress made of some iridescent green fabric that stopped a little below her knee, just high enough to show off the matching three-inch heels and the calves that went with them. I was still wearing my smoke-stained clothes I got blown up in twelve hours earlier.

I looked down at the tattered jeans and They Might Be Giants tour shirt and called up a little power. *"Glamourfage,"* I whispered, and released energy into the air around me. Suddenly, I was decked out in a spotless tux with tails, complete with top hat. I kept my Doc Martens visible, though. I guy has to hold on to some piece of his personality.

"Good enough?" I asked a frowning Glory.

"Too much."

I waved a hand, and the tux turned into a sedate charcoal gray pinstriped suit, still with my Docs. "Better? Now I'm dressed like a banker."

"That's exactly what we need to look like, Harker. A couple of parent volunteers here to chaperone the dance. Which is what we're doing, after a fashion."

"Yeah, except we don't give a shit who's spiking the punch or feeling up their date on the dance floor, and we're a lot more concerned about accidental demon summoning."

"I bet if those soccer moms knew it was a real thing, they'd be plenty concerned about accidental demon summoning," Glory argued. She had a point. Out of all the people I'd told about demons, none of the ones who believed me were ever unconcerned. That's because they were usually about to get eaten by something they thought didn't exist, but her point was still valid.

We walked up the long sidewalk to the school, a monument to 1980s prison architecture, complete with cyclone fencing around the perimeter, and I held the door for her. She gave me a surprised nod, and I decided now was not the time to remind her that I was raised among the upper middle class of English society back when there were things like English society and an upper middle class. I have great manners, I just usually don't drag them out for anyone to see.

We glamoured our way past the kids tearing tickets and moved into the gym to see if anyone was trying to suck souls out through the teens' supercharged libidos. The gym was massive, the kind of shrine to athletic endeavors that could house five thousand basketball fans easily. Every inch of the place was decorated with streamers, glitter, and LED lights softly circulating through a set of preprogrammed colors. There was the requisite disco ball casting little dots of light all over everything, and dozens of round tables scattered around the perimeter for the tired or unpopular to recover or while away the night.

My feet thudded onto wood, and I looked down at the little arched bridge that ran over a faux river by the door. A flash of light blinded me for a moment, and only Glory's hand on my arm kept me from yanking the pistol out of the back of my pants and shooting whatever was coming after us. Good call on her part, since the only thing coming at us was a portly man with a salt and pepper beard holding a massive camera rig.

"You can order prints and digital photos of your special night from my website tomorrow morning," he said, passing me a business card.

"Do I look like a teenager?" I snarled at him.

"Look around, pal," he shot back. "Most of these kids look like they're twenty-five. Besides, a lot of the hottie teachers like your girl there like to have pictures of themselves all dressed up. What does she teach? Home Ec?"

Glory's eyes blazed and she looked at the douche photographer with murder on her face as she said, "I teach calculus and physics, asshole. Haven't you ever seen *Hidden Figures?* Women even get to use computers nowadays." Then she swept past him and made a beeline for the refreshment table.

Nothing about the place made my Spidey-sense tingle, so I dropped my Sight over my regular vision to take a peek in the supernatural spectrum. Wow. So there was *definitely* something going on at this dance because almost every single person radiated some level of magic, from a light dusting to a few kids who lit up like neon billboards. Most of the glow seemed to come from two places: the refreshment line and one table near the edge of the dance floor.

None of the magic smelled like demons, and it didn't look like any kind of attack or harmful magic I'd ever seen, so I figured Glory wasn't going to run into anything she couldn't handle at the punch bowl. I meandered through the sea of writhing youth and made a big

137

arc to end up just a little behind the table where most of the magical energy was concentrated. It was hard to focus on their conversation with the music blaring, but a whispered filtering spell and the bass line dropped to merely a dull roar and I was able to eavesdrop.

One girl, a stereotypical goth kid with long black hair, pale makeup, and more eyeliner than an eighties metal band, leaned over to talk to another kid, this one sporting dreadlocks with sparkly tinsel wrapped around them and a corset that kept her from sitting back in her chair.

"It's not working," Goth hissed.

"Give it some time. It hasn't even been an hour," Corset replied.

"This is boring," chimed in a third girl, a pixie-ish type with pink hair shooting out from her head in all directions and a purple tulle skirt sparkling with glitter in the dance floor lights.

"Give it time," Corset said. "The Goddess doesn't work on our timetable, she works on her own. Besides, the old man at the magic shop said it might take as long as two hours. Why else did we get here so early? It sure wasn't to watch these lame assholes grind on each other."

"So why did you get here early?" I asked, pulling out a chair and sitting down at the table with the startled girls. "Because if you didn't want to watch these lame assholes grinding on each other, I have to assume that you did something stupid. And judging by the amount of magic on these kids before and after they visit the refreshment table, I'm guessing you spiked the punch with something a little stronger than bottom shelf vodka."

"Who the fuck are you, pervert?" Corset said, starting to stand. I slapped a hand on her shoulder and pressed her down into her chair, giving myself a little mental pat on the back for taking the chair next to the one most likely to be the leader.

I called up a little power and let it leak out in the form of a purple glow from my eyes. "I'm the motherfucker that's going to make sure your graduation party takes place in the Ninth Circle of Hell if you don't answer every one of my questions right fucking now. Now what did you little idiots do?"

22

Pink Hair squealed a little, bounced out of her chair, and ran off toward the nearest exit. Goth Girl leaned back in her chair, crossed her arms over her chest, and glared at me, making me very happy I never had kids. Corset, however, stood up and started waving her hands through the air and chanting. She wasn't actually casting a spell, at least not any that I'd ever heard, just calling on someone called The Blessed Mother to protect her and sanctify her body to her service, whatever that meant. She was calling up less power than a park bench, so I leaned over to Goth and asked, "Does she do this often?"

Goth rolled her eyes at me so hard I'm surprised they didn't pop out. "Dude. Like, all. The. Time. Pop quiz in Trig? Call on the Goddess. Extra homework in US History? Ask the Goddess for guidance. Can't decide whether or not these socks are cute enough for those shoes? Beseech the Goddess for her blessings. She talks about religion more than my stepdad, and he's a Baptist preacher. It gets old, lemme tell you."

I stifled my laughter and said, "You might want to tell her to calm down a little. People are starting to stare."

"That's kinda the point. She's the middle kid, so not a whole lot of attention at home, so she does some weird shit to get noticed at school. If she can do something to get people talking about her on Monday, she's in."

"Is that why she spiked the punch?" I guessed.

Goth's eyes widened just a hair, then she nodded. "Yeah. She got this potion from a creepy old store over in the industrial part of town. Said it was supposed to lower inhibitions and make people reveal their true feelings. I think she's hoping one of the football team will come out of the closet in the middle of prom or something."

"Would that be so tragic?" I asked. "I mean, it is the twenty-first century."

"And it's still Tennessee, so it might as well be 1920. Nobody would kick his ass or anything, but he probably wouldn't be on the team anymore. And nothing will fuck up your social standing in high school like being different."

"Says the girl with Robert Smith's makeup," I said.

"Who?"

I didn't bother explaining. If she wore that much kohl eyeliner and didn't listen to The Cure, it wasn't on me to educate her. I looked up at Corset, who was still waving her hands in the air to absolutely no effect. Even the three or four people that had been watching her were back to dancing or making out, so I decided to put an end to the farce. "It's not working," I said, just loud enough to be heard over the music.

Corset ignored me, focusing on her "spellcasting." I called up a tiny bit of power and flicked a little ball of energy at her nose. A tiny spot of purple light burst across her face like a soap bubble, and she dropped her hands. "Did you just put a curse on me?"

I held my hand to my ear, feigning deafness. She frowned and stepped closer. "DID YOU JUST PUT A CURSE ON ME?" she said, very slowly and distinctly.

"I couldn't hear. I'm not stupid," I said. "And no, I didn't put a curse on you. I just wanted to get your attention."

"Then what was that?" she asked.

"What was what?" I made my eyes as big as possible and put on my best innocent look. I've been told that my best innocent look falls somewhere between Charles Manson and Hannibal Lecter on the creepy scale, so I wasn't at all surprised that Corset didn't look at all relieved.

"What did you do to me?"

"Why don't you have a seat? I'll explain it, but I'd rather not shout."

She gave me a long look, then sat down. I watched in amusement as she tried to slump down in her chair like Goth and hit the grumpy teen slouch, but her corset wouldn't let her, so she had to sit up straight. "Okay, I'm sitting, Now, what did you do?"

"I flicked a little ball of magic at your nose," I said.

"I know that, but what did you *do*?"

It was my turn to feel superior and treat her like the idiot. "I. Flicked. Your. Nose. With. Magic."

She opened her mouth to say something, probably something rude, but I held up a finger. "That's it. That's all I did. I called up a little bit of magic, and I threw it at you. I needed to get your attention, and you were pretty wrapped up in your prayer, or your meditation, or whatever. So I booped your nose."

"Spell," she said primly. "The word you're looking for is 'spell.'"

"Not if I'm referring to you waving your hands around and mumbling to yourself. I think it's more likely the words I'm looking for are 'psychotic break.' You weren't doing anything. That wasn't a spell, you're not a witch, and you don't have a magical bone in your body. You can learn some things, anybody can. But it will be hard, and you'll never be particularly powerful. In almost every case, it will just be easier for you to do something the mundane way than it will be to do it with magic. Sorry." I added the last bit because I saw her face start to crumple, and I didn't want to deal with interrogating a crying teenager.

She stiffened her upper lip, almost visibly, and curled it into a sneer. "And how exactly would you know, old man? I suppose this is the part where you tell me you're a wizard?"

"Sure, we can use that term if you like. It keeps the terminology clean. I don't like labels, myself, but whatever."

She stared at me. "You're serious."

"Yeah," I replied. "What do you think made the glowy eyes? Gas? Because that's not how that works. And the whole flicking your nose with magic thing? Kinda hard to do if I don't have any magic."

She looked skeptical, but the logic I was putting out was pretty hard to refute. "Okay, Mr. Wizard—"

"That's a different guy," I said, thinking back to the old black-and-white TV days.

"What?"

I stopped trying to use pop culture references on children more than a century younger than me and motioned for her to go on.

"Okay, Magic Dude, what do you want with us? Because we're not into that tantric stuff." Corset cocked an eyebrow at me like I was supposed to be impressed, or maybe shocked, that she knew about tantric magic.

I wasn't. "Good. Because I'm not into jailbait." I left off the fact that they were about the right age to be my great-grandkids. "I want to know what you put in the punch, how to get rid of it, and who gave it to you. Then I want you to swear not to mess around with magic you don't understand because it looks like you got lucky this time and didn't do anything that will get your soul filleted by a demon from now until Judgement Day, and I'm pretty sure you'd prefer there wasn't a next time."

"You're just trying to scare us," Goth said.

"You're damn right I am," I replied. I leaned forward. "Look, kid. Magic isn't something you want to screw around with. It's not some-thing you can turn on and off like a faucet. It's more like a raging river that you can dam up for a time, but it always finds a way to get loose. And when it does, it's pure chaos. Magic can do anything you can imagine, but that also means it can do anything the worst people you can think of can imagine. If that doesn't scare the shit out of you, then you're too stupid to live anyway, and if we're all lucky, you just get yourself killed when you stick your finger in the mystical light socket again."

Corset's eyes blazed, but Goth put a hand on her arm. "Listen to him, Ruthie. He's not messing around."

"How do you know?" Corset asked.

Goth looked me straight in the eyes, a braver act than she knew, and said, "Look at him. He's seen some shit. I've seen that look on my uncle's face. The one that did three tours in Afghanistan. He looks like that when he remembers some of the bad things he saw over there."

Corset gave me a long look. "Okay. If you're serious, then I'll tell you what you want to know about the magic shop. But I'm not promising to give up Wicca."

"I'm not asking you to," I said. "I've got no problem with Wicca. It's a perfectly fine religion, less harmful than most of them. Do all the rituals you want. Dance naked under the full moon whenever it's warm enough if you want to. Bless the shit out of the harvest and burn all the candles and sage you like. Just don't fuck around with the real magic. If it feels like it's doing something, it's probably not going to end well for you."

"So you're sayin' Wicca isn't magic?" Goth asked.

"I'm saying it's not magic like I do magic. There's power in their rituals, just like there is in all belief systems. It's every bit as much magic as Communion or any other religion. But what I do is different. Neither of you have a particular gift for it, so you shouldn't have any trouble avoiding the real stuff, as long as you don't go looking for it. And if you do..." I let my voice trail off and ran a little purple energy back into my eyes. "Well, let's just say that dabblers sometimes have to be taken care of."

"Oh, for Dad's sake, Harker, stop trying to scare the poor girls." Glory pulled out a chair and sat down beside me. "I'm Glory. I'm an angel. If you tell us everything we want to know, and promise not to screw around with putting love potions in the punch again, I'll show you my wings. How does that sound?"

Goth's eyes got huge, like a girl in an anime. "Seriously? You're an angel? A real one?"

"Yep. Been to Heaven and everything. And he's right." She jerked a thumb at me. "The kind of magic he messes with is bad news. It leaves scars. If you can stay away from it, you're better off."

I thought about that for a second, and the truth of what she said hit me like a jackhammer. If I'd never touched the magic the first time, how different would my life have been? Would I have lived a mostly normal life? I would still have my vampire blood, but would I have died at the normal time? Would any of the people I cared about died if I had just left well enough alone?

That was not a question to be asking myself in the middle of a case, especially not one taking place in a high school gymnasium. There are places specially designed for that kind of deep thinking, and they're called bars.

"So," Glory went on. "Who sold you the potion? It won't work, by the way. I purified the punch. Took out the booze while I was at it, too."

"Jesus, Glory," I said. "You're a real buzzkill."

"Angel, remember? One of us has to follow a few of the rules."

"Fair enough." I turned back to the girls. "Okay, kids, spill it."

And spill they did. Ten minutes later, we were out the door, no further along in our search, but with a description of the magic shop owner who sold them the "truth serum," and an empty vial that I could scan for magical signatures and hopefully track back to the bracelet or one of the other artifacts. I figured worst case, maybe it would lead us to the shopkeeper and we could beat some answers out of him.

I had no idea what the worst case really looked like, but I was about to find out.

23

W ell, that was a bust," I said as we walked out of yet
another prom.
"Yeah," Glory replied. "I guess it was wishful think-
ing, but when we found those girls right off the bat, I hoped we would
be able to stumble onto our guy just as easily."

That hadn't happened, of course. What had happened was me and
Glory wearing through a fistful of high school dances, dodging
parents, principals, and puking prom queens for three hours en route
to a bad case of tired feet and throbbing eardrums. I guess they're
right—it was too loud, and I was certainly too old.

"This sucks," I said, getting into the truck and turning over the
tired engine. My truck sounded like I felt—old and worn out. Just like
me, the old pickup had a few too many miles on it and more dents in
the bumpers than was exactly healthy. But like me, it kept plugging
along. "What's next?"

"There are five more dances tonight, and more tomorrow night,"
Glory said, pulling the door closed with a rattle. "Why do you drive
this heap of junk, Harker? I know you have money. You own the
building you lived in when we were in Charlotte. You haven't gone
bankrupt in half a year."

"I just don't like to spend money on cars. That's Luke's thing. Daisy gets me where I'm going, and we have an understanding." I patted the dash lovingly, like I would a vehicle I'd had for significantly more than six months.

"You have an understanding with your junker pickup truck?" Glory looked skeptical.

I understood. It's not everyone who can easily comprehend the relationship between a man and his truck. I finally let my smile crack through. "Yeah, we have an understanding. She doesn't break down on the side of the road, and I don't drive her rusty ass into the Mississippi. I just haven't cared enough about a car since I've been here to need anything better."

To be honest, the first couple of months after I left Charlotte, and everything good in my life, behind, I hadn't cared about much of anything. It was just a few weeks before Glory showed up that I pulled myself out of the depths of self-pity and tried to get back to at least pretending to give a shit about living.

"So what's the plan, boss?" Glory asked, snapping me out of my reverie before I went too far down the rabbit hole of depression and regret.

"We've got time to hit one more tonight. Let's see which one's closest." I pulled out my phone and opened up a navigation app. The nearest school on our list of potential targets was about twenty minutes away, and across the river in Arkansas. "I dunno, Glory. The closest one is in West Memphis. I think our asshole would stay a little closer to the city center."

"Why?" she asked. "He's already shown he likes the riverboat casinos, why wouldn't he go across to the other side for a little recreational murder?"

I didn't have a good answer, so I just put the truck in gear and drove. Glory flipped on the radio, but I snapped it off again.

"Hey! I like that song!"

"That's what I was afraid of," I said. "We are not riding through Memphis, Tennessee, one of the greatest blues towns in history, with Katy Perry blasting through my pickup truck."

"You love Katy Perry, Harker," she protested.

"You're not wrong," I agreed. "But it's a matter of propriety. There's a time and a place for everything. And this," I said as I slid a CD into the dash, "is a time for the King."

The opening riff of "Jailhouse Rock" filled the cab, and we laughed our way to the next dance.

I could feel the magic the second I stepped out of the truck. "This must be the place," I said.

"No shit, Sherlock," Glory said. "What gave it away? The wave of energy that almost knocked you down?"

"Yeah, that pretty much did it," I said. "We've only got half an hour before the dance ends. If our guy hasn't done his thing yet, he will soon." We hurried up the walk toward the school, yanking the front doors open.

A skinny kid with an ill-fitting suit and bad acne stood up as we walked in. "Sorry, folks. The dance is for students only. The radio station's Second Chance Prom is next weekend. And it's at the Peabody, so you're way off."

I didn't say anything. I just called up a little power and slammed him in the chest with it, shoving him back into his chair and his chair backward onto the floor. Glory and I never broke stride, peeling right around the ticket table and following the sounds of Vanilla Ice down a long cinderblock hallway.

"I mentioned I hate the way Americans build schools, didn't I?"

"Only about, let's see…six times tonight, Harker. Once per school, except for the third one, where you said it twice."

"Well, that place was particularly prison-esque. It's like these people don't want their kids to like anything about school. Look at this place! There are hardly any windows, the colors are disgusting, and the flooring looks like the kind of tile you'd put in a bathroom. If you hated yourself and everyone who would ever use your toilet."

"Next, you're going to start bitching about the fluorescent lighting and I'm going to have to ban you from ever watching home improvement shows again," Glory said. "Now can we focus? Just a little?" The entrance to the gym stood in front of us at the end of the long hallway. Two sets of double doors flanked a huge trophy case, decorated for the night in streamers and glitter, with a banner hanging down in front of it that said, "Welcome Pirates to your Dream Voyage!"

"I'm gonna go out on a limb here and say that the school mascot is a pirate?" Glory asked.

"Either that, or someone has confused the prom with a hacker convention. But I don't think they play Vanilla Ice at hacker conventions."

"I didn't think they played Vanilla Ice anywhere anymore."

"Retro is in, apparently," I said. "Can you get any kind of bead on our guy? There's a *lot* of magic pouring out those doors. I'm afraid if I go in there with my Sight open, it'll overload me and I won't be able to see shit in either spectrum."

"I'll take a look," she said, then blinked out of view. She popped back less than a second later, but it wasn't a clean disappear/reappear thing like she'd done to me hundreds of times. This time she came back looking for a second like she was made of static, and when she solidified beside me, she almost fell over.

I caught her around the waist and held her up, suddenly worried about what the hell we'd gotten ourselves into. Glory wasn't an Archangel, but she had some mojo. If something was able to knock her loopy in that short a time, we might not be able to take it down.

"What is it?" I asked. "Demon? Angel? Worse?"

"Worse," she said. "Far, far worse."

"Well, what is it? I don't have much with me in the way of weapons, but I bet we can dig up some salt or other ingredients in the cafeteria to use as spell components." I put one of her arms over my shoulders and started to lead her up the hallway, back the way we came. I was pretty sure I'd seen a sign for the cafeteria near the entrance.

"It's...Harker, it looks like an orgy."

I stopped. There was no way I heard her right. "Are you sure you said what you meant to say?" I asked.

"Yes, I meant orgy."

"Not to be funny, Glory, but do you even know what an orgy looks like? I mean, I'm thinking your education might have been lacking in certain areas."

"I've seen a lot of Hieronymous Bosch paintings, Harker. And you have high-speed internet. I know what an orgy looks like. And I'm pretty sure what's going on in that gym is either a full-blown orgy, or it's about to be."

"That can't be good," I said. "They're...kids. They shouldn't even be thinking about...well, they're kids, they probably don't think about anything else, but they damn sure shouldn't be *doing* anything about it, much less in the middle of the school gymnasium." I don't have the American sensibility toward sex, which borders on prudish at its most liberal. I was raised to pretty much do whatever you like, just don't scare the horses. And people certainly came of age much younger in my time. But nothing about the idea of a few hundred randy teenagers re-enacting their favorite games of naked Twister seemed like a good idea to me.

"We've gotta get in there and stop it," I said. "Can you stand?"

"Yeah, I'm good. It just surprised me, that's all. And Harker?"

"Yeah?"

"I didn't see the wielder, but I certainly *felt* that bracelet. There is an artifact in there, and it's working overtime."

"That's probably what's causing the orgy," I said. "Well, that and the whole being a teenager thing." We didn't need spell components, we needed speed, so we skipped the side quest to the cafeteria and marched down the hall toward the sound of music. As we reached the doors to the gym, I felt what Glory was talking about. The power was palpable, almost visible as it coursed through the building. It rolled over me, and I felt...well, to be honest, I felt horny as hell. I felt like I wanted to fuck pretty much everything, and I'd be perfectly content to murder anything that got in the way of my pleasure. I took the sensations and choked them down, getting myself under control and whispering a quick spell of warding.

"Holy shit," I murmured.

"Yeah, exactly," Glory agreed.

"We gotta get in there. If it affected me that much, I hate to think what it will do to a bunch of teenagers with shitty impulse control." I flung the doors open before Glory could make any wisecracks about my own shitty impulse control and stepped into a scene out of a mother's worst nightmare and a pornographer's wildest dreams.

There were bodies everywhere. People were making out on every horizontal surface, and a fair number of vertical ones. I saw at least half a dozen tables overturned by the vigorous writhing of people on top of them, and that did little or nothing to dissuade the couples from their...well, their coupling. Most of them weren't actually having sex yet, but there were a lot of people on a lot of laps that I couldn't really be sure about, and everyone had most of their clothes on, but there was definitely a lot of grinding, humping, moaning, kissing, licking, and plenty of other things going on.

The place looked like something out of a cheesy movie version of a sex club, with red lights flashing and moving over everything, strobe lights going off, and Nine Inch Nails blaring through the speakers. "That's all I needed tonight," I shouted to Glory.

"What?"

"Watching a bunch of teenagers hump like goats while Trent Reznor tells the world he wants to fuck somebody like an animal."

"We've got to cut this off, Harker," Glory yelled over the pounding bass line.

"Yeah, I know. I can feel the magic building. I don't want to know what happens when it reaches a crescendo."

"If it works anything like the ring was supposed to, it's going to harvest the souls of all these people," Glory said, waving a hand around the room. There had to be four hundred people in there, all in various stages of foreplay and undress.

"Okay," I said. "Let's see if this gets their attention." I raised both hands over my head, called up enough power to make my magic-shrouded fists glow brighter than the stage lights, and shouted *"Disperire!"* at the top of my lungs. Purple light streaked from my upraised hands toward the DJ booth, striking the sound board and turning it into nothing more than a shower of molten plastic and shattered metal.

The sound shut off abruptly, and everyone in the room froze in place. The DJ picked himself up from where the explosion hurled him, and I got my first look at the bracelet glowing crimson on his left wrist. He pointed that hand at me and shouted, "He shut off the music! He wants to make you stop! Get him! Kill him!"

The eyes of every man, woman, and student in the gym glowed with the same red as the bracelet, and they all turned as one to glare at me. Then they surged toward me, and I knew I'd just found worst case.

24

You know we can't kill them, right?" Glory said to me.

"I don't want to kill them, but I sure as hell don't want them to kill me," I replied. A couple hundred angry teenagers and about a dozen chaperones were advancing on us, their pace slow and determined. They looked like a pack of zombies creeping across the polished gym floor, disjointed and shambling.

"They aren't in control."

"I get that, Glory. The DJ's driving them somehow. I'll go take him out. You keep the kids from tearing the building down around our heads while I do."

"Not a problem. But…where did he go?"

I looked to the DJ booth. "Shit." She was right. The DJ was gone. A few seconds before, he'd been standing behind the turntables wearing Elton John glasses and a light-up jacket with LEDs blinking down the sleeves. Now there was nothing there but empty air. "I'll find him. You try to keep the horde occupied."

"Got it."

I dropped my Sight down over my eyes, and a red light blazed from behind the DJ stand. "Gotcha, assclown," I muttered, then started off in that direction. A forty-something man in a tan sport coat, his belly bulging out over his belt, stepped in my path, a red gleam in his eyes and a little hint of drool running down his face.

I didn't break stride as I dropped him with a shot to the jaw. He went down like a ton of bricks, and I glanced down to make sure he was breathing. He was, so I kept up my pursuit. I heard repeated thumps behind me as Glory beat up teenagers, but I knew she was going a lot easier on them than I would.

"Come out, come out, wherever you are," I called in a singsong voice as I passed the DJ booth. Nothing visible, so I looked through the supernatural spectrum again. I spun around in a circle, looking for the telltale crimson light, and finally caught sight of it around the corner of a stack of bleachers pushed back to the wall. "Got you, asshole," I whispered, switching back to mundane vision.

Three prom goers were closing on me, snarling with rage at my impromptu music critique. I gathered my legs under me and sprang into the air. I leapt twenty feet over them, leaving my attackers to slam together and go down in a jumble of arms and legs. I was at the bleachers a breath later and slipped into the narrow space behind the stacked metal seats.

"Ollie Ollie Oxen-free," I called, then paused. "I have no idea what that even means." I changed gears. "Hey, asshole! Get out here before I get pissed off and decide to hurt you."

"You threw lightning at me!" The voice came from about midway down the row, but I couldn't get a good line of sight on him to blast his ass to pieces.

"You turned a high school dance into a fetish party!"

"I just gave them the freedom to do what they really wanted all along," he called back, and it sounded like the voice came from a little farther away now. I pushed further into the confined space, glad for once that my weird genetics kept me trim.

"Look, pal. I just need the bracelet. Nobody needs to get hurt." I tried to soften my voice, make it less intimidating.

"Fuck you!" Okay, maybe the soft-sell ship sailed when I threw magic at his face. That's fine, I suck at polite persuasion anyway.

"I'm taken, sorry," I called back. "Why don't you just come out and we can talk about this. You can give me the bracelet, I can punch you until my hand hurts, and you can pass out. That sounds fair, right?"

"Fuck you!" As bad guys go, this one was not winning any points for originality.

"You gotta work on your witty repartee, pal. How are we going to have epic Spider-Man battles if you won't say anything but fuck you?"

"Fuck you, asshole!"

"That doesn't count as a new line." I was about two-thirds of the way through the bleachers and couldn't see my quarry ahead of me anymore. He must have already slid out the other side. I pressed on. "Come on, dude. We both know how this ends. Let's cut out all the chasing and get right to the punching."

"I said, fuck you!" The voice came from a lot closer, right on the other side of the stacked-up bleachers now, and as he spoke, the whole mass of metal creaked and groaned, and I felt the space around me shrink. "Crush him! Don't let him stop the party!"

Shouts erupted from the other side of the bleachers, and I could hear fists banging on the metal around me. The collapsed bleachers were going to turn into a sheet steel coffin if I didn't get out of there. I tried to call power, but the din of people hammering on metal and screaming at me blew any hope I had of concentration. The pressure on my ribcage got greater, and my space grew tighter and tighter, until finally, just before I turned into a greasy spot behind a wall of metal and used chewing gum, I gathered my scattered will and yelled *"IMPETU!"* at the top of my compressed lungs.

A wave of pure force shot out from me in all directions, and the screech of metal was nearly deafening as the bleachers reversed course and flew out from the wall. Bodies, supports, and folded bench seats flew back as my magic slammed into the kids trying to kill me and ripped the wall of metal from their hands. The metal opened up in front of me like a twisted flower, and I stepped through, scanning the fallen bodies in front of me for the DJ. I spotted him about ten feet away, sitting on his butt in the middle of what used to be a round banquet table but now looked a lot more like a box of varnished toothpicks.

Bodies littered the gym floor like bowling pins after a drunken league night, and more than one dress or tux was showing the telltale blooms of bloodstains. I was pretty sure I was responsible for blowing more than one security deposit. I bent over and rested my hands on my knees, gasping for breath while I kept my head on a swivel. The fire seemed to have gone out of the room, since no one rushed to attack. I saw Glory across the room thump a stocky kid on the tip of the head with the butt of her sword, then she was standing alone in a darkened gym. Stage lights and disco ball reflections still sparkled all over us, making strange shadow dance across the wreckage.

"*Lumos*," I said, opening my hand to the sky like I was tossing a ball underhand. A globe of white light coalesced in the air and floated to the ceiling, dispelling the last of the prom night magic and casting a cold blue-white light across the gym, or what was left of it.

The place looked like a bomb went off in the middle of an orgy. Aside from the shrapnel I created, there were people lying everywhere in varying states of undress, some like the DJ lying in the shattered remains of tables that looked like they hadn't been powerful enough to withstand their vigorous coupling. At least a dozen kids lay unconscious in front of the bleachers, obviously part of the mob that tried to crush me, but there were at least that many scattered around the nearby floor that looked like they had just fucked themselves insensate, or worse.

I stalked to the splintered table, bent down, and hauled the DJ up by his no-longer-blinking LED jacket. "What the fuck were you thinking?"

He looked at me, his eyes rolling wildly in his head, and just laughed. It was the ululating cackle of a truly shattered mind, and I worried that I'd never get any useful information out of him. I looked at his wrist, where the bracelet glowed with an unholy fire. I reached down to snatch it off his wrist, or maybe to snatch his wrist off the end of his arm, but the circle of metal sizzled and scorched my palm.

"Ow, goddammit!" I jerked my hand back, and the skinny bastard wriggled free of my grasp.

"Can't catch me, I'm the gingerbread man!" he yelled in a singsong voice as he skipped through the trail of destruction across the gym. He made it almost halfway to the far door before he ran into Glory's outstretched forearm and clotheslined himself. The little bastard sprawled flat on his back and just lay there, giggling up at my floating globe of light.

"What the fuck is wrong with him?" I asked as I got to Glory's side and looked down. "Seems like the lights are on, but nobody's home."

"Oh, I'm home, alright," he said, rolling to his hands and knees. He got to his feet and dusted himself off. "I'm home, and I've already won! You didn't know you were doing me a favor, did you?" He held up his arm in front of his face and shook it, making the bracelet swing around his arm like a tiny magical hula hoop.

"What the fuck are you talking about, asshole?" I asked, reaching for the bangle. I hissed and jerked my hand back as the metal seared my hand. "Owww!" The bracelet, which looked like a snake eating its own tail, glowed and writhed like a living thing, and its amber eyes flashed a radiant yellow, then grew brighter and brighter as we stared at it.

"Harker, get down!" Glory yelled, knocking me to the floor in a flying tackle. I sprawled on my back, but I saw nothing but white feathers and yellow light as Glory spread her wings over my entire body, making a shield over me from whatever the bracelet was throwing off. I heard a hum that grew into a high-pitched buzz, then a shriek like metal fingernails down the world's largest chalkboard, a cacophony of horrific noise that split the air for long seconds until finally a huge thunderclap rent the air, and even with Glory's wings covering my face, I was flash-blinded from the intense yellow light and felt a huge blast of power wash over us.

Then it was over. Just as quickly as it began, it was over. Silence fell like a curtain, and I looked up into Glory's face, disturbingly close to mine. "Hey, Glory, you...might want to get off of me now."

No answer. I pulled back a little and saw that her eyes were closed. She'd passed out, either from the sound, the light, or the pressure wave, but something definitely took her completely out of the fight.

"Shit." I pushed up as gently as I could and rolled the unconscious angel over onto her back, careful not to put too much pressure on her wings. Her eyes didn't even flicker open as I laid her down on the hardwood floor.

I looked around, trying to get a bead on the assclown with the bracelet. The gym looked like a damn bomb went off, and not just where I blew the bleachers apart. There was a crater where I'd last seen my buddy the DJ, and it went all the way down to the foundation and through it to the dirt below. Splintered wood, twisted conduit, and shattered concrete lay in a circle around a four-foot pit with a very dead DJ lying in the bottom of it, the arm where the bracelet had hung blown completely off. It wasn't just severed, it was *gone*. I saw nothing but a chunk of bone sticking out of his shoulder, and a few scraps of meat lying around the bottom of the crater. There was no sign of the bracelet.

"Fuck." I turned around in a circle, taking stock of the damage. The place was fucked, to put it mildly. There were bodies strewn everywhere, and I couldn't tell how many of the promgoers were killed by the blast, or my escape from my steel prison, or just screwed themselves to death in a frenzy of hormones and sweat. I looked at the wreckage through my Sight, but there was nothing to see. No trace of magic anywhere, just death and destruction in all directions. Whatever magic the DJ had wielded, it vanished with the artifact.

"Harker?" Glory's voice came from the floor behind me.

I turned and knelt by her side. "I'm here."

"I don't think we won this one."

"No, Glory, I think it's pretty easy to say we can chalk this one up in the Loss column. Can you walk?"

"I think so."

"Good. We gotta get out of here before people show up to find out why the gym just exploded." I reached down and hauled her up, then pulled one arm over my shoulders and started walking her out of the building.

"Wait," she said.

I stopped. "What is it?"

Glory was silent for a moment, and when I looked over at her, there were tears streaming down her face. "Can you hear it, Harker?"

"Hear what?"

"All these kids...I can hear their guardian angels crying."

I blinked back my own tears and hauled her out into the night so we could chase down the motherfucker that just murdered a gym full of teenagers.

25

W hat the fuck happened back there, Glory?" I was sitting on the bed in my room back at Zeek's, my back pressed against the wall and my feet stretched out in front of me on the bed. My ears still rang from the explosion at the school, and I couldn't get the smell of charred flesh and burned hair out of my nostrils. I had a bottle of Jim Beam in one hand and a glass on the bed next to me. I hadn't touched the glass since I twisted the cap off the bottle. Sometimes you need to just go straight for the source.

"I'm not really sure, Harker, but it seems like the bracelet over-loaded somehow."

"Overloaded? On what?"

Her face was bleak as she looked at me. "Souls. It was harvesting souls, and I think there was enough death and destruction that it couldn't hold them all. Or maybe whoever set the thing to siphon souls also built a safeguard into it to keep the artifact from falling into the wrong hands."

"Wasn't it already in the wrong hands? I mean, don't get me wrong, I love a good disco as much as the next person, as long as the next person hates everything about disco. But that demented DJ and his bizarre orgy didn't seem like anything I'd call the right hands."

"I'm with you there. But what if you were a demon?"

I opened my mouth, then stopped. She was right. Good and evil were often a matter of perspective. Even Hitler was a hero in his sick, twisted mind. That's how bad people get to sleep at night: they convince themselves they're doing good. So if whoever was using the bracelet to harvest souls felt like they were doing the right thing, then we would be very much the wrong hands.

"So it sucked the souls out of the kids at the dance?" I asked, remembering the blank stares of the teens trying to crush me in the bleachers.

"Some of them. Some of them screwed themselves to death, and giving in to the sex magic, or spilling blood in the middle of that much magic being thrown around...I think it sucked their souls into the bracelet."

"And then what?" I asked. "I mean, I know what happened, but what was *supposed* to happen? I can't imagine the whole point was to suck souls into this bangle and then just leave them there. There had to be something else, right?"

"Yeah, but I don't know what."

"Well, think, dammit!" I slid off the bed and stomped across the room. There wasn't enough space to get a good stalk on, there wasn't even enough real estate to pace in, so I just kinda stood there turning around in circles for a minute before I sank back down on the bed. "What do we do now?"

Glory looked up at me, her expression bleak. "I don't know."

"What do you mean, you don't know?"

"I mean I don't know what the next step is, Harker. I'm no more omniscient than you are. I can't see everything all the time, and I don't know where we're supposed to turn next. I just know that there are a bunch of dead kids, teachers, and parents, and all we've got to show for it is the pinky finger off a dead magic-user." She held up the finger in question, a charred sliver of flesh and bone that looked a lot like a half-melted candle.

"That's nasty."

"Yeah. It's also all we've got."

"Then what fucking good are we?" I let my head crash into the wall again with a thud.

"What do you mean?"

"I mean what are we doing here, Glory? What have we done? We stopped some third-rate wizard from conning a couple of people out of their souls, but when a half-assed card cheat got his hands on a magic toy, we couldn't find him fast enough to keep him from dropping a nuke on a high school dance. Now we're no closer to any answers than we were two days ago, and the body count is a lot higher. Why are we even bothering? Seems like we do more harm than good lately."

She looked at me, her brow furrowed. "You know better than that, Q. We hunt down the things that go bump in the night, and we make sure they don't bump again. That's what we do. We saved the Robbinses, and there are probably some kids at that school who are alive because we stopped the music before it got completely out of hand. We do good work, Harker. Don't give up hope."

"Hope?" I laughed, a short bark that had about as much humor in it as a root canal. "You think I have *hope*? Jesus Christ, Glory. Are you fucking high? I walked away from everything and everyone I love because I have exactly zero hope. I looked fucking *Lucifer* in the eye, and he promised to end me and everyone I've ever cared about. Hope flew out the window a long damn time ago. For me, and for anybody I've tried to help."

I stood up again and moved toward the door. She put herself between me and the door, and I glared at her. "That's not somewhere you want to be, Glory."

"What are you going to do, Harker? Blast me to pieces?"

"No. I'm just going to move your ass." I picked her up and set her to one side. "Now let me go, Glory. I need to clear my head."

She looked at me with my pain reflected in her face. "But you're coming back, right? Because you can't hide from me, Harker. No matter how hard you try. You're stuck with me."

"I'll be back," I said. Then I pulled the door open and said under my breath, "Maybe." Then I walked through the bar and up the stairs without looking back. I knew the look I'd see on her face, the mixture of hope and disappointment that was becoming the standard for anyone looking at me lately. I couldn't handle that look tonight. Not when every time I closed my eyes I saw dead teenagers strewn across a gym floor, their prom dresses and tuxedos splattered with blood and empty eyes staring at me from lifeless faces.

A warm wind hit me off the river when I stepped out of Zeek's door, and I turned left to walk up the banks. It didn't take me long to pass out of the streetlights and be alone with the shadows and my thoughts, each vying to see which would be the darker. My thoughts won.

I walked for an hour or more, the Mississippi lapping at the shore beside my left elbow. There isn't really a beach or much of a riverfront in Memphis, just one long park and a couple of wooded areas, but I walked north from Zeek's place to the top of the Riverwalk, across the concrete landings all the way up to the welcome center across from Mud Island. Every so often I'd pick up a rock and skip it across the water, sometimes giving it a little extra magical song, sometimes just flinging it as far as I could.

I heard the music long before I saw the old man, the mournful slide of old blues snaking through the thick air, hanging in the mist off the river like a snake of sound that wrapped around my feet and pulled me forward. The slide wailed through the night like a banshee, lyrics indistinct but the pain of the notes touching something deep inside me.

I stepped out of a small patch of trees, gravel crunching under my boots, and looked at the old man sitting on a low concrete wall under the harsh blue-white light of a streetlamp. He looked up at me and smiled. "Hey there," he said, a bright smile splitting his dark face. He held up a bottle and waggled it at me. "Want a slash?"

"I won't say no," I said, walking over and sitting down next to him. I took the bottle and poured a slug down my throat, my eyes going wide at the taste. It burned like fire going down but tasted like the sweetest honey mead I'd ever tried. "What is this?"

"Just a little home-brew," he said with a grin. I took a better look at him, trying to figure out why he looked familiar. I was pretty sure I'd never seen him before, but I felt safe around him, like there was no way in the world he'd ever hurt me.

He was an old man, his skin furrowed by deep wrinkles that showed decades of laughter. His brown eyes were set deep in his craggy face, and the red roadmap of broken blood vessels across his nose told me this wasn't the first bottle he'd knocked back in his day. He was dark-skinned, but his features spoke more of Middle Eastern descent than African-American, with a little Asian mixed in around the eyes for good measure.

"I've got a little bit of everything mixed in me, sonny," he said, still smiling. "No, don't be embarrassed. I get it all the time. People all like 'what are you?' and I'm just me. I ain't white. I ain't black. I ain't nothing else. I'm just me."

"I think that's fine, old-timer. More people oughta focus on just being themselves and stop worrying about what everyone else wants them to be."

"Good advice, son. You any good at taking it?"

I chuckled. "Hell no."

"Most folks ain't. Why you out walking the river in the middle of the night? Your clothes too nice for you to be living out here, even if you are nasty as all get out."

I looked down at myself. I was still pretty gross, with soot and bloodstains all over my jeans, and flecks of stuff I didn't want to iden-tify all over my boots. I called up a little energy into my hands and held them out, palms down. "*Emundabit*," I said, releasing the power in a slow breath. White light shone around my body, and all the night's debris cascaded off of me like a waterfall. I looked up at the man. "Better?"

"Much. Now why don't you have a seat, since you don't stink of dead people no more?" He patted the wall next to him, and I sat, the smooth concrete hard under my butt.

"That didn't freak you out?" I asked.

"What? Magic? Son, you live in this world as long as I have, you see some shit." He held up a hand. "No, don't go doing that."

163

I stopped before I called my Sight down. "You saw what I was doing?"

"I've seen it all at some point, boy. You don't need to know what I am. You just need to know I don't mean you no harm. There ain't a whole lot of folks telling you that nowadays, are they?"

I shook my head. "No, there aren't. If we're gonna get all meta-physical, you're gonna need to share that booze again." I held out my hand.

He slapped a bottle into it with a grin, and it looked like we hadn't even made a dent in the contents. I did my best to change that, slug-ging down a healthy drink before coming up for air and passing the bottle back. "That's good stuff."

"Be careful, son. It'll knock you on your ass if you ain't paying attention."

"I've got a high tolerance."

"Not for this stuff."

"I think I'm a little hardier than you think," I said.

"Suit yourself," he replied. "You got any requests?" He gave one of his tuning pegs a little twist and settled the guitar on his knee.

"Nah. Play whatever you like."

He picked out a low melody on the guitar, and I lost myself in the music and the smells of the river. The old man's song reached down inside me and shook something loose that I'd been holding wrapped up tight for months. I felt all the despair, all the loneliness, all the fear, and anger, and pain well up inside me, and before I knew what was happening, I was sitting on the ground with my back pressed up against the wall weeping like a motherless child as an old man's blues coiled around me in a hug that was as much therapy as comfort.

I don't know how long he played, or how long I wept, but the moon had moved halfway across the sky when I next looked up.

"Seems like you needed that," he said.

"More than you know," I replied.

"I doubt that, Quincy Harker."

I looked into the eyes of the kindly old man and wasn't even worried that I'd never told him my name.

26

U sually this is the point where whoever I've just met that knows more about me than they're supposed to know shows me their black eyes, or red eyes, or yellow eyes, or just throws a fireball at me, or tries to kill me somehow. If you're going to do that, can you at least make it quick? I've got a long eternity of torment ahead of me and I'd rather not dilly-dally," I said. I didn't meet his eyes again, just stared up at the stars wondering if it was time to die. I was at peace with it. I didn't want to die, but it seemed like lately a big chunk of the world would be better off if I wasn't alive. At least then I wouldn't fuck anything else up.

"Do you want me to kill you, Quincy?" The old man started playing again, softly, just a trickle of melody under his words.

"I don't think so."

"You're not sure?"

"No." Like I said, I didn't want to die. I certainly didn't feel suicidal. I was just…tired. So goddamn tired. Something about tonight, something about screwing up and getting those kids killed, had a bigger effect on me than most of my fights. I'd lost innocents before, watched people die because I wasn't fast enough, or strong enough, or just plain good enough at the hero bullshit to save them. Hell, I'd watched the woman I loved more than life itself die in a storm of blood and fury in the mountains of France the better part of a century ago. Even that didn't hit me like tonight.

I fucked up. I fucked up, and a bunch of kids weren't going home to their parents. I got myself trapped behind the bleachers and had to use lethal force to get out, and when I did, I played right into the trap of whoever was using these artifacts to collect souls. I got too laser-focused on chasing down the asshole in front of me that I completely ignored the fact that there's always a bigger asshole further up the food chain.

"Well, I'm only going to kill you if you're sure you want to die," the old man said, still picking out his little melody. "You got any good reason to live?"

I thought he was playing the devil's advocate a little too well, but it worked. I barely let the words get out of his mouth before I said, "Flynn. She's why I do everything. She's why I keep going, she's why I left, she's why I came back from Hell."

"So why are you here when she's all the way back yonder?"

"Because it's too dangerous to be around me right now. I've got a pissed-off Lucifer just waiting in the wings for me to slip up, then he'll swoop in and destroy everyone I care about. I can't risk that happening to Becks."

"That sounds all noble until you realize it's bullshit."

"I have been surrounded by potty-mouth angels lately," I remarked.

"Who said I was an angel?"

I paused. He had a point. "I guess I just assumed Glory sent you when I walked out on her."

"You think you can talk to a guardian angel like you did and she'll still give a shit about you?"

"Yeah," I said. "I do. Glory won't give up on me. She can't. It's not in her nature. There's nothing she won't do for somebody she cares about, no matter how little that person deserves it."

"Oh sure, because everybody just waltzes into Hell with an army of Archangels for their friends. You know what your problem is, Quincy Harker?"

"You've narrowed it down to just one?"

"Well, aside from hubris, poor decision-making, a complete inability to think more than thirty seconds ahead, and a total disregard for the property of others, this is the main one."

"Okay," I said, turning around to sit cross-legged on the grass looking up at him. "Teach me, oh wise one."

"I apparently left out horrible smartass. No, your problem is that you can see everybody and everything way too clearly, but when it comes to looking in the mirror, you are blind as a motherfucker."

"Huh?"

"You are one of the least self-aware creatures I've seen on this earth, and I promise you I have seen a *lot* of creatures. You talk about how loyal Glory is, you talk about how caring Detective Flynn is, you'll even talk about the strength that your uncle Vlad has. But you can't see that they get that from you. Your uncle was the original vampire, a revenge-obsessed psychopath with a demon riding inside his soul until you came into his life. Glory was a mid-level Cherubim with no chance of ever doing anything impactful in the universe, and now she's helped save the world more times than either of you know, just by associating with you.

"And Detective Flynn? She would be dead half a dozen times over if it weren't for you. Yes, she has encountered danger greater than most mortals can even comprehend thanks to being with you, but she also didn't get shot by a mugger two weeks after getting her badge, which is what would have happened without your influence in her life. It's the small changes that matter the most, Quincy. Of course the big events are important, but people of substance, people like you and your friends? You change the world just by walking through it. You make the world a better place, whether you believe it or not."

"You're full of shit."

"Not the first time that accusation has been made." He smiled and took a long pull from his bottle, then passed it to me. I looked at it, not saying anything about the fact that he'd been sipping from it pretty steady for the better part of two hours and it seemed to be at exactly the same level as the first time I touched it. I drank and felt that same burning-into-sweetness sensation going all the way down to my toes.

"So what do I do, wise one?" I asked. "I don't know how to stop this guy. I don't even know if I'm actually chasing a person, or a demon, or some kind of monster I've never seen before. I just know I've got one artifact, I missed my best shot at laying hands on another one, and I have no idea where to find the others. But Glory is pretty concerned about Tennessee sinking into the earth if the wrong guy gets his hands on all four pieces of magical bling, so I guess I'd better figure something out."

"Yeah, that all sounds pretty bad."

"This is the part where you're supposed to give me some guidance, in case you missed that memo."

"Oh. Yeah, I don't really do that. I mean, who wants to listen to me? I'm just an old blues man with a bottle of booze that never seems to get empty. What would I know about cosmic stuff?"

I just looked at him, not speaking. After a minute, he chuckled. "Okay, fine. Maybe I can help. What would you usually do if you had one piece of a set and wanted to find the other pieces?"

"Usually I'd have Dennis do a bunch of research for me in about ten seconds of internet scanning, but he's busy being an Archangel now, so I guess I'm on my own for the library shit. If I didn't find anything there, I'd try to examine the piece I have...I'm a moron."

"I wouldn't go that far, but I also wouldn't hold you up as an example of the pinnacle of human intellect."

I showed him the hangnail I'd developed right at the base of my middle fingernail and clambered to my feet. I looked down at the slender man sitting there picking out the blues on a battered old guitar, bottle sitting on the stone wall next to him and the glow of a streetlight cascading down around his head and shoulders. "Thanks. For listening. I appreciate it."

"It's what I do, Quincy. I listen, I drink, and I play the blues." His fingers danced across the strings in a lightning-fast run that turned into a mournful wail as he ran the slide down the neck of the guitar.

I turned and headed back the way I'd come, then stopped. I turned around and looked back at the old man. "Why the blues?"

He smiled at me, and it was one of those smiles that says, "You're an idiot, but I love you anyway." The kind of smile only a lover or a parent can give you, completely adoring, and highly amused all at the same time. "Son. You been in Memphis for months, and you got to ask me that? The blues is life, boy. It ain't just the heartbeat of this country, it's the heartbeat of the *world*. The blues has got everything. It's got joy, and pain, and understanding, and rage, and heartbreak, and love, all wrapped up in something that's halfway to Hell but sent straight from Heaven. The blues is everything, boy. Once you get your head wrapped around that, you'll be able to walk through the world with a lot less scars."

"What if I like my scars?"

"You've earned them, that's for damn sure. Get out of here, Quincy Harker. Go save the world, or at least your little corner of it."

"Yes, sir." I raised two fingers to my brow in a little salute, and he nodded back to me as another song started pouring from his fingers across the strings of that old sunburst guitar. I turned around and headed back to Zeek's, ready to shove what little pride I still had down into the deepest part of myself and apologize to Glory. She didn't deserve any of the shit I gave her, and I was going to need her help if we were going to find the rest of the artifacts before any more people died. And I'd be damned if the body count on this one was going any higher on my account.

27

I knew something was fucked up the minute I walked through Zeek's front door. Nobody in the joint would meet my eye, and Henry literally ducked behind the bar as I walked up. I just leaned over and said, "Hey, Henry. What's up?"

He studied the floor very carefully, and being down on all fours must have made it much easier to see. "Nothing. Everything's fine, Harker. Why do you ask?"

"Because you're on the floor behind the bar about to piss yourself and nobody will look me in the eye, so I know something's up. I'm old, Henry. I'm not stupid."

"Jury's still out on that one, bud," Zeek chimed in from down the bar where he was cutting limes.

"What's going on, Zeek?"

"In your room," was all he said.

I shook my head and walked past the left-hand side of the bar to my room. The wards I had set up around the door were still intact, so nothing with ill intent had tried to get through. That was one of the first things I did when I set up shop in Zeek's back room—ward the door. Even before I had an apocalypse-level magical ring in my desk drawer, I still didn't want to come home from the grocery store to find any unpleasant surprises in my room. And yes, I shop for groceries. Man cannot live by beer and whiskey alone. I know. I've tried it.

So I cast a series of warding spells on the door at varying levels of strength and aggression based on the power level of whatever was trying to get through. If it was a human, they were probably trying to rob me, or maybe stab or shoot me. That would trigger an electric shock and a force push to fling the intruder back into the bar. If it was a were or other cryptid, I used more force and more electricity, but basically the same warding. Vampires were another story. Vamps are a lot more dangerous than weres, even Alphas, but don't let a wolf hear you say that. So I set up much stronger defenses against vampires.

If a vampire came through without disabling my protection spells, it would be bound in place by magic and bathed in fire until there was nothing left of it but ash. The binding spell had a shield built in to keep the fire from spreading, but honestly, I was a lot more worried about torching a vamp with bad intentions than with keeping Zeek's bar safe.

Demons and magic-users got the highest level of protection, basically a small nuke's worth of explosion that would probably blow the back half of the bar into the Mississippi, and me along with it if I happened to be sleeping in the room at the time of the break-in. There was fire, holy water, silver nitrate, and pure magical force, all designed to hammer any bad guys all the way through the floor and send any demonic intruder back to Hell, with extreme prejudice.

But none of my wards had been touched, so if there was someone waiting for me inside, they were either human, or a friend. I couldn't think of any reason Henry would be pissing himself over that, so I pushed open the door and stepped into the room, ready to apologize to Glory for being a dick. Again.

My mouth clicked shut as I saw exactly zero pissed-off angels waiting for me in my room. Glory was gone. The only hint that she'd been there at all was a note sitting on my desk. I picked up the scrap of paper and read it.

Dear Asshat,

Since you're too busy pissing and moaning about your existential crises to actually get anything done, I'm going to go save the world. Try not to get dead without me around to watch over your sorry behind.

G

I gotta say, when she took to profanity, it was like a duck to water. That was an ass-chewing the likes of which I'd rarely gotten in a two-sentence letter. But now she was out there hunting down a dangerous artifact on her own, and I had to find her before shit went even further sideways.

"How do you hunt down an angel in a city of blues and barbecue?" I mused, looking around the room for inspiration. My eyes lit on the drawer where I had the ring tucked away, and I had an idea.

I opened my desk and got out the ring, placing it on the floor of my room. Then I drew a circle around it with some chalk I keep around for just such a purpose, and inscribed some Enochian runes around the circle, starting at the north cardinal point and writing widdershins. When my circle was scribed and sealed, I turned to the door and threw a quick ward on it to keep *anyone* out, not just those with ill intent. It wouldn't do to have Zeek sense me throwing around magic and come in to check on me in the middle of these spells.

I sat down cross-legged by the southern point of the circle and called power. I reached deep beneath the bar, carving a thin slice through Zeek's warding and fighting my way through the natural resistance of running water. The effort was incredible, and coupled with everything I'd endured over the last few days, I was sweating and shaking by the time I felt like my connection to the earth was solid. But I reached down, grounding myself and pulling energy through me, and drew a symbol in the air over the ring.

The glyph shone with a bright yellow light, and beams of brilliance spun out of it in querulous fingers, dancing through the air until one locked onto the ring and several others twined around to strengthen it. I leaned forward, my Sight fully open, and one of those tendrils of power tapped the center of my forehead.

I felt a tingle as the magic spread over me, growing stronger as more of the shafts of light wove themselves around to touch my face. Power rolled over me like a wave, sliding down my face, to my neck, across my chest, down my back, and all the way to every inch of my skin. I felt tiny bits of me flowing back up the line and watched as slivers of my essence danced through the air, coursed around the glyph, and flowed down into the ring. My aura was red and blue and gray, with a very few hints of white or yellow shining through, but as it touched the ring, flecks of the ring's energy broke off, deepest black and blood-red, and flowed back up the streams of power to the glyph, and down into me.

Little bits of my soul lodged deep in the recesses of the ring's magic, and tiny hints of its power crept into the darkest nooks and crannies of me, and I felt every bit of it. I felt the corrupting power of the thing, the hunger of it, the rage of it, the lust and sheer hubris of the thing, and I knew. I knew I could find any piece of this awful magic as sure as I knew I could always find myself. Because I was now a part of this power, and it was a part of me.

I severed my connection to the glyph and dropped the conduit of power I held to the earth. The glyph winked out, and the energy forming the boundary off the circle dissipated into the air. I leaned forward, trying to get my stomach under control, then lurched for the wastebasket as I realized it was a lost cause. I puked up everything I'd eaten for at least a week, and maybe a little piece of my spleen just for good measure. When I was finished turning myself inside out, I closed my eyes and reached out with my mind for the ring.

There it was. I could feel it, like a sonar ping, a deadly note of contact with a magical mine. And if I wasn't careful, the damn thing was going to blow me straight to Hell. I reached further, and off in the distance, I felt three more vague, tenuous contacts, slightly different, but all coated with the same malignancy that I felt roiling deep within my soul. If this shit didn't kill me, I was definitely going to have to get Glory to do something about that. If she ever spoke to me again, that is.

Now that I could locate the other artifacts, it was time to find

Glory and make sure she didn't do anything that I would be likely to do. My guardian angel had a serious pile of heavenly mojo, but my bad decision-making could counteract a whole lot of divinity. I drew myself up from the floor, emptied out the puke bucket into the toilet, gave it a quick rinse in the tub, and left it in the bathroom. Then I headed out into the bar to find myself a tracker.

"Henry!" I called from my doorway, grinning as every eye in the place spun to look at me. "Time to go, pup! We've got some world-saving to do!"

Zeek walked over to me, his face a thundercloud. "What the hell do you think you're doing, throwing around power like that in my place? You shouldn't even be *able* to draw that much power through my protections, much less wield it here."

I cocked my head at Zeek. "Zeek, old pal. Did you really think I didn't carve myself a back door into your wards within the first week of being here? I swum around and carved a glyph on the underside of the floor to my room, giving myself a weak spot. Then, when I needed to cast here without you taking down the rest of the wards, I just set my circle on top of the glyph, and *voila!* Instant portal. Think of it like cutting a hole in your wall so you can steal the neighbor's cable signal."

"I think of it as an affront to my hospitality." His eyes were dark, and I felt the sting of sand blowing against my legs as Zeek's true form bled through his illusions.

"For that, I apologize," I said, completely sincere. "But I needed to be safe from external assault while I worked, and this seemed like the best way. If we need to have a more in-depth 'conversation' about this, we can do that when I get back. But right now, I need to find Glory before she locates the next artifact and gets her divine ass blown to pieces. These things are potent, and nasty. She shouldn't touch one, like ever. I don't know how it would react to her, but I bet it wouldn't be good."

Zeek relaxed, just a hair, and some of the tension eased from his shoulders. "I accept your apology, on the condition that when you have finished with this matter, you remove your back door from my wards. I cannot have my protections compromised, even by a...friend."

I noticed the pause. He meant for me to notice the pause, and I didn't blame him for it. I deserved a pause before he claimed me as a friend, because I certainly didn't act like one. Hell, I barely acted like an employee most of the time, and I still wasn't quite sure if I was fired or not. But those were matters for a latter conversation, one that would require a lot of good whiskey, or a *whole* lot of cheap whiskey. "I can live with that. And again, my sincere apologies."

"Liar," he said, but he smiled a little as he said it. "If your apology was sincere, you would regret breaching my wards. And you don't."

"No, I don't," I agreed. "But in my defense, I very seldom regret any of my bad ideas." I turned to the bar. "Henry, get over here!"

The skinny werewolf hopped over the bar and trotted over. "Yeah, Harker?"

"Go get changed. I need your nose."

He looked to Zeek, who nodded, then back to me. "You sure? I'm not exactly inconspicuous when I'm changed."

"I'll handle that. You just get into your furry suit. We've got to go track an angel."

28

There are places in the world where walking around with a giant wolf off-leash by your side in the middle of the night draws attention. Beale Street is not one of them. Well, Henry drew attention, of course, but not *attention*. There was no running and screaming, no mindless panic at the wolf in their midst. It was more "ooh, puppy!" and "can I pet him?" than "holy shit." Of course, with as many record company producers as have operated in Memphis over the years, they might just be accustomed to having predators roaming their midst.

Either way, Henry was a babe magnet. It felt like every U of M sorority girl with more daiquiris than sense wanted to scratch behind his ears or take a ride on his back. I allowed the first and dissuaded the latter, to the disapproving glare of my wolf companion.

"Sorry, buddy. I need you to stay focused. Glory could be in trouble, and we need to stay sharp." Now that I had bound myself to the artifacts, I didn't need Henry's nose to help track the next little chunk of trouble, but I did want a little backup, just in case things went sideways. Again.

Okay, I'll admit it. I was expecting for things to go to shit, and I wanted someone with a lot of natural weapons at my side when it did. I'd already had to deal with hellhounds, a demon, and an army of hormone-enraged zombified teenagers since I started this stupid adventure, and without Glory, I needed somebody to watch my back. Zeek would have been a more potent choice, but I kinda wanted him back at the bar to keep an eye on the ring hidden in my desk.

Not to mention the fact that Zeek was pissed at me, and strolling through a potential war zone with an irritated djinn sounded like a really good way to find out which one of us was stronger before the night was through. If anything went totally to shit, I knew I could take Henry. I had no such confidence about being able to kick Zeek's ass if he turned on me or got brainwashed or possessed.

I parked down at one end of the street across from the Orpheum Theatre and started heading up one of the most famous streets in the blues. Music wove around me like dazzling threads of its own magic, tinkling piano, brassy trumpet, mournful slide guitar all jumbled together in a stew of sounds that made me hungry to sit down and listen for a while. I looked around with my Sight, and my suspicions were confirmed: there was a little bit of magic in all the really packed clubs.

Sometimes it came from the stage, and I could see the blue-and-yellow power dancing along the sound waves. Sometimes it was a warm purple mist permeating the sidewalk around a barker-like doorman. Some places just glowed with amber warmth and safety and tones of home, wherever home may be. Henry leaned against my leg and whimpered a little at one door, but I twined my fingers into the fur at the scruff of his neck and held on tight.

"Not tonight, buddy. I'll bring you back when you have thumbs and we can go in there and get a couple beers." He looked up at me with those big expressive wolf eyes, and I sighed. "Yes, I promise. What, do you want me to pinkie swear?"

He plopped right down on his haunches and lifted a paw. I guess he did want me to pinkie swear. Wolves don't have pinkies, but lycan-thropes sometimes have remarkable control over their shifts, and we were far enough from the full moon that Henry was at the apex of his control. So it only surprised me the slightest bit when he shifted the paw into a hand and extended his pinkie.

So I took it and made a pinkie swear with a werewolf that I would come back to a blues bar and buy him a beer.

"Satisfied?" I asked.

Henry gave a contented *whuff,* and we resumed our trek eastward toward the heart of the blues. I paused at the Elvis statue, looking up at the man they called the King of Rock n' Roll. The statue was young Elvis, not long after he got back from the war, with his hips cocked, his lip curled, and the heart of rock n' roll beating loud in his chest.

"I met him, you know," I said to Henry. The wolf looked up at me as I stood there, staring up at the man who looked so different immortalized in bronze than he had close to fifty years ago when I saw him backstage at Madison Square Garden. Back then he was young, and wouldn't get very much older, but he was still a mesmerizing performer.

I didn't meet him by chance. No, I was summoned to the King upon his arrival in New York City. He and Luke had met once or twice, and he knew how to get in touch with me if he needed anything of the supernatural bent. I was spending a lot of my time around Studio 54 and was perfectly capable of getting people mundane things that made them *feel* magical, but Elvis wanted the real thing.

He was sitting on a small couch in the dressing room when I walked in, his long leg thrown over to one side, his head down as he picked out a tune on a battered acoustic guitar. This wasn't ELVIS. This wasn't the King. This was Elvis Aaron Presley, a farm kid from the South, noodling around on a guitar and picking out an old Robert Johnson tune. Then he looked up at me, and I literally took a step back from the intensity of his presence.

Yeah. I hang out with an angel, I've gone toe to toe (kinda) with the Devil himself, and I've given the middle finger to Dracula more times than I can count. But Elvis's personality was like a force of nature. His gaze was a hurricane of personality, and when his face broke into a wide, genuine, smile, he warmed places in me that had been chilled for decades.

He stood up, set his guitar very carefully down on the couch, and stepped over to me, hand extended. "Thank you for coming, Mr. Harker. I appreciate it."

I took a step forward without even really knowing I was doing it and shook his hand. A *frisson* of energy flowed through him, and I stepped back. "Holy shit," I said. "What was that?"

His smile twisted into a rueful, self-effacing one, and he said, "That's why you're here, Mr. Harker. That's the music. It's burning me up inside, and if I don't find some way to hold it all in, it's gonna kill me."

Then I got the whole story. The story of a young man from Mississippi who was born feeling guilty because his brother died and he lived. A young man raised in a strict Assembly of God church that never approved of his secular music. A man who loved his mother more than any other woman in the world and mourned her death almost twenty years later.

"I never sold my soul, Mr. Harker. I know some people talk about me making a deal down at the crossroads like some of them old blues men, but I never did that. I need you to believe me." I did. I looked in his eyes, and I believed him.

"Okay, I believe you. You didn't make a deal with the devil. But there's something more at work here than you're telling me. If it's not a demon causing the magic to cook you from the inside out, what is it?"

He looked over to the couch, sadness filling his deep eyes, then looked back at me. "It's Jesse."

"I know this is going to seem anticlimactic after what feels like you just told me something really important and personal, but who's Jesse?" I asked.

He laughed. He threw back his head and laughed long and hard. "Oh man, I can't tell you how good that felt," he said, walking back over to the couch. He motioned toward an armchair and I sat. "You want a drink?"

"I'll never say no. Scotch?"

"Bourbon." He picked up a crystal decanter and poured two

179

glasses. I raised mine to him and sipped. "Man, you can't imagine how long it's been since I met somebody who doesn't know every little thing about me. Seems like reporters, fans, even other musicians have all read up on Elvis Presley. They all want to ask me something ain't nobody ever asked me or dig deep and get to know the real me. But you don't care about all that, do you?"

"Not really, no," I agreed. "Look, I'm impressed. I like some of your songs. Not crazy about your movies, but you seem like a good person, and Luke says you need help. And more, deserve help. So I'll do what I can for you. But no, I didn't go to the library and look up newspaper articles before I met you. Not to be a dick, but you're the one asking me for help. I'm not the one in the room who needs to impress anybody."

He watched me through that whole little spiel over the rim of his glass, his eyes tight on my face. When I was finished, he knocked back his drink and held up the empty glass in my direction. "Well, cheers to that, Mr. Harker. You're right. I need your help, because I think my brother's dying, and if he dies, my music dies with him."

"I didn't know you had a brother. I assume that's Jesse?"

"Yeah. Jesse Garron Presley. He was my identical twin, and he was stillborn."

I was confused, and it must have shown on my face, because Elvis held up a hand. "I know, it sounds crazy. But hear me out."

"Mr. Presley—"

"Elvis, please."

"Okay. Elvis, let's take a minute here to really think about who you're talking to. If there's anybody in the world who will believe in some crazy-sounding shit, I'm the guy. So your dead brother is dying again, and you're afraid that will take away your music. Is that pretty much it?"

He nodded. "Yes, sir."

"If I'm going to call you Elvis, you can call me Quincy. Besides, people calling me sir reminds me that I'm pushing eighty. Okay, this is not the craziest thing I've heard this year. It wins the month, but it's early yet. So how is Jesse still alive at all?"

"Well, I don't rightly know how it happened, but I ain't never felt alone. I've always felt like Jesse's with me somehow. Like he was a part of me. And when I got to Memphis, I met an old man in one of them blues clubs down on Beale Street, and he told me he could see another soul living inside of me, and that's what made my music so special. He said I was living two lives at once, and that extra soul meant I was gonna do great things."

I closed my eyes and opened my Sight. When I opened my eyes again, sure as shit there were two men sitting on the couch across from me. There was Elvis, looking just like he did in the real spectrum, but there was a shadowy figure along with him of a thin man with very slightly sharper features, slicked-back hair, and the same dark eyes.

He looked like Elvis, but like Elvis with sharper edges, an Elvis that had never smiled, or felt the adoration of a crowd, or his mother's touch. This was Jesse, the darker parts of Elvis. The dangerous, hip-swiveling parts that made mothers worried and fathers outraged. The parts that led Baptist preachers to burn albums and small-town sheriffs to threaten arrests for lewd behavior. Elvis was right. Jesse was the part of him that was the King of Rock n' Roll. And as I watched the ghostly figure flicker in and out of view, I knew that he wasn't long from vanishing completely.

"Son of a bitch," I murmured.

"You see him? Your eyes are all funny, and you ain't looking at me no more, so you must be seeing Jesse."

"I see him all right," I said. "I see him, but I don't know what to do about him."

"I need you to keep him with me," Elvis said. "He's my brother. I can't lose him. He's been with me forever. He's the only one…"

"The only one who knows who you really are?" I asked.

Elvis nodded. "I don't know what I'd be without him."

I didn't either. But I knew one thing for certain: if I couldn't figure out how to keep Jesse Presley's soul tied to his brother, the King of Rock n' Roll would never play again.

29

O kay," I said, clapping my hands together and rubbing them briskly. "I'm gonna need to call in some backup."

"Now hold on just a minute," Elvis said, standing up and holding his hands out in a "stop" gesture. "I don't know about letting on to a whole lot of people just what's going on here. It was hard enough getting you back here without folks making a ruckus, but we start—"

"Shut up." He stopped in mid-sentence like I'd slapped him across the face. His eyes bugged out, and he stood there for a second with his mouth hanging open. "Now close your mouth. You look like a damn trout."

His jaw clicked shut, but his eyes stayed wide. "Now I guess it's been a while since anybody's told you to shut up, or told you much of anything, you being the King and all," I said.

"You better believe that. I—"

I cut him off again. "But you called me, remember? Not the other way around. Now I'm not some screaming schoolgirl, or her fainting mother. You go out on that stage, and it's your world, and you're the King of Rock n' Roll. But back here, dealing with this shit? This is my world, sonny. So you can shut your mouth and do as you're told, or I can go back to the bar and get good and drunk like I'd planned on tonight. Now which is it going to be?"

He opened and closed his mouth a couple of times, and I'll one hundred percent own up to the fact that I enjoyed it, probably more than the situation warranted. But while my behavior may have been rude, the logic behind it was sound. I needed him to focus and do what I said. And I needed him to be in the habit of doing what I said, as soon as I said it, without argument. I didn't know quite what we were trying to do, but it was definitely going to be some messing with the fabric of reality shit, and that's not the kind of stuff where you can call time out and explain the play to the second-string quarterback.

He sat back down on the couch, his eyes locked with mine the whole time. My gaze didn't waver. I'd stared down scarier things than a grumpy rock star before. Like that morning, when my girlfriend was pissed off I drank all the milk again and put the empty carton back in the refrigerator. She was serious about her milk, that one.

"Now," I said. "Tell your security guards there's going to be a nun coming to visit, point me to a telephone, and see about getting some decent Scotch in here, will you?"

It took Sister Lucia nearly an hour to get to the dressing room. It only took the stage manager fifteen minutes to get me a bottle of Scotch, so I was feeling pretty good when the rotund little nun toddled through the door. She was only old back then, not ancient like she is today, but the hairs peeking out from under her wimple were already steel gray and on their way to snow white.

"Quincy Harker, are you drinking in the middle of the day again? I have told you more than one time that is going to lead to your downfall, boy!" She stalked over to the chair where I stood, snatched the highball glass out of my hand, and drank down my Scotch like a true professional. Which, as a Catholic nun, I guess she kinda was.

"That's good, son. Who you working with got enough money for good liquor like this? I know you too cheap to buy it." She looked around the room and froze when her eyes landed on Elvis, sitting in another armchair watching television.

He stood up and came over to her. "It's a pleasure to meet you, ma'am. I'm Elvis Presley."

She looked up at the smiling man with the pompadour and said, "I reckon I know that, child. I wasn't born a nun. I saw you a long time ago. You was with Johnny Cash and that Perkins boy. It was a National Guard Armory in some little podunk town in Mississippi. The archbishop was trying to start a church down there and sent me, of all the nuns in the damn country, to go down there and try to bring some of them rednecks to Jesus. I think I might have damned more souls than I saved."

"Mississippi wasn't a good place for colored folk or Catholics back then, ma'am," Elvis said, his eyes serious.

"Son, it ain't a very good place for either of them now," Lucia said with a nod. "But you didn't call me here to talk about race relations twenty years ago in Mississippi. What do you need, Quincy Harker? What's going on with this boy that's so bad you have to call on the Church to cover your narrow behind? Again."

I let her digs slide right off. Lucia was a little crass, and a lot prickly, but she was one of the very best people I'd ever had by my side when shit went sideways. And believe me, there was a lot of sideways shit in New York in the early seventies. "Elvis has a problem. And I don't have the slightest damn idea how to fix it."

She looked the King up and down. "He looks fine. Put on a little weight since he spent all that time in Las Vegas, but that's understandable. We all carry a few extra pounds as the years move on."

"Look at him again," I said. "And this time *look* at him."

Lucia's eyes went wide, and she shot me a questioning look. I nodded, and she closed her eyes, and I watched as her brow knit for a moment, then she opened her eyes. Now I knew what Elvis meant when he said my eyes had "gone funny." I'd never looked at anyone using the Sight before, unless I was using mine at the same time. It's not usually something I have much opportunity to observe, what with there not being very many practitioners in the world anymore, and with so many of them wanting to kill me.

The nun's eyes didn't glow. Not exactly, but they did seem to be lit from within just a little bit. She looked Elvis up and down, and I let a little smirk escape as I saw her eyes widen. "What in the world..."

"That's Jesse," I said. "Elvis's twin brother."

"He died as we were being born," Elvis said. "He's been with me all my life."

"His hold on this world is weak," Lucia said. "He needs to move on. That boy don't need to be hanging around here watching you live. That won't do a soul no good, sitting by while everybody around it lives, and it can't ever draw a breath itself. You got to let him go, son."

"But I can't, ma'am," Elvis protested. "I ain't got no music without him." He looked around, and reading the confusion on our faces, continued. "Whenever I'm about to go on stage, I get real nervous. But then I close my eyes, and I reach out to Jesse, and once I can feel him with me, I'm okay. I ain't got no kind of swagger, that's all Jesse. I'm just a country boy who can pick a couple gospel tunes. He's the King of Rock n' Roll."

Lucia blinked, and when she opened her eyes, they were clear of Sight, and blazing. "Elvis Aaron Presley, you hush that talk. You are the man all those people been coming to see all these years, not some dead brother who ain't never drawn breath in this world. Now I don't believe in kings and queens, except for the one upstairs, but if anybody is the King of Rock n' Roll, you are it. I knew it in 1955 in Mississippi, and I know it today. There has not been a soul in this city that hasn't been talking about Elvis playing the Garden for a month. You can't buy a ticket to tonight's show for any amount of money, and that does not have a single thing to do with the ghost that you've been dragging around for almost forty years. That is what you have done. You have taken the gifts the Lord gave you and brought joy to millions of people in this world, and you will continue to do so after we let your poor brother loose to go on to Heaven to be with his mama."

"Mama..." Elvis's face went soft at the mere word. I'd heard that he loved his mother more than anybody in his life, and now I could see

185

the truth of that in his eyes. He took a breath, then another. He closed his eyes for a long moment, then he straightened up his shoulders. When he opened his eyes, there was a little hint of fear in them, but it was buried behind a wall of steely resolve. "You're right, Sister Lucia. Jesse never got to be with Mama here on Earth, and it ain't right for me to deny him being with her in Heaven. I'm gonna miss him, and I ain't half as convinced as you are that I can do this without him, but you're right. It's time to let him go."

He looked at me. "What do we need to do?"

I walked over to the bar and poured myself a fresh drink. "I have no idea. This isn't an exorcism. You're not possessed. None of the rituals I know how to do have anything to do with helping ghosts pass on to their rest. I'm more the guy you call when you need to blast them to oblivion. This is her scene, man." I gestured with my glass at Lucia.

He turned to the stocky nun. "Ma'am? What do we need to do to let Jesse get to his rest?" You could see the fear in his eyes. It was so different from his lip-curling, leather jacket-wearing stage and screen persona. This was just a boy who coveted family more than anything, trying to be brave as he gave up the only person who had known him his whole life. This was going to cost him something, and I hoped that he'd be able to fill the void left in his heart with music, or something, at least.

"Well, I reckon one time you said you like the old spirituals, didn't you?" Lucia asked. She wore a gentle smile, and I could see the comforting Sister Lucia now, not the ball-breaking Church enforcer that I usually dealt with.

"Yes, ma'am. Them old gospel songs are my favorites."

"Well then, I suppose there isn't any more fitting ritual for you to use to say goodbye than that. Quincy, bar the door. We don't need anybody interrupting this."

I did as I was told. Even back then, Lucia was a force. When she gave an order, I hopped to with vigor. I pulled a chair over to the door, slammed it up against it nice and tight, and sat down to watch the show.

Elvis picked up that same beat-up acoustic guitar he'd been noodling on when I walked into his dressing room and sat down on a low coffee table. After a couple second's tuning, the familiar strains of "Peace in the Valley" came from the instrument. He played through the melody once, then circled back around, and started to sing.

Look, I knew who Elvis was. I'd seen some movies, even heard plenty of his records and songs on the radio. But I promise you, there aren't very many people alive who saw Elvis like I did that night. This wasn't the King. This wasn't a performance. This was a man playing his mother's favorite song to lay his brother's spirit to rest, and when Lucia came in on the chorus, her sweet soprano coming from somewhere I could never even imagine, I closed my eyes and let the song wash over me. Their voices blended perfectly, even though neither one of them was perfect. Elvis was a little fast, Lucia was a little sharp, but you could tell that they *felt* every note they were singing, and there was a magic to that like nothing I'd ever felt before.

For just one moment, in a dressing room under Madison Square Garden, probably less than ten feet from enough drugs to get all of Queens high, mere hours before Elvis Presley took the stage at the most famous performance venue in the biggest city in the United States, I experienced something absolutely holy.

I didn't open my eyes until the last note faded away, and when I did, I wasn't surprised that my vision was like looking through a rainy windshield and my cheeks were soaked with tears. I dropped my Sight into place and smiled as I saw Elvis sitting there by himself. Jesse was gone.

"Is he...?" Elvis asked.

"You tell me," I replied.

"I can still feel him. But it's different. It's the way I can feel Mama. He ain't here like he used to be, but he ain't completely gone, neither."

I looked over to Lucia and raised an eyebrow. She gave the slightest shake of her head, telling me not to disillusion the boy, so I didn't. "The ones we lose are never really gone, Elvis. They're always looking over us, guiding us, helping us find our way. Jesse's finally at peace, but he'll never truly be gone."

It was a complete crock of shit, of course. Jesse was gone like a robber fleeing the scene of a crime, but if it helped Elvis play to believe all that bollocks about dead loved ones looking out for us, who was I to shatter his worldview? I mean, yeah, I usually like nothing better than shattering someone's worldview, but not this time. He needed those illusions to get by, and I didn't need to be known as the reason Elvis Presley never played the Garden.

He stood up, laid the guitar down on the couch, and held out a hand to Lucia. "Thank you, ma'am. Thank you very much."

She batted his hand away and pulled him down to her for a fierce hug. "You take care of yourself, son. You're a good boy, and the world needs all the good boys it can get."

"Yeah, it balances out all the bastards like me," I said, walking over and putting out a hand.

"I wasn't going to *say* that, Quincy," Lucia said with a grin.

"You don't have to, dearie. I know where I stand." I got serious for a moment. "Thank you, Sister. I owe you one. Another one."

"I owe you both," Elvis said. "Tell you what. Why don't you come to the show tonight as my guests? I don't think there are any seats, but you can stand on the side of the stage and watch."

Just as I opened my mouth to regretfully decline, I got a very pointed elbow in my ribs, and a voice from beside me said, "We would love to, thank you." I glared down at Lucia, who smiled up at me and mouthed, "You owe me."

And that's how I came to see the first time Elvis Presley played Madison Square Garden.

30

Henry looked up at me, then pawed at my leg as if to say, "Cool story, bro. Now can we get on with this shit?"

"Okay, okay," I said, looking up at the statue of a young Elvis. I've always wondered if, when we laid his brother to rest after all those years, Elvis just couldn't handle being truly alone for the first time in his life. He was already well down the path of addiction that took his life when I met him, but he died less than five years after our encounter, and I've always wondered if some of that was on me.

I gave myself a mental shake, telling myself not to invent things to blame myself for when there were so many things that really were my fault, like Glory being out on her own chasing down artifacts with enough stored magic to level a building. She had her divinity back, but I still wasn't sure she could withstand the blast if one of those things went off right next to her. She might be an angel again, but parts of her were decidedly more human than they had been when we first met.

And those were the parts I was looking for, walking down Beale Street in the middle of the night. In most cities, the crowds would be thinning by now, but Memphis isn't most cities. Throngs of humanity still crowded the doorways of B.B. King's place, and the bar at Silky

O'Sullivan's was stacked three deep with a mix of hipsters, bikers, rednecks, and middle-class blues lovers that had a uniquely Memphis feel to it.

What I didn't feel was any magic. Oh, sure, there was the odd tingle of talent as I walked past an open door. There was a guitar player with a slide haunted by an old bluesman, or a piano player with a hellhound laying sprawled atop his upright piano, just watching the man play and biding his time. Some of these bits of magic were good, some were bad, and a couple were downright nasty, but they were all small-time evil. The kind of bad that comes from one or two bad decisions, not the kind of bad that comes of millennia of working to completely fuck over all of humanity.

No, I couldn't feel hide nor hair of Glory or the artifact anywhere on Beale, so I sat down at the base of the W.C. Handy statue and leaned back on the famous horn player's shins. Henry sat by my leg and laid his head on my knee, looking up at me as if to say, "What now, asshole?"

"I don't know, buddy. I can feel it, but it's faint, like it's hidden, or diffused somehow. Maybe all the other little magics running around down here are confusing the scent. You know what I mean?"

Henry pawed at my leg and nodded. He totally knew what I meant. He cocked his head to the side just seconds before an ear-splitting howl of feedback ripped through the night air. The couple dozen people milling around the Beale side of Handy Park all froze, their heads whipping around to the amphitheater. I slowly leaned to the side and peered around the base of the statue at the stage and saw a sheepish guitar tech wave to the crowd.

"A little late for a concert, isn't it?" I asked Henry. The wolf didn't answer, just shrugged, a movement I didn't know dogs could make. My eyes landed on a tent set up at the back of the seating pavilion, with a big sign saying, "CD Release Concert - Mississippi Paul Lloyd - FREE - One Night Only." There were people rushing around setting up more tents and tables, and like the feedback was a beacon, people started streaming into the park through the big brick pillars on the sidewalk.

I closed my eyes and felt for the thread of power that led me there. It was hard to grab hold of the artifact's magic with everything else floating around, but finally, I managed to filter out all the junk and lock on to the red and black twisted cord of power weaving through the air back toward Zeek's place. Surprising me not at all, the line of magic floated over the crowd, through the late-night air, and disappeared into the wall at the back of the stage. The artifact was here, and I was willing to bet my life that it had something to do with this concert going on in a public park in the middle of the night.

"Okay, pal," I whispered to Henry. "Time to go to work. I'm going to look for the magic, you keep people off my back and get Glory out of there if we find her. Got it?"

Henry held up a paw, and I gave him a high five. We walked out the front gates of the park and around the block to where a pair of rented Penske moving trucks and a battered Econoline van were parked. A beefy guy with a long red ponytail and a laminated card hanging around his neck leaned on the passenger door of the van, his thick arms folded across his chest.

I walked up to him, Henry a step or two behind me, and looked up at him. "Hey man," I said. "You seen Jerry?"

The muscle looked a little startled, like maybe I snapped him out of deep contemplation of astrophysics, or maybe he was dozing. "Who the fuck is Jerry? How did you get back here?"

I looked around. "There ain't no gate, man. What's gonna stop me? And you know Jerry. He works in production. Or was it catering? I don't know, man. I just know I've got to deliver his package, you know?" I waggled my eyebrows like I had a secret.

Muscles didn't catch on. "No, I don't know. And I don't know anybody named Jerry. You got to get the fuck out of here." His eyes widened, and he looked past my elbow. "Hey! What are you doing? Get off that!" He pushed past me, and I turned to see Henry on top of a big road case, sprawled out with his head on his front paws. Muscles got about eight feet from the werewolf when he stopped, apparently just now taking in exactly how *big* Henry was.

191

"Good dog," Muscles said, holding up both hands in the universal gesture for "Please don't eat me."

I took the opportunity to move further into the backstage area, following the trail of magic. The trail led me into a concrete block building with a metal roof and a sign on the door that said, "Authorized Personnel Only." I quickly authorized myself and slipped through into a brightly-lit hallway. I blinked a few times as my eyes adjusted, glad for once that using my Sight to follow the trail of magic obscured my mundane vision.

As the sparkles faded from my eyes, they focused on the two grumpy-looking men stomping toward me with stun sticks in their hands and violence in their eyes. Since I still had my Sight active, I could see they weren't actually men at all, but demons in disguise.

"Guess I found the right place," I said, and dropped my Sight while I called power into my fists. I coalesced energy around my left arm with a muttered "*Scutum*." An oblong shield of pure power stretched from my fist to my elbow, and about eight inches on either side of my arm. I caught the first overhand strike from the lead demon on my shield and poured raw power from my right fist into his midsection.

His eyes went wide as he flew backward, bowling over the demon behind him and losing his grip on the stun stick. Neither of them stayed down long, and nasty grins stretched across their faces as they got to their feet.

"We heard there might be trouble from some busybody mage, but I didn't think we'd be lucky enough to find somebody that stupid," the front demon said, his voice sounding like lava rolling over gravel, all hisses and rumbling. These weren't terribly impressive demons, just run of the mill hellspawn. They wouldn't be as fast and vicious as Reavers, and thankfully not as strong as Torment Demons, but a pair of them was still more than I wanted to tangle with in a hallway where mundane humans could wander through at any second.

So I did the most valiant thing I could think of: I turned around and bolted out into the parking lot. Muscles was back at his post leaning on the van, and he snapped upright as the cheap metal door sprang open and slammed into the cinderblocks.

"Hey!" Muscles shouted. "What are you doing in there?"

"I told you, dickwhistle," I said as I ran straight at him. "I was looking for Jerry. Now get the fuck out of here—the security guards are demons."

He held out both hands to me, stopping my flight and wasting precious seconds where I could keep him from being fed his own testicles. "Now hold on a minute, pal. What makes you think they're demons?"

"Horns and fangs, twatmonkey, now let's *go!*"

"I don't think I should let you go anywhere, buddy. You might need a doctor. Did you slip in there and hit your head?"

"It's okay, Curtis," came a rumbling voice from behind me. "He's a mage. He knows what's up."

Muscles, whose name was apparently Curtis, looked at me and smiled. "Oh. Okay, *Dad*. What should I do with him?"

I looked at Curtis with my Sight but saw nothing out of the ordinary. Then he reached up with a thumb and licked it, then rubbed the digit across his forehead. The half-demon form swam into view, and I let out a muttered, "Fuck."

"Yup," Curtis said, his pointed teeth shining as he grinned at me. "A little Nephilim blood, and we can hide who we are."

I knew that, but it wasn't something I ran into often enough to look for. Most Cambion don't know what they are, and they sure as hell don't know enough about magic and their demonic nature to know that they can use the blood of an angel-human hybrid, or Nephilim, to mask their presence from magical detection. Then there's the other challenge of knowing where to get Nephilim blood, which isn't exactly sitting on the shelf at your local Walgreens.

I was surprised, but probably less so than Curtis was counting on. I'd fought Cambion before. More than once, and I knew that while they had certain advantages over mere humans, armored nutsacks weren't one of them. So I planted a knee right in Curtis's balls and stepped aside to let him collapse to the asphalt parking lot.

I turned to the two demons and let a little grin slip out. "Guys, I'm going to give you one chance to get the fuck out of here. I've had a long day and a shit night, so blasting you stupid fuckweasels back to the Third Circle might be the best thing that's happened to me in at least twenty-four hours. But I've kinda got shit to do, so if you'll run away, I won't turn you into little smears of demonic assclown all over this parking lot."

The larger of the two demons, the one I hadn't blasted in the hall-way, cracked his knuckles and smiled at me. It was a cold smile, the kind a monster gets when it's spent a lot of years causing a lot of pain. I had a brief concern that I might have underestimated the demons, then decided that it didn't fucking matter because I was going to kill them no matter how high up on Lucifer's food chain they were.

"Who the fuck do you think you are, little wizard?" the demon said, starting toward me.

He froze when I smiled and gave him his answer. "I'm Quincy Fucking Harker, shitstain, and I'm the hero you deserve."

Then it was on.

3 1

The first demon stopped his advance, and I smiled as his feet actually slipped under him a little as he tried to backpedal. The second one either had never heard of me, or I'd blasted him harder than I thought, because he just kept right on coming. I turned to focus on him and immediately went down to one knee as a heavy blow slammed into my left shoulder.

I spun around and pushed up to my feet, scrambling to get away from whatever had just hit me. Apparently "Muscles" wasn't that bad a nickname for my friend Curtis the Demonspawn Douchebro because he stood there grinning at me with his fists up.

"You gotta deal with me first, asshole," he said.

"Okay," I replied. I pointed over to a big concrete ashtray full of sand by the door of the backstage area and said, "*Volant!*" I released power in a stream of bright blue light, and tendrils of magic curled around the ashtray. It wobbled a little as it lifted, but with a sweep of my arm, it flew across the parking lot to slam into Curtis's chest and take him clean off his feet.

The butt can pressed against his ribcage, he flew back through the air to crash into the van's hood and windshield, shattering the safety glass in a huge spiderweb. The ashtray rolled down his torso and crashed to the pavement, leaving Curtis stuck with his ass shoved through a windshield and most of his ribs shattered to shit.

Curtis dealt with, I turned to face the oncoming demon, lowering my shoulder to catch his charge and throw him over my back. He saw it coming, though, and stopped short, bringing a knee up as I brought my head down. Pain flashed white across my vision as my neck snapped in the opposite direction, then it blared red as he slammed a fist into my nose.

If you've ever been punched right square in the nose, you learned one thing really quickly—that shit *hurts*. My eyes teared up, my vision blurred, and I had to drop to my knees to keep the demon from knocking my head off with his next punch. Fortunately for me, I wasn't just armed with my good looks and magic. I also had a Glock 19 in the back waistband of my jeans. I drew the pistol, jammed it up into the demon's belly, and squeezed off five quick shots.

It's hard to miss when the barrel is literally pressed up against your target, no matter how fucked your vision is. So I didn't. I poured five rounds of hollow-point ammunition into the demon's belly, and he went down with a bloody *thump*. Since we were on about the same level, I put three more into his face before I stood up to deal with his much larger partner, the one Curtis called "Dad."

"You killed Grinthat!" the demon howled.

I raised the pistol and pointed it at his face. "And guess who's next if you don't get the fuck out of here."

He just looked at me for a second, then said, "Grinthat was an asshole. Now I get his car. After I rip your fucking face off, of course."

I pulled the trigger on the Glock, but this demon wasn't interested in any new orifices today, apparently. He sidestepped the first two bullets and swatted the next pair to the ground. That was new. I'd only ever seen much higher-level demons move with that kind of speed. Something had to be amping him up...the artifact. It was upping the ante on the demon juice. This was definitely going to be more of a fight than I expected. I didn't have a lot of time to ponder the jacked-up demon, though, because it very quickly became time to *fight* the jacked-up demon. He was on me in a flash, barely giving me enough time to get my shield back up around my arm.

I fell back onto the pavement and skidded along under the creature's momentum, but his claws and teeth just scraped off the surface of the shield. I was kinda safe, but since he was on top of me, with my shield between us, I couldn't get my other hand free to do anything. So I just kinda lay there with a demon slamming his fists and face into the glowing energy around my arm and really wished I hadn't pissed off my guardian angel.

Apparently I hadn't pissed off my guardian pooch, though, because a huge gray blur slammed into the demon's side and knocked it off me. I rolled over and sprang to my feet as Henry shifted to his half-wolf form and prepared to throw down.

"Henry, get out of there," I called, drawing power into my hands. I had to let my shield go to do it, but if I could do enough damage with one big alpha strike, I wouldn't need defense. That's the saying, right? The best defense is turning your enemies to a greasy spot on the pavement?

Henry's head whipped around, and he gave me a quick *whuff* as if to say, "I got this," right before the demon stepped up to him and proved that he didn't have shit. The hellspawn stepped up to Henry and laid an uppercut on the point of the werewolf's jaw that would have knocked Andre the Giant halfway to the moon. Henry was big in his partly shifted form, but he wasn't stout enough to withstand a direct hit by a demon amped up on evil artifact mojo.

I heard the sick *crack* of Henry's jaw and watched him straighten up, then topple backward to the ground, out like a light. He was completely human by the time he hit the ground, all his wolf knocked clean out of him. The demon stepped forward with his claws in the air, grinning down at Henry's prone body.

"I'm gonna eat his heart in front of you, Reaper. Then I'm gonna rip out your guts and hang you from the flagpole with them. Maybe if you beg enough, I'll let you die before I send you to Hell to face Lord Lucifer. But probably not."

His hand flashed down as both of mine flew up, palms pointed straight at the demon's chest. *"Fulgur RELIDO!"* I yelled at the top of my lungs, then cut loose with a primal scream and lightning coursed down from the cloudless sky, struck me full in the face, and routed out through my hands to slam into the demon's chest. I felt the electricity sear all the hair off my arms and my mystical tattoos bled from my skin as they tried to contain the primal power of the lightning. They failed, and my tattoos were burned right off my arms, too. But I didn't die, and my eyeballs didn't melt, so I called it a win.

It felt a lot more like a win when the bolt of lightning struck the demon right in the solar plexus and lit him up like a Christmas tree. He flew back fifteen feet to slam into the side of the van, shattering every window down the driver's side and shaking the unconscious Curtis loose from his precarious perch ass-first in the windshield. Demon and Cambion both hit the ground with a *thud*, and I sagged to my knees, smoke rising up from the sleeves of my tattered hoodie. I lose more clothes to my own spells than I do to the bad guys, I swear.

"Henry?" I asked. Nothing. The werewolf was out cold and butt naked on the asphalt. I took off my hoodie, leaving me in a freshly scorched Jason Isbell t-shirt with a bunch of new burn holes in the front, and wrapped the hoodie around Henry so he didn't get arrested for indecent exposure. I wasn't worried about the immense vandalism, or the apparent murders I'd committed. I just didn't want Henry to get busted for laying on the ground in public with his little werewolf flapping in the breeze.

Henry dealt with for the moment, I went to look at the demon. He was out, but he wasn't dead. Demons don't leave a whole lot of their meat suits when their earthly shells are destroyed. That's why I wasn't really sweating the guy I filled full of holes. He'd already turned into kind of a puddle of flesh-colored soup in cheap black clothes, and if Zippy the Super-Demon was dead, he would be doing the same. That probably meant that he was—

I didn't even have time to properly think the phrase "playing possum" before the bastard's eyes popped open and he launched himself at me. He sprang up from a sitting position way faster than he should have been able to, and I went back ass over teakettle. I managed to get one foot between the demon's chest and me and give it a kick as I rolled over backward, but that maneuver is a lot harder than it looks on *Monday Night RAW*. Probably because the demon didn't know what I was going to do and wasn't cooperating with me at all. He flipped over, all right, he just didn't have the courtesy to let go of my arm as he went over, so when he flipped hard enough to land on his feet, he had my left arm trapped in both his hands.

He jerked me to my feet, then twisted my arm out to the side and gave me a vicious headbutt that left me seeing stars, and not the ones overhead. I let out a scream as he ground the bones of my wrist together and went down to one knee. I looked up at the demon's grinning maw and in the span of half a second managed to catalogue an extensive list of things I regretted about my very long life.

Well, the only good part of this is I won't be able to add anything to that list now, I thought as the laughing hell-spawned asshole raised his clawed hand high in the air.

Only to stare in shock as that same hand tumbled to the ground with a meaty *thump*. The demon stared down at its severed hand for a full second before it let out an ear-splitting scream, which was quickly cut off by the flaming silver sword that protruded from his neck. The blade gave a little twist, and with a sound like tearing wet paper, the demons head popped right off. He finally let go of my fucking hand as he toppled to the side, and from the *splat* he made as he hit the tarmac, I'd say he was already well on his way to dissolving.

I looked up at Glory, standing there looking down at me with a flaming sword in her hand and ice in her eyes. "Hey, Glory," I said. "Glad you could make it."

"I'm still pissed at you, Harker."

I paused for a second, trying to figure out which approach wouldn't get me bitch-slapped with a burning blade. I went for honesty. "I was a dick. I'm sorry."

It worked. She didn't hit me. Instead, she reached down and helped me up, just like she always did. I stood up and looked her in the eye. "I mean it," I said. "I'm sorry."

"I know. Doesn't change the fact that you're a dick."

"Yeah. I'm glad you stuck around." I meant it, too. Glory had told me I'd had other guardians over the years, but she was the only one who'd ever voluntarily become part of my life. And she was a damned important part of my life. Outside of Flynn, she was probably my best friend.

"Oh, for fuck's sake, Q. If somebody stopped being your guardian every time you were an asshole, you would have run through every cherub in the Host before you hit thirty. Now wipe that mopey look off your face and let's find this fucking magic doodad before anybody else dies."

Just then we heard a guitar chord from the stage and the roar of a crowd, and when we looked at each other, we knew there was a very good chance we were already too late.

32

There were three more demons between us and the side of the stage, but none of them were prepared to deal with an angel on a mission with a sword of pure channeled divinity. They didn't even break Glory's stride, and the human security took to their heels when they saw the crazy blond woman with a flaming blade and the tall man with glowing purple hands stalking in their direction.

We got to the stage and stopped to assess the situation. Glory let her soulsword disappear while we looked around, and I turned off the fireworks on my fingers. There was a young man on stage, a quartet of female dancers, and a DJ on a riser upstage tapping on a computer and occasionally scratching on a digital turntable. The performer was a blend of a rapper and singer, prowling the stage like a jungle cat in cutoff jeans and an untucked white tank top, a Grizzlies cap sideways on his head, and what looked like jailhouse tattoos crawling up and down his skinny, fish-belly-white arms.

"There it is," Glory said, pointing.

I followed the line of her arm but didn't see anything. "Is it on the singer or the DJ? I don't know if my musical karma can take it if I blow up another set of speakers tonight," I said.

"Look around the singer's neck," she replied. "And can we really call that singing?"

"I still think Glenn Miller is contemporary," I said. "I might not be the best judge. I see it now, the necklace, right?"

"Yes. Do you see the magic spinning off that thing? It looks foul."

She wasn't wrong. When I slipped back into my Sight, the nasty black-and-red tendrils of power that I followed to the park led right to the stone at the young man's scrawny throat, then split inside the amulet and scattered back out across the crowd, multiplied into a thousand tiny fingerlings of badness.

"Nothing about this looks good," I said. I looked around for a solution that didn't end up with me knee-deep in corpses, and after a few seconds of wracking my brain, I saw the answer. "I've got an idea. Stay here, and if he's still going in sixty seconds, go cut that necklace off him."

She looked down at the blade in her hands and gave me a nasty grin. "Not a problem. I'll just imagine your face overlaying his."

Yeah, that sentence wasn't going to give me trouble sleeping for the next forever or anything. I turned and followed the line of heavy-duty electrical cables from the dimmer racks at the side of the stage around to the big power panel behind the amphitheater. Three sets of thick feeder cables ran across the asphalt and plugged into the main breaker panel, and I had no idea which one was the most important. But after a couple seconds of looking over the panel, I found a huge red handle sticking out of the side of the box with the word "MAIN" on a label by it.

"This must be it," I muttered and took hold of the handle. I pulled down on it, encountering a surprising amount of resistance. That thing was seriously stuck. I put my back into it, and on my second try, the red handle slammed down with a loud *ka-chunk!* Every light in the park went out, and the sound cut off instantly. Loud boos rose up out of the crowd, and with the electricity disconnected, I took the opportunity to slice through all the cables with a concentrated line of pure energy.

Satisfied with the destruction I had wrought, I stepped back with a slight smile across my face. "Finally, one for the 'W' column."

"Not yet it ain't, asshole," came a voice from behind me. "Put your hands over your head and kiss the wall." The telltale sound of a hammer being drawn back told me that whoever was back there was either human, or a supernatural creature too weak to kill me with their bare hands.

I raised my hands, still glowing purple, and channeled more power through them into a blinding flash of light. I spun around and dropped to a knee, just as a bullet *spang*ed off the concrete about where my lung would have been. Seems like it's a very good thing I have no faith in humanity's ability not to shoot first and ask questions later.

The shooter was a Memphis beat cop with his Sig Sauer pistol in hand, gun now pointed at the sky as he blinked furiously to clear his eyes. I stood up, snatched the pistol out of his hand, and punched him right at the hinge of the jaw. He stopped blinking as I knocked his ass clean out, and I had to catch him as he slumped to the ground. I ejected the magazine, then ran the slide to clear the round from the chamber, slid the bullet back into the magazine, and snapped the empty pistol back into the holster on his hip. Then I slipped the magazine into the pocket on his uniform shirt, patted him on the cheek, and stood up. "Sorry about that, Officer, but you really don't need to be part of this."

I walked back to the stage, dodging scurrying stagehands and screeching managers, to where Glory stood watching the chaos. "Not bad," she said.

"I didn't even have to kill anybody," I replied. I was pretty proud of that fact.

"How many people did you injure?" That's angels for you. Always getting in a dig where they can.

"Permanently? None. I can't see our little Justin Bieber wannabe. Where did he go with the amulet?"

"He's over on stage left yelling at somebody who looks like she might be his mother."

I looked where Glory pointed, and sure enough, there was Bieber Lite yelling at a woman of maybe forty over on the side of the stage. The woman had her hair tied back in a ponytail and a clipboard in her hands and kept waving her hands at Bieblet to shush him, to no avail.

After half a minute or so of this, Bieber Jr. reached over to someone out of sight, then turned and stormed the stage.

"Oh, shit," I said as I saw what the little shit had grabbed. "Glory, how worried are we about this guy talking to the crowd?"

"The artifacts seem to be able to reach victims through sound, so I'd guess pretty worried. Why?"

I pointed to the stage, where Bieblet now stood down center with what looked like a battery-powered megaphone in his hand. "That's why."

"Son of a bitch," she said. Her sword appeared in her hand again, and she started toward the stage.

I grabbed her arm, and she turned to me, eyes blazing. "What are you doing, Harker?"

"Do you really want to walk out there and chop that guy to pieces in front of a couple thousand people?"

"No, but I also don't know what choice I have."

Well, this was different. Now I was the one advocating a solution that didn't involve killing someone. "Let's at least try something that isn't lethal first," I said.

I called up a ball of energy the size of a softball into my palm and narrowed my eyes as I concentrated on it. As I tightened the focus of my magic, the orb shrank in on itself more and more. Finally, it was about the size of a marble and glowing so bright it was hard to look at. I held it up between my thumb and forefinger, and as Baby Biebs raised the megaphone to his mouth, I hurled the energy pellet at him while I said, *"Recte fereo!"*

The ball of purple brilliance streaked across the stage, only to fly off course and splash harmlessly against the ceiling when one of the backup dancers stepped forward and stuck her hand out, smacking the little marble of power as she shot me an evil grin. *Another damned demon. Shit.*

"Okay," I said to Glory. "Plan B." I took two steps toward the stage and froze as the Wannabieber shouted out to the crowd.

"Okay, fam, we ain't done! We gone take this party back on my bus, but I ain't got room but for about ten of y'all. So what I want to know is, who wants to party wit' Big Daddy Beale?"

A roar went up from the thousand or so people randomly gathered in Handy Park in the middle of the night, and I felt myself go pale. Glory and I sprang into motion, each of us sprinting toward center stage, but we were both tackled by security before we got ten feet. I lay on my stomach, my right arm wrenched around behind my back in a hammerlock and a knee jabbed into my kidney, and all I could do was watch.

The kid, who I now knew as Big Daddy Beale but still looked like a Justin Bieber impersonator, raised the megaphone back up to his mouth. "What I need to know, is who out there is willing to do *anything* for a private concert with the BDB?"

Another roar from the crowd, followed by the sight of two girls in the front row who couldn't have been more than twenty yanking their shirts over their heads and throwing them onto the stage at Beale's feet.

"Nah, nah, nah, y'all," the kid said, shaking his head. "I ain't talking about that. I can get booty whenever I want. I'm a legit player, yo. What I need is your *devotion.*"

Screams from the crowd.

"What I need is your *undying love.*"

Screams, louder this time.

"What I *need* is your *soul!*"

The screams were at a fever pitch now, and I could feel the magic building. All the hair on my arms stood up, and power rang in my ears like a siren.

"Will you give it to me?"

I could almost see the vocal chords tearing as the crowd screamed itself hoarse. It had gone past just fandom now, way past just adoration of a rock star, or whatever Big Daddy Beale styled himself as. The magic had a hold on their passion for whatever they thought this kid stood for, whatever he represented to the most devoted or desperate of the crowd, and it was spinning them up into a cyclone of frenzied shrieks that made Beatlemania look like tepid applause.

"Who will give their very *soul* to be with me?" The kid held his hands out over the edge of the stage like he was blessing a crowd, and this time when they screamed, the gem at his throat glowed. The artifact shone with a blood-red inner light that shot out from the gem like a laser split into hundreds of tiny beams, all streaking out to the most fervent fans in the crowd, the ones with blood flecking their lips and tears streaming down their faces.

They promised their souls for the chance to be with him, and the magic granted their wish. I heard a new, hoarser screaming as the souls of a hundred young fans flew into the amulet along laser beams of magic, leaving empty bodies behind to collapse on the grass. I heard a screaming in my ears even over the laughing of the demon who held me, and I realized the screaming was my own. I squeezed my eyes shut against the growing crimson brilliance as more and more souls poured into the necklace until finally, with one gigantic eruption of magic, the amulet exploded, sending a bomb blast of magical force out from Big Daddy Beale in a sweeping circle that blew the singer into a thousand bloody chunks. I had half a second to register the immense wave of power coming toward me before my vision filled with white and went dark.

33

I woke up staring at the stars, the sound of water lapping against a shore in my ears and the not-so-fresh scent of the Mississippi River in my nose. Always eloquent, I rolled up onto on elbow and looked around. "What the fuck?" I asked.

"You're awake, good." Glory's voice came from off to my left. It sounded as flat and lifeless as a desert highway. I pushed myself the rest of the way to my feet, groaning a little as I found new bruises and what felt a lot like a pulled muscle in my right shoulder from the demon wrenching that arm behind my back.

Glory sat a few feet away on an artificial chunk of jig-sawed ground made to look like a spur of mud sticking out into the water. Her back was to me, and it looked like she had her knees pulled up to her chest with her arms wrapped around them. I limped over to her, looking around and trying to figure out where we were.

"Are we...at Mud Island?" I'd only been to the riverside park a couple of times, but the faux mud bars that stuck out into the edges of the river were distinctive.

"Yeah," she said. "I needed to get you out of the blast radius, and we really didn't want to be around there when the cops showed up, so I ported us here."

I sat down next to her and started pulling off my battered Doc Martens. "You can teleport? With a passenger?"

"Not often, and not for very far, but yeah. If my charge is going to die unless I do something extreme, I can push myself and carry you along with me when I jump. But only you. I can't carry anyone who isn't my direct responsibility, which is why I haven't ever told you about it before now."

"Because you figured I'd use you as a 'Get Becks Out of Harm Free' card, counting on you to teleport her out of trouble, you wouldn't be able to do it, and…"

"And bad things would happen. Either she'd die, and you'd hate me, and potentially go dark and make things *really* bad for the world. Or you'd tap deeper into your power than you ever have before to save her, get seduced by that much power, turn dark, and make things really bad for the world. Or I'd do it."

"I thought you said you can't."

"I can't. Not and stay a guardian."

"What would happen if you did something that made you stop being a guardian?" I was pretty sure I knew the answer, but I wanted to make sure I understood all the consequences of Glory's potential actions.

"I'd Fall." She said it simply, like "I'd stub my toe," or "I think I'll have lox on my bagel." But I could tell from the tension in her jaw that this scared the ever-loving shit out of her. This woman, or angel, rather, had literally gone into Hell by my side, fought more demons that I've drank beers, and stared down Lucifer himself. But the thought of Falling scared her silly.

I took a deep breath and let it out, then rolled my jeans up a little and stuck my feet in the cool water. "Well, I'm glad I never pushed you to do that, then. I like you a lot better un-Fallen."

She relaxed a little, and that was all it took for the emotions to pour out. She buried her face in her hands and began to cry these great, wracking sobs that made her whole body shake. I pulled her to me, wrapping my arms around her as she poured out her anguish against my chest.

"I felt them, Q," she whispered, her face buried in my t-shirt. "I felt every one of them die. That happens, you know? We can feel you short-lived, accident-prone, monumentally stupid bastards when you die."

"Shit," I said. "I didn't know." I was learning a lot about Glory tonight, it seemed.

"Not all the time," she said, sniffling a little and wiping her nose on my shirt. "But if we're distracted, or tired, or fighting something big when a human dies near us, we feel it. And of course we feel it a thousand-fold if our charge dies before their time."

"Fuck," I muttered. "That must have been brutal, then."

"Worse for the guardians nearby. A dozen or more of them were in Memphis when the people they were supposed to protect had their life force suddenly snuffed out."

"Because of me," I said. "If I'd been a little faster, or a little stronger, I could have—"

"Oh, shut up, you arrogant prick," Glory said, sitting up and nailing me with a murderous glare. "You think *you* feel guilt for those people dying? How about the cherubs whose whole existence was dedicated to keeping them alive? They had one job, and because we fucked up, *they* feel like they failed. We failed, and hundreds of people are dead."

"Well, now what? My tracking spell is blown to shit. It ended when I lost consciousness, so I can't find the artifacts now. Not that having the damn spell did us much good in the first place. Where do we look for these things now? We've got one of them, but two of the others have sucked in a fuckton of soul energy and blinked out of existence, and we have no leads on the last one."

I noticed that it was getting lighter and looked around. "What time is it? How long was I out?"

"It's about seven. You were down for several hours. That was a *big* wave of magic, Harker, and you caught some of it before I could port you away. You're lucky you heal fast."

"Well, I guess we go back to Zeek's and recast the locator spell?" I asked. "I can't really think of anything else to do. Oh shit, Henry!" I

209

said as I remembered the werewolf I'd left unconscious backstage with my jacket covering his junk.

"Henry is fine," Glory said. "I put in a call to the local Alpha, and he sent someone to take Henry to a safe house downtown where he can heal up."

"Okay, then," I said, standing up. The water was ankle deep but felt good on my sore feet. I held out a hand to Glory. "Are you good?"

She looked up at me, her eyes red from crying. Fucking angels, man. They don't even recognize the term "ugly cry." Glory had just rubbed snot all over my favorite shirt, and she was still model-gorgeous.

"I don't know," she said. "This has been a bad one, Q. The body count is really high, and like I told you, I *feel* those. It's...it's a lot." She reached up for my hand, and I pulled her to her feet.

"If you need to sit the rest of this one out, I understand," I said, then let a little smirk escape. "I know how delicate some of you womenfolk can get."

She put both hands in the center of my chest, picked me up by my shirt, and flung me over her head into the river. "How's that for deli-cate, asshole?"

I came up spluttering and laughing. I swam a couple of feet forward until it was shallow enough to stand up in. "That's pretty good, I guess. You feel better?"

"Yeah." She gave me a rueful grin. "Prick."

"True enough," I said, walking up out of the water and muttering a quick burst of Latin to dry myself off. I sat down to put on my boots when something buzzed in my pocket. "Hey, look at that," I said. "My phone really is water resistant."

I pulled the slim plastic rectangle out of my pocket and looked at the screen, miraculously unbroken after the night's activities. I slid my finger across the screen to answer the call. "Hey, Zeek. What's up?"

There was a pause on the other end, then a faint voice rasped, "Quincy...come...fast...taken...." Then I heard a thump, and nothing else. After a few seconds of me yelling into the phone, I hung up and slid it back into my pocket.

"We gotta go," I said. I finished tying my boots and started off down the riverbank toward where I left my truck. Then I stopped. "That's going to take too long. Help me steal a car."

"What was that?" Glory asked, grabbing my elbow. She turned me around and gave me a shake. "Q, talk to me! Was that Zeek? What's wrong?"

"I don't know, but he sounded *bad*."

Glory took half a step back, her eyes widening a little. "Zeek's a djinn, isn't he?"

"Yeah."

"Djinn are among the most powerful creatures on Earth, and more powerful than a lot of things from other planes," Glory said.

"I know that. So we need to haul ass and get back to his bar to help him."

"Harker?"

"Yeah?" I asked. I looked at her face, and what I saw pulled me up short. My guardian angel was *scared*.

"What can vanquish a djinn? And if it can beat up Zeek, how the hell are we going to handle it?"

I took a deep breath, then let it out slow. "Same way we handle everything else, kiddo. Dumb luck and lots of profanity. Let's roll."

34

Zeek's place didn't *look* destroyed, until we got to the door and noticed there wasn't a door there. There were a lot of splinters that used to be a door, but there wasn't anything hanging out in the frame, just three hinges swinging in the breeze. Glory and I exchanged a look, and I slipped my Sight back over my eyes. There were traces of heavy magic strength around the entryway, but some of that could have been from Zeek's shattered wards.

That door was nothing to sneeze at. It was a physically heavy thing, a solid slab of wood reinforced with steel bands, but it was the magic scribed into the wood and all around the jamb that really gave the whole place its feeling of impenetrability. Zeek had wards layered on top of wards, and protective sigils woven in between the layers of magic. If anyone had asked me before that moment, I would have said that nothing short of a nuclear blast could take down that door, and I only gave the nuke about a fifty-fifty shot.

But there was no door anymore, just a bunch of oaken toothpicks and some scattered scraps of cold iron that used to hold the wood and magic together. The walls surrounding the door even looked blackened, like whatever had blasted the entryway wasn't contained in one spot, but damaged the whole structure. This was some serious mojo. I didn't have a whole lot of faith in my ability to survive an attack from anything that could brute force its way through Zeek's front door and still have enough juice left to kick his ass, but I also didn't have a whole lot of options.

Zeek provided me with shelter when I needed it, a sanctuary in which to begin the process of rebuilding my life. I owed him for that, and I was going to repay that debt if it killed me. I just really hoped it didn't.

"Let me go first," Glory said, but I shook my head.

"Nah. I want you back there to save my ass if it's still there. You go first, if anything gets the drop on you, I don't have a snowball's chance of taking it down. If something surprises me, you've still got enough firepower to send it back to wherever it came from."

I could almost feel the disapproving glare burning twin holes into my back, but I didn't turn around to see. The light was out over the door-hole, and the steps leading down to the bar entrance were pitch black, so I called up a little trickle of power and whispered, "*Lux.*" A sphere of white appeared floating a few inches above the palm of my right hand, and as I blew on it, it floated down the steps, casting the whole stairway into cold blue light.

"That's not good," I murmured.

"Why?" Glory asked. "At least now you can see."

"Yeah, but it also means that every ward Zeek had in that stairwell is blown to shit. No way a puny little light spell should survive more than two seconds in there before getting dispelled with extreme prejudice, and with a nice chunk of backlash into my face to boot." I waved my hand down the corridor. "But there sits Tinkerbelle, glowing away by the door like a good little fairy." Sure enough, the orb was floating down at the bottom of the steps, waiting for further instruction.

"Oh well, nobody lives forever," I said. I drew my pistol, shrouded my left arm in my magical shield, and started down the steps.

"You know that we have literally met people who live forever, right?" Glory said, manifesting her soulsword and following me down.

I didn't answer, concentrating on trying not to fall through the battered steps. Whatever blew out the door did a number on the whole stairwell, and I wasn't looking forward to trying to maneuver through the bar if the floor wasn't stable. There was a lot of water running underneath this place, and I really didn't want to get dumped into the Mississippi with the entire building on top of me. The stairs creaked and groaned, but they held, and when I put my palm on the door, it swung open freely.

I slipped through the door and rolled left, my shield in front of my face and my gun sweeping the room as Glory came in behind me and peeled right. The place looked like a bomb had gone off in there, but there were no hostiles that I could see in either the magical spectrum or the mundane one. As a matter of fact, I couldn't see anyone, living or dead. Including Zeek.

"Zeek? You in here, buddy?" I called, bringing my pistol around in front of me as I turned right to check the rest of the room.

There was a clatter from behind the bar, a bottle rolling across the wooden floor, and I motioned to Glory. She and I split and moved through the room without a sound, stopping on opposite sides of the wooden horseshoe. I looked across at her, and at her nod we both leapt from the floor to the bar top. My boots slipped a little in spilled beer, but I kept my balance and aimed my pistol down where I'd heard the noise.

"Holy shit, man," I said, holstering my Glock and hopping down to the floor. "What the fuck got hold of you?"

Zeek looked like twenty miles of bad road. I'd been blown up twice in the last twenty-four hours, and I didn't feel as bad as he looked. His bottom lip was split, his left eye was swollen almost shut, and there was a gash on his eyebrow that ran all the way up his entire forehead. His scalp wound had obviously poured blood because a dark brown mask covered his face.

He sat on the floor with his back to the bar, his left leg folded underneath him and sticking out at an angle that made me wince just to look at it, and he didn't seem to be able to move his left arm. It lay against his stomach, and he was holding it in place with his right.

When my boots *thumped* to the floor, he tried to open his eyes, and I was pretty sure I saw vitreous fluid seeping from the swollen left. Whatever was here had done a number on him the likes of which I'd barely ever seen anything walk away from.

"Harker..." he said, and I could see the tops of broken teeth as his voice rasped, barely audible.

I knelt beside him, putting one hand on the side of his face. "I'm here, dude. I'm here. Don't try to talk. Just let me get..." I started to say, "let me get you out of there," but I wasn't honestly sure how much I could move him without doing more damage. There was a fresh trickle of blood at the corner of his mouth, and I couldn't tell if it was coming from his busted lip or if there was some internal bleeding going on.

"Glory?" I looked up and got even more concerned when I saw the worry on her face. "Can we move him? Can you heal him? Fuck, can he even *be* healed?"

"Yesss..." he whispered. "River..." His eyes fluttered shut, and his head lolled to the side.

I looked back to Glory. "Djinn are elementals, magic by nature and tied to one of the five elements."

"Five?"

"Yeah, five. Fire, earth, water, air, spirit. Why do you think a pentacle has five points? Come on Harker, think a little. But that's not the point. Yes, he can be healed, but we need to get him into the water."

Now the bar's location made even more sense. Not only would the running water screw with most practitioners like me, but the nearness of his primary element would heighten Zeek's power, putting him at an even greater advantage. Smart.

"Okay," I said, standing up and walking around the corner of the bar. "Hop down there and grab him. Maybe do a little laying on of hands or something."

"Pretty sure my magic and Zeek's don't work the same way. What are you doing?"

I held up a glowing hand. "I'm going to open a door to the river."

215

"Harker, stop!" Glory shouted.

I looked at her, letting the light around my fist wink out. "What?"

"Look around, jackass. You want to bring the whole place down? You were so careful thirty seconds ago. Now at the first opportunity, you want to start blowing holes in everything." She shook her head. "Jesus, the shit I put up with…"

"Are you allowed to take the Lord's name in vain?" I asked.

"It's not in vain if you used to change his diapers," she replied. "Now get over here and help me get him down the trapdoor."

"Trapdoor?" I looked to where she was pulling up the non-stick floor mat to expose a square of floor with a ring set into it. "How did you know that was there?"

"It just made sense," she said. "I mean, the first thing you did when you moved in was to make yourself a bolt hole, and Zeek's been alive a lot longer than you, so it stood to reason he'd have done the same thing."

"Yeah, but how did you know which side of the bar it was on?"

"I didn't. If there was nothing over here, I was going to have you pull up the mats on that side. I just knew it wouldn't be along the front because that's where Zeek holed up after calling you. He knew he was hurt, so he wouldn't block his own escape route."

"You've put a lot of thought into how injured people act," I said.

Glory looked at me like I was stupid. "It's literally my entire reason for existence—keeping stupid humans from doing stupid human things. Figuring out how you people behave when you're at your worst is kinda my thing. And Zeek might not be human, but he's spent a lot of time pretending to be, so he's going to react like a human in most cases. Now get over here and jump down this hole."

I was halfway to the trapdoor before I stopped. "Why am I jumping down the hole?"

"So you can catch him when I slide him down to you. I don't want to take a chance on hurting him more. And you smell like demon guts."

Both of those were valid points, so I just stepped forward and dropped straight through the three by three hole in the floor. I plummeted about eight feet and landed with a splash in the shockingly cold river. It didn't feel that cold when I put my feet in it an hour ago, but it also wasn't up to my waist then, either. I wiggled my feet from side to side to get my footing as firm as possible, then held both arms over my head.

"Send him down to me," I said.

Glory's face disappeared from view, and over the lapping of the water on the bank, I heard the unmistakable sound of a body being dragged. Zeek's head appeared in the hole, then his shoulders, then his arms flopped down. I took half a step back as Glory lowered him as far as she could by his ankles, then I caught him under the arms and staggered under his weight.

I lowered the unconscious djinn into the water as gently as I could, holding his face up so he could breathe. Did djinn breathe? If water was his element, could he breathe water? There was a lot I didn't know about djinn. Honestly, all I really knew was they came from the Middle East, and they wielded some seriously potent magic and could fight like the proverbial whirling dervishes.

That meant that whatever kicked Zeek's ass was even more powerful, and I wasn't exactly batting a thousand in my fights this week. I watched as the water washed away the blood on his face, then saw the cut on his forehead begin to knit closed. As I stared at him, the swelling around his eye subsided, then his lips returned to their normal, unpunched shape. I heard a *crack* from under the water and looked down to see his leg now extending straight out from his hip like normal, and his left arm pulled away from his side and floated in the water, apparently mended.

After a few more seconds, Zeek reached up with his right arm, gripped my shoulder to hoist himself up a couple of inches, then flopped over face first into the water with a huge splash. I let out a startled yelp, then stepped back as he stood up, scrubbing water and dried blood from his face with his hands. He bent at the waist, washing the last traces of the battle from his cheeks and chin, then stood up straight and turned to face me.

Zeek looked like nothing had happened, like we were just two buddies taking an early-morning swim fully clothed in the river under his bar. "Thanks for coming," he said. "I appreciate it."

"I do still technically work for you," I said with a lopsided grin. "So, it's poor form to ignore your calls."

He smiled back at me. "Still. It is appreciated. Now let's get inside. There are some things you need to know."

"Like what beat the shit out of you and where we can find it?" I asked.

"More like what came in here, beat the shit out of me, stole the ring from your room, and is going to destroy half the United States if we can't figure out how to stop it." Zeek bent his knees, then sprang straight up, catching the edge of the trapdoor with his fingers and pulling himself up and out of sight.

"That's okay," I called. "I'll go around."

I'd taken about two steps when Glory's face appeared in the trap door and stretched an arm out. "Get up here Harker, we've gotta go save the world."

"Again?"

35

Glory hauled me up through the trapdoor, which I flipped closed behind me. I know me, and I could just see me falling halfway through and dangling there with one leg and one arm swinging in the air while my guardian angel laughed her ass off at me. Zeek was sitting on a stool on the customer side of the bar with a bottle of Maker's Mark in front of him, no glass.

"You want a straw with that, pal?" I asked. I grabbed a highball glass and a bottle of Gentleman Jack and walked over to sit next to him. Glory leaned on the bar from the business side and sipped on a Yuengling.

"So, what's the story, Zeek?" I asked as I sat down. "Something beat the ever-loving shit out of you, and I have to admit, I'm a little worried about what might have that much horsepower."

Zeek didn't look up, just sat there with his elbows on the bar, staring at the wood, his hands spinning the bottle of bourbon slowly against the polished wood. "I've never been hurt that bad before, Harker. I've lived for thousands of years. *Thousands*. And I've never had anything handle me that easily. Sure, I've lost fights. Not many, but it happens to everybody. A Yeti caught me off guard in Nepal once and broke both my legs, and I was too far from water to heal. Took me a day and a half to drag myself to a mountain stream and get right again. I battled a Torment Demon at Sinope during the Crimean War, and he almost had me until he made the mistake of trying to drown me. Hell, I even went toe to toe with that snotty prick Gabriel a few years before the Battle of Hastings, but even he didn't hit as hard as she did."

"She?" I asked. "Who was she? Hell, *what* was she?"

"She's a dragon, Harker."

I didn't fall off my stool, but I certainly had to put a foot down to steady myself. "Dragons aren't real, Zeek. Trust me, I spent a lot of time looking for them in Europe in the early part of the twentieth century. There's no such thing as a dragon."

"But demons, vampires, werewolves, and djinn you don't have a problem with?" He raised an eyebrow at me. "Come on, Harker. Why should one set of mythical creatures be real and another not?"

"I don't know, because that's kinda what the word 'mythical' means?" I replied. "Anyway, how do you know she's a dragon? I'm guessing we're not talking something the size of Smaug, since your bar still has a roof."

"Dragons can change shape and, even in their human forms, are incredibly powerful. They have magic oozing from their very pores, and strength, speed, and nigh-invulnerability to boot."

"Did you just reference *The Tick* while we're talking about dragons?" I asked, pouring myself a healthy slug of Jack and tossing the amber liquid down my throat.

"Just because I've lived for thousands of years doesn't mean I don't appreciate good literature," Zeek replied. "But that's beside the point. She came in here and mopped the floor with me. I got the feeling she only threw me around the room as long as she did because she was feeling playful. She could have ended me at any time and taken the ring. But she *knew* she could take me out whenever she wanted to, so she took her time and made it last."

"Fuck," I said. "I forgot about the ring." I moved to stand, but Zeek held up his hand. "Don't bother. It's gone. She made a point of showing me the ring glittering on her finger as she sashayed out the door."

"Well, what do we do now?" I asked. I looked between Zeek and Glory, but neither seemed to have any suggestions. "We've lost the one artifact we had, two more have killed literally hundreds of people tonight and vanished, and we've never had so much as a sniff of the fourth one. I think as far as world-saving goes, we kinda suck."

"We'll get there, Q. It's been pretty awful, but we'll figure it out. We just have to—" Glory stopped in mid-sentence and dropped to her knees, agony written across her face. I had just enough time to register what happened to her before I was taken down myself by a wave of magical energy that felt like it wanted to turn me inside out. I gripped the top of the bar with both hands, barely managing to keep my stool upright as the world flipped on its axis a couple of times, then twisted around like a funhouse mirror before everything settled back in its proper place.

"What...the fuck...was *that*?" Glory asked as she dragged herself up to her feet.

"Fuck if I know," I said, standing up from my stool and holding my arms out from my sides as my balance threatened to go sideways again. "But it didn't come from in here." I moved to the door, using the backs of the few chairs still upright as touchstones to keep my balance as I crossed the bar. The floor rolled back and forth like I was on choppy seas, but by the time I got to the door, I had pretty much stabilized. I looked back, and Glory was helping Zeek navigate the floor, so I booked it on up the stairs.

I made it out to the parking lot, thanking everything I'd ever prayed to or cursed at for the man who invented the banister, and scanned the area for threats. The gravel lot was empty except for Zeek's sports car and my pickup, and there wasn't another soul in sight. I turned back to see Zeek and Glory come through the door, and as I did, I saw what caused all the commotion.

"What is it, Q?" Glory asked, then she turned and looked at the sky, following my gaze.

I didn't say anything. I just pointed.

Zeek turned to look, then nodded. "Yeah, that's probably what we're looking for."

Djinn are apparently masters of understatement because the "that" in question was a column of red light streaking up to the sky in the distance, looking for all the world like a low-rent Luxor plopped down on the banks of the Mississippi. "What's over there?" I asked. I could see something at the bottom of the beam, but I couldn't quite make it out.

"That would be the Pyramid," Zeek said. "Memphis's most bizarre attraction, and this coming from a town that houses Graceland."

"You think your dragon's there?" I asked.

"Part of me hopes not," Zeek said. "But if being around you the last few nights has taught me anything, it's to hope for the best, and expect an absolute shitstorm."

"Well," I said, looking from the beam to my friends. "Let's go stir some shit up."

It wasn't my first trip to the Pyramid, the giant arena-turned-outdoor megastore/hotel/restaurant/bowling alley/psychedelic monument to human hubris and poor taste, but it was the first time I'd ever been to the Pyramid when a giant beacon of hellish magical power streamed up from its tip to roil against the clouds like a really creepy *Ghostbusters* imitation. We got out of my truck, and I looked at Zeek and Glory.

"I think this is probably the place."

"Yeah," Glory said. "But the place for what?"

"Hopefully the place where we find all four artifacts and some way to destroy them, before whatever that is," I gestured at the beam shooting up out of the ridiculous Bass Pro Shop, "does something even nastier than we've seen tonight."

"Okay, so what's the plan?" Zeek asked.

I let my Sight slip down over my mundane vision and peered up at the top of the Pyramid. Shifting back to normal vision, I said, "It looks like all the excitement is coming from the observation deck, so I think that's where we go. You two come up the sides, and I'll come up the elevator shaft."

"You're just going to ride the elevator up, Q? Don't you think they'll be watching for that?"

"Yeah, I do. I expect the elevator to be disabled at either the top or the bottom. But I don't think they'll be expecting someone to climb that stupid glass tower they've got the elevator in, which is exactly what I'm going to do."

I'd gone to check out the Pyramid in my first week in Memphis, and I'd ridden all the way to the glass-encased observation deck at the very tippy top. I remembered the elevator as being basically a jungle gym of exposed girders, pretty simple to climb. As long as there wasn't anything trying to knock me off, of course.

"And you want us to go up the outside of the huge glass pyramid?" Zeek asked.

"Don't act like it's such a big deal. Glory's got wings, so if you don't have some way to magic your ass up there, she'll carry you."

"I can make it on my own. I just wanted to know why we weren't all going up together."

"Because this way you guys hit them on opposite sides from outside, and I come in from below inside, and whoever is in there might not be able to take out all three of us before we can wreck those artifacts."

"Don't you at least want to find out what they're planning?" Zeek asked.

I looked at him and felt my face go grim. "Not really, no. Two of these things killed a gym full of teenagers and a park full of music fans tonight on their own. If all four of them are up there, and there's a dragon, that's a lot of fucking juice. I don't give a fuck what they're trying to do, I just want it stopped any way we can."

"If we can," Zeek said.

"I was trying hard not to phrase it that way," I replied.

"I'm very, very old, Harker. I know what an impossible situation looks like."

"Well, if you know that from experience, then you've obviously misjudged the impossibility meter at least once. Here's hoping you did this time, too." I didn't think he did, but we were all trying to look brave for the others. All any of us really wanted to do was join the throngs of people in pajamas and bathrobes streaming out of the lower floors of the Pyramid as the hotel evacuated. There had to be three hundred people running our way, all in the kind of hurry that you don't get from a false alarm in the middle of the night. They knew this was a bad scene.

And just as they started their escape, the scene got much, much worse. The light from the beam flickered in my peripheral vision, and I looked up to see a pair of giant wings obscure the column of energy for a second as a huge golden dragon burst through the glass of the observation deck and flew down toward the fleeing hotel guests.

"Holy Khaleesi, Batman," I muttered as I took in my first sight of an honest to God dragon. It had at least a thirty-foot wingspan, maybe more, and it did nothing but get bigger as it flew forward. A head the size of an office desk sat atop a sinuous neck, with a pair of thick ridges coming down the front of its skull over its narrow eyes. Long fangs lined its jaws as the monster opened its mouth and belched a huge gout of flame down onto the fleeing tourists.

I held both hands above my head and called power. I caught sight of Zeek out of the corner of my eye as he waved his hands toward the river. As he did, a column of water six feet in diameter rose from the water's surface and streaked through the air at the fireball.

"*Restinguendum incendium!*" I shouted at the top of my lungs, flinging the summoned power like a ball at the dragon's mouth.

Zeek's water turned the fire to steam, and my spell flew into the gaping maw of the creature and exploded in a shower of green-blue energy, cutting off the last tendrils of flame lingering in the dragon's mouth. The creature whirled around impossibly nimbly, pinwheeling one wing almost to the ground and coming about in a lightning-fast turn.

Then it landed, and we were standing in front of a huge, very angry dragon with teeth the size of my forearms and a bloodthirsty look in its eyes.

Not for the first time I wished that one of my brothers had been born with magic instead of me. Then the dragon opened its mouth and drew in a huge breath to incinerate us where we stood.

36

Except nothing happened. The dragon's mouth opened wide, it thrust its neck forward, it let out a terrifying roar. But no fire.

"Huh," I said. "Looks like the extinguish spell was pretty solid."

Glory whipped her head around to gape at me. "You didn't know if that would work?"

"Work?" I asked. "Jesus fucking Christ, Glory. Two hours ago, I didn't believe dragons existed. So no, I had no goddamn idea that spell would work on one."

Before our eyes, the dragon change form, shrinking from a giant winged beast to a human-sized woman with a very large sword in her hands. She stood nearly six feet tall, was broad through the shoulders, and her dark hair was pulled back into tight cornrows. Her clothes looked like some kind of leather armor, and she held her sword like she knew how to use it.

"Let's finish this, djinn. When last we met, there wasn't room to swing my blade. Now I'll teach you the meaning of the word pain." The smile that crept across her dusky face was chilling, made not the least bit less terrifying by the fact that her eyes still shone with the golden color of her scales.

"When last you met, he didn't have backup, either. You want to dance? Let's dance, bitch." Glory's soulsword flared to life in her hand, and she dropped any façade of humanity. She grew several inches, her body adding mass to match her foe, and brilliant white wings appeared on her back. She flew straight at the dragon, Zeek by her side. As she sprang into the air, she shouted, "Get upstairs, Harker! We'll handle the dragon!"

I had my doubts about their ability to do together what Zeek hadn't been able to even realistically attempt a few hours ago, but looking to the peak of the Pyramid, I had zero doubts that something exceptionally fucked up was happening atop the building. I looked to Zeek and Glory, both charging at the dragon with a determined look on their face, and nodded. She was right. If they beat the dragon or didn't, somebody needed to stop whatever was happening upstairs, because there's no world in which a random pillar of eldritch power streaking from the ground to the sky is a good thing.

I sprinted right, taking a big arc around the dragon as I ran to the front door of the oddball structure. The flood of people running out was down to a trickle by the time I got there, and it was a simple matter to turn sideways and slide past a woman in bunny slippers and a UT sweatshirt into the entrance of the huge store.

I stopped cold a few steps from the door, momentarily stunned at the magnitude of the Redneck Mecca I was in. There were huge fresh-water fish tanks scattered here and there with giant catfish in them, a faux river wending its way through the entire store, and an honest-to-God bass boat with a mannequin holding a shotgun floating in the river. There were more fishing lures than I ever knew existed, and a climbing wall that must have gone twenty feet vertical.

I shook myself out of the consumerist trance as a security guard walked up to me, waving his arms. "I'm sorry, sir, you've got to—"

I cut him off, flipping out my badge holder and saying, "Homeland Security," in my most official voice. The badge was so expired as to not even be funny, and I was probably breaking three federal laws just holding it, but mall cops aren't usually the most perceptive or the most diligent.

This one might not have been either of those things, but he was stubborn. He shook his head and pointed to the door. "Sorry, sir. I haven't been cleared to let anyone through, so you'll have to take it up with my boss outside."

He reached forward to take me by the elbow, and I shook him loose. "Son, if you don't want to end up in Gitmo with every hint of your very existence erased, you'll get the hell out of my way. You think being a rent-a-cop is bad? Wait until you're in a federal prison and somebody decides you need to be the back section of the human centipede. Now you go help the rest of the civilians. I'm going upstairs to see what the hell is happening here."

I took a step forward to push past him, but this time he did grab my bicep, and his grip was pretty tight. He lowered his voice into that really annoying "authority" voice that people with no authority what-soever like to use, and said, "Get the fuck out. Now." Then he tried to spin me around and shove me into the dwindling crowd of people slowly heading out the double glass doors.

"Okay, shithead, I've wasted enough time on you," I said. I turned back to him and locked eyes. "*Somnus*," I said, and let out a little whisper of power, just enough to send him to Dreamland for an hour or two, not enough to knock out the whole lobby. To my surprise, he didn't go down. He just raised an eyebrow at me and smiled a little.

"You must be the guy who's been trying to fuck up the boss's plans all night. We were told somebody might show up, but I didn't think I'd be the lucky one who caught your ass." Then his grip got a *lot* tighter on my upper arm, and with a jerk, he flung me over his head deeper into the store.

I crashed through a display of Carhartt shirts and went to the floor in a tangle of 3XL denim and more flannel than I've seen since Seattle in 1993. I disentangled myself from the clothes and the rack, getting to my feet and reaching around behind my back for my pistol. My hand closed on empty air. *Shit.* After getting thrown around all over town all night, the poor clip on the holster finally gave up the ghost.

I caught sight of the guard headed my way with two of his buddies in tow. I guess they'd decided that they wanted me in the store after all. Of course, now they were in position to cut off my route to the elevator, so I wasn't any closer to my goal. I slipped on my Sight to take a look at exactly what I was dealing with.

Big fucking surprise, it was demons. Still not anything really heavy duty, just random pitchfork-pushers from the middle Circles. They were strong, and fast, and resistant to at least some of my magic, though, so I needed to figure out this weapon situation, and fast.

Fortunately, if you ever find yourself in a retail establishment and needing to fight off demons dressed like security guards, or even just real security guards, I highly recommend a sporting goods store. I knew I didn't have enough time to get a gun out of the case, find the ammo, load it, and fire before the trio of assholes ripped my throat out, but I could sure as hell sprint across the store to the hunting section.

So that's exactly what I did. It wasn't quite directly away from the demons, so my route did give the right-most critter a chance to cut me off on the diagonal. That's when I took advantage of the fact that the Memphis Bass Pro Shops is fucking gigantic. A former basketball arena and concert venue, there's a *lot* of empty space inside. We were on the bottom, or on a false floor built over top of a fake river that ran through everything, but that meant there was at least forty feet clear overhead. I planned to use every fucking inch of it.

I took a hop onto a shelf, leapt off the top, and shouted, *"Volant!"* at the top of my lungs. No, yelling didn't give the spell any more power, but it made the few stragglers by the front door turn and look, and I'm vain enough to want an audience every once in a while, and mature enough to own that fact. If only barely mature enough. I poured willpower into *myself*, which is a lot harder than it sounds. The magic wants to go somewhere, and if it's already inside you, it's pretty hard to get it to turn around and affect you instead of rushing outward.

That's why it's much easier to blast something to pieces or cast an illusion than it is to change yourself magically. That and the fact that most spells wear off eventually are why nobody uses magic to make themselves thinner, stronger, or taller. At least not more than once or twice. But I've been playing around with forces outside of the natural world for a long time, so I could control the power enough to get airborne for a good forty yards.

I landed right in front of the counter at the hunting section and smiled. I didn't do the whole superhero landing thing for a couple reasons. One, there was no one around to see it. The onlookers by the door couldn't see past all the merchandise, and the store was pretty well deserted by this point. Two, that landing is hell on the knees, and I'm not as young as I used to be. So I just channeled power out of my palms to counteract my momentum and dropped down on my feet, soft as you please.

I found what I was looking for in seconds, in a glass case about five feet away. No time to screw around with unlocking things, so I just drove my elbow through the glass and reached down to pluck my new toys from the red faux-velvet display shelves. I turned around just about the same time the first demon skidded to a stop at the end of an aisle about fifteen feet away.

"I got him, guys! Get over here!" he shouted. He cracked his knuckles together and smiled. "We'll probably get fresh human meat for killing you. This is gonna be fun *and* rewarding." Then he dropped his human form, sloughing off the flesh and ripping through the guard uniform in a truly nauseating transformation. He grew to about eight feet tall, and his gangly arms stretched down almost to his knees. He gave himself a shake, and the last scraps of meat and fabric clinging to his gaunt, red-skinned frame flew off to land on the tile floor with a *splat.*

His buddies arrived then, already transformed. I guess with the mundanes out the door, they decided there was no need to be inconspicuous. So now I was looking at three demons coming at me down the aisle of camping gear and fishing rods, all in their true forms with gaunt frames, overlong arms, yellow eyes, horns, and claws on their freakishly long fingers.

"One against three," I said, twirling around the pair of tactical tomahawks I'd pilfered with a satisfying *whish* through the air. "Seems about fair. You guys want to surrender now, or do you want a story to tell the baby demons when I send you back to Lucifer in pieces?"

"Who the hell do you think you are, human?" the nearest demon asked, scraping his claws against the floor with a bone-splitting *screeeeeeesh*.

"Who am I?" I asked. I smiled, and as I did, I channeled power into the hilts of the axes, wreathing the weapons with purple fire. "I'm the one they whisper about in the dark corners of Hell. I'm the guy Lucifer has wet dreams about getting his hands on. I'm the mother-fucker that waltzed into Hell, kicked your boss in the dick, and danced out again giving all of you pit-dwelling fuckwits the big middle finger as I left. Who am I? I'm your worst fucking nightmare, you piece of soul-sucking shit. I'm the thing that you really hope isn't behind you when you hear something scrape across the pavement. I'm the face you see right before you wake up screaming and soaked in piss. I'm Quincy Fucking Harker, and I'm going to show you why they call me Reaper."

37

My name didn't send the demons scurrying back to whatever hole they'd climbed out of, but it did give them about half a second's pause in their advance, and that was the opening I needed. I flung both axes at the lead demon of the pair right in front of me, catching him square in the chest. He toppled back into the monster coming up behind him, and they went down in a tangle of elbows and assholes.

I whirled around to the shattered display case, reached in, and came out with a pair of kukri-style machetes. Turning my head to the last demon standing, I grinned at him and said, "Let's dance, motherfucker."

Then I leapt at him, pushing energy out through the soles of my boots to give me a little extra oomph. I streaked through the air, throwing my weight forward at the last second into a flip so I planted both feet square in the demon's chest and sprang over his head like a luchador, only without the funny mask. I landed, then spun around as the demon slammed to its back just a couple of feet away from me. I swung both machetes down at the same spot, pushing power through them to wreath the blades in the same fire I wrapped the tomahawks in, but the asshole moved too fast for me to bury burning metal in his skull.

I did nick its left shoulder, though, and it glared at me as it got to its feet. Purple sparks danced around a gash near the demon's collarbone, and I could almost smell the sulfur as part of the creature's essence cooked away.

"That's not going to stop burning," I said, a casual smile dancing across my lips. "It's actually a cooking spell, meant to purify meat. But since you nasty bastards are a plague upon the very plane you inhabit, it's going to burn and burn and burn until every last vestige of your corrupted soul is consumed."

The creature smiled at me, an obscene expression on its elongated face, showing far too many teeth. "You think I'm afraid of fire, Reaper? I was born in flame! I have danced along the lakes of fire in Hell itself and lived to tell the tale. I have felt Lucifer's flaming lash dance across my flesh, and I thanked him and begged for more. Fire doesn't harm me, you idiot. Like steel, it only makes me stronger!" Then the demon stretched both obscenely long arms out in front of itself and charged me.

It stepped forward, claws ripping through my chest, except my chest...wasn't exactly where it seemed to be. As the demon's hands shredded air, I let the masking spell I was holding drop, and the faux-Harker the demon was fighting vanished. I was, at that second, running at full speed toward the demon, and when it looked up at me in shock, I dove through its legs in a baseball slide that would have made Jackie Robinson proud. As I passed under the stunned monster, I sliced through both hamstrings with my glowing machetes, then scrambled out of the way as the demon crashed to the floor like an overturned box turtle.

Its arms flailed wildly for a couple of seconds, then they flopped around on the floor after I chopped them off at the elbows. Unable to stand, with no arms, the demon still didn't give up. It snapped at me with its jaws until I shoved a two-foot blade through each eye and turned it into a melting pile of black and red-streaked sludge. The demon's true form on Earth is still an invader, like its meat suits, and it still turns to goop when the creature is destroyed, as much as any of them can actually be destroyed here. It just turns into goop of a different color, that's all.

"One down, two to go," I muttered, just in time to hear the scratch of claws on cheap vinyl tile behind me. I spun around and dropped to one knee, flinging the machete in my right hand overhead to bury in the demon's gut. I called power and channeled it into the streaking blade, shouting, *"Volare!"* at the top of my lungs. The machete sped up on the jet of magic and buried itself in the demon's solar plexus, piercing all the way through the monster with several inches of point sticking out the back. The blade came even further through as the demon toppled forward, pushing the blade the rest of the way into its chest.

I thought it was dead, but I didn't want to take any chances on it getting back into the fight, so I strode over to the fallen demon and chopped off its head. That sealed the deal, and the corpse began to decompose immediately. I looked down at the machete in the bubbling pile of demon goo and decided that I could probably make do with the one weapon I had left.

Which I promptly dropped when a sledgehammer crashed into my spine and sent me hurtling to the floor. I managed to push off a little with my feet, so I didn't land face-first in demon carcass, but there was enough splashing that I was pretty sure I was going to have to douse these pants in holy water. And burn them. If I survived the night, of course.

I got to my hands and knees and crawled forward before whatever knocked me down, the third demon I assumed, could stomp my lungs flat. The claw that came down missed my vital organs, but it did bury four needles of hot agony in the back of my thigh, setting my leg aflame and pinning me to the floor like a butterfly in a display.

"Gotcha." The last demon's raspy voice was hot in my ear, its breath moist on the side of my neck.

"Yeah, you did," I gasped. "But then you had to go and get close, you dumb fuck." I rolled over, willing myself to ignore the fire shooting up my leg as the monster's claws ripped out of my thigh. I locked my fingers around the creature's throat and slapped my right hand down on its forehead. I channeled power straight through my palm, not trying to shape it or guide it, not even adding a snazzy purple flair. No, I just poured raw elemental energy through myself into the demon's head, blasting a beam of blinding white light through its eyes and straight out the back of its skull.

The demon's head blew apart, as did the shelf behind it, a metal and plastic sign that read "Hunting/Fishing," and a mannequin in a duck blind hanging from the rafters. I released my hold on the power and scooted back on my butt, trying to get out from under the demon before it turned into shithead soup.

I tried to stand, but my leg was having none of that bullshit. I couldn't see the wounds, but it felt like someone jabbed a screwdriver into the back of my thigh and was trying to tighten my hamstring that way. In four separate but equally agonizing places. I managed to get to one knee, then I used the shelf of camping equipment to haul myself upright. I could barely put any weight on my leg, at least for the moment. I knew it would be mostly functional in a couple hours, thanks to the accelerated healing I inherited from Luke, but given the light show atop the building, I wasn't all that confident in there being a couple of hours to give it.

But I couldn't walk, much less fight, so I had to do something, and fast. I hobbled down the aisle, keeping as much weight off my bad leg as possible and using the shelves as support. When I reached the end of the row, I hopped across the few open feet and dragged myself around the counter to sit in a lopsided office chair by the key machine. Then I sat down, and with a long sigh for my poor devastated wardrobe, I grabbed a knife from the counter and cut the left leg of my jeans all the way from my ankle to my ass.

With the wounds exposed, I could almost see what was going on, and it wasn't good. There were black streaks running up and down the back of my leg from the puncture wounds the demon's claws left behind, and the blood that seeped from the holes I could see was thick and running with black goo. Just what I needed, a demon infection.

"This is gonna suck," I muttered. I broke another display case and yanked the sliding mirror door out of it so I could see what I was doing, then I made a deep "X" over each of the four wounds in the back of my leg. It hurt like a mother, and I couldn't decide which I wanted to do more, scream or pass out, so I settled on just gritting my teeth and translating the word "motherfucker" into every language I knew. When I had opened each wound and let it bleed out a little, trying to flush the poison out of my system like a snakebite, I focused my will on the knife in my hand and whispered, "*Calor.*" The blade warmed, then began to glow red as I poured more energy into it. I wiped the blood off each wound with the tattered remnants of that pants leg, then pressed the red-hot blade into each wound, searing the flesh and hopefully destroying the last little remnants of demonic taint in my blood.

When I finished cauterizing the last hole in my leg, I flung the knife away from me and laid my head down on the counter. The cool glass felt good on my cheek, which ached from holding in my screams, and I felt like I could lay there and sleep until the Sporting Goods manager showed up for work the next day and found me amidst the wreckage of his once-fine department. But I couldn't really do that. There was something on top of the Pyramid blasting a fuckton of energy into the sky, and I was one hundred percent sure it had really bad intentions for the city of Memphis.

And probably the whole world, but I get tired of saving the world all the time. It's a really big burden, and nobody ever seems to notice, anyway. So I was just going to save Memphis. If that saved the world, awesome. But my focus was to not let the home of some of the best blues and barbecue the world had ever seen be turned into a magical apocalyptic wasteland. And that meant I had to stand up.

It sucked, but not as bad as before. My leg hurt like a son of a bitch, but I could feel the power in my blood working overtime to repair the damage. I might not have gotten all the demon rot out of my thigh, but I got it clean enough to get me through the next hour. And let's face it, after that I'd either be in a position to get Glory to heal me fully, or I'd be dead and wouldn't give a shit about my leg.

So I drew one of my own knives this time, not one from the

display case, and cut off the shreds of denim hanging around my left leg, leaving me in half jeans, half Daisy Dukes. Just the look I wanted to show up to a boss fight in. Nothing screams "Fear Me!" more than your Captain Marvel boxer briefs sticking out of your booty shorts.

I limped over to the elevator and pressed the button, taking a quick mental inventory before I rode a glass box up a hundred feet or so to meet my possible doom. I had about half my magical reserves left, one bum leg, a pistol with two full magazines, a pair of silver-and-cold iron-bladed daggers, a pair of blessed brass knuckles, and a fuckton of attitude. And I was going to go fight an unfamiliar opponent on unseen terrain for unknown stakes at way less than full strength.

Yup, felt like another goddamn Saturday night.

38

Why is it that no matter where you go, no matter how rich the musical culture of a city, when you get into an elevator, you know that at some point you're going to hear *"The Girl from Ipanema"*? There I was in Memphis, home of Sun Records, birthplace of Rock n' Roll, one of the greatest blues towns in the world, and halfway through my trip to battle whatever monstrosity was atop the Pyramid, here comes that damn song. I wasn't sure which was worse, that the last song I ever heard might be *"The Girl from Ipanema,"* or that no matter whether I lived or died, that stupid song would be stuck in my head for at least a week.

The doors *dinged* open, and I stepped out into what I thought would be a nice little observation deck at the top of a giant pyramid with a Bass Pro Shops in the bottom of it with no real connection to Egypt whatsoever. But now it was even more surreal. I was expecting something like the Empire State Building—a gift shop, a bunch of windows, and some of those telescope things you put a quarter into. I was not expecting the elevator to open up into a full restaurant with a giant circular bar backed by another big-ass aquarium.

And that was the stuff that was *normally* there. That doesn't even address the fact that floating in the middle of the room, inches off the bar and right in front of that huge aquarium, was a skinny man wreathed in magical energy. The crimson glare was almost blinding at first, but as my eyes adjusted, I could see the ring stolen from my room at Zeek's floating in the air around him, along with the bracelet I last saw on the DJ's arm at the school dance. There was a golden locket on a thin chain, which I assumed was made from the cursed gold Glory told me about that came from the golden calf Moses smashed way back in the day. But the *piece de resistance* was the amulet.

Floating above the guy's skull was a blood-red stone set into a simple golden loop. Energy flowed from the other three artifacts into the man, then up through the top of his head and into the amulet as a beam of purest white. Those must be the souls stolen from all the people who died at the dance and the concert. This fucker was channeling them through himself, and as the light flowed through the amulet's gem, their energy turned from brightest white to blood-red. I didn't know what the fuck this guy wanted all that power for, but nothing good was going to come from hundreds of souls passing through the stone Cain used to invent murder. Then the man on the bar looked up, and as the lank brown hair fell away, revealing his face, it was all I could do not to pass out from pure shock.

Grinning at me under his waterfall of unwashed hair was Charlie the Creeper Welch, last seen heading for a beer at Zeek's bar with his idiot brother Bart. Charlie had the essence of literally thousands of people flowing through him as a conduit and pouring into one of the darkest artifacts in the history of mankind, and he was *smiling*. "Hi there, Quincy. So glad you could join the party. Some things just aren't as good if nobody's there to see it, and this is one of them."

"Charlie?" I asked. "What the fuck?"

"Oh, is this the part where I'm supposed to explain everything to you while you come up with some sneaky plan to blast me in the middle of my soliloquy? I think we'll take part of that off the table. That work for you?" Charlie extended his right arm straight out from his body, and glowing chains of red energy streaked out from his index finger and wrapped around me, slamming me up against the closed elevator doors and holding me firm.

"Now you sit there and be a good boy while I finish my ritual, and I'll tell you a story. It's a story about a boy who grew up in a bad place. It wasn't bad for everybody, just for him. Because the old man that lived next door didn't like boys with blue eyes, like Bart. And he didn't like boys with hazel eyes, like Waylon. No, he had a very special place in his heart for boys with green eyes. And this boy had pretty green eyes."

Charlie didn't have green eyes. As far as I could tell, he didn't have eyes anymore at all, just glowing white orbs full of soul energy. But the message wasn't lost on me. He went on, his voice crackly like static on a phone line. His body was being blown out by all the energy passing through it.

"When the boy's mother was at work, sometimes the man who lived next door would invite the boy and his brothers over to play video games. Sometimes he'd fix supper for the boys, and that was nice, because there wasn't much food in the boy's house most of the time, and it was usually yucky like vegetables. But when the man cooked for the boy and his brothers, there were hamburgers, and French Fries, and even *dessert*."

"Little Charlie didn't like it when there was dessert, though. If there was dessert, it would mean that his brothers would get sleepy right after supper because the man always gave them a special dessert. But Charlie was awake, and that's when he and the man would go upstairs to play their special games…"

"Look, Charlie," I started, but a wave of his hand and Charlie sealed my mouth with more of that red energy.

"You don't get to talk, Quincy. You talk too much already. But not Charlie. Charlie never talked. He never told anybody about the games he played with the man. Because he knew if he told anybody, the man would stop, and nobody would ever make Charlie feel special again."

My eyes went wide as the horror of what he said sank in. The sick fuck hadn't just abused this kid, he'd warped the poor boy's sense of self into thinking that he *liked* the abuse. I didn't want to kill Charlie anymore. I wanted to dig up the bones of the man that did that shit to him, piss on his bones, and haul him up out of Hell so I could banish him again and again.

Charlie went on. "But then one day, the games stopped. Charlie didn't want to stop playing, but the man said he was too old for those games now, and Charlie would have to find someone else to play with. And Charlie was sad for a long time. But then Charlie found the internet, and he found *lots* of people to play with. There were plenty of people to make Charlie feel special online, and sometimes they could even meet up in real life, and Charlie really liked that.

"He played different games now, though. And sometimes the people he played with didn't like the games, and they cried. It's not good when people cry. But Charlie always helped them stop crying, because Charlie is a good boy. He's the best boy. Then he found someone who told him he could help him, that he had a magic spell and if Charlie learned to cast it he could go down to where his first friend was, the man who taught him how to play the game all those years ago, and he could play with him *forever.*"

Charlie's face took on an almost rapturous expression, and he started to tremble as the power coursing through his body struggled for release. I don't know if it was his delusions and paranoia that finally pushed him around the bend, or if something triggered him going off the deep end, but there was not a shred of sanity left in Charlie's eyes. He'd always been creepy, but I never thought he was truly dangerous. I'd been around him dozens of times in the bar, and he looked as normal as anyone who visited Zeek's. Even at the Robbins's, he was a lech, but he didn't seem insane. Channeling the power of all those souls must have hammered on the cracks in his mind, and with this mysterious "mentor" pouring poison into his ear, he finally shattered under the weight of the imagined slights and injustices. I almost felt sorry for the poor stupid fuckwit, but I was way too busy worrying about how I was going to get myself free of the bonds restraining me to take Charlie down and stop whatever he had set in motion with the power of all those souls.

As I watched and schemed, the last flickers of power ran out of the floating artifacts and into Charlie. The white lights vanished, the three artifacts other than the amulet crumbled to dust, and the nimbus of power surrounding the almost skeletal floating man shifted totally to red.

"It is complete!" Charlie said, standing up in thin air and grasping the amulet. The stone flared even brighter red, and I had to close my eyes against the light for a second.

When I opened them again, Charlie had one hand raised overhead, holding the amulet and streaming soul power into the night sky. With his right hand, he pointed to the floor of the restaurant and extended his index finger. A line of red energy streaked from his finger, and as he moved his hand through the air, a casting circle appeared on the floor, burned into the wood by Charlie's power.

The circle was about six feet in diameter, a pair of concentric rings, with glowing Enochian script ringing the barrier between them. I couldn't see through the glare to read them all, but it looked like a pretty reasonable facsimile of a Gate to me, and I'd had way more experience looking at doorways to Hell than I ever wanted. The last symbol drawn, the floor inside the circle disappeared, and through it I could see back into the last place I ever wanted to see—Hell itself.

A pair of huge clawed hands gripped the edge of the inner ring, and my heart sank as a demon began to pull himself through the circle. Not just any demon, but a red-skinned demon with overlong arms, legs that ended in hooves, huge swooping horns jutting out from his forehead, and more teeth than the crocodiles in the tank downstairs. The demon dragged his body up through the circle, and Charlie waved a hand in the air. The only barrier between the demon and the rest of the world blinked out of existence, and a pair of black, pupilless eyes locked on mine.

Asmodeus smiled, and my blood ran cold. "Why, Quincy Harker, imagine seeing you here. The last time we met, I think you promised to ass-fuck me with a piece of the true cross, didn't you?"

I didn't remember saying that, but it sounded like me, so I just grinned. "Sorry, Az. I left all my sex toys at home. But I bet we can improvise a good rogering with a magnum of Dom if you're really desperate."

Asmodeus laughed. This was a laugh I'd be hearing in my nightmares for years to come. It was an echoing cackle that promised lingering pain for a long, long time. "I have waited so very long for this, Quincy Harker. I am going to make you hurt, then I'm going to torture everyone you love in front of you until their hearts and brains turn to jelly, then I'm going to hurt you even more. Then I'm going to walk around this little slice of paradise Father created for his favorite miscreant children, and I'm going to turn it into a scorched wasteland to rival Hell's Eighth Circle. And just for the fun of it, I'll wear your soul in Cain's stone around my neck so you can watch every second of it, as helpless as you are right now."

"You've obviously put some thought into this," I said.

"No one summons me to clean up their errands, forces me into a bargain, then threatens me in full view of a mortal and the spawn of that shitbird Orobas! That insult must be repaid in kind, and I am very, *very* good at payback."

That explained it. It wasn't so much that I summoned him and made him kill Jacob Marlack five years ago. It was that Smith, the Cambion son of the demon Orobas, saw it. That meant Orobas knew about it, which meant that word had been out in Hell for five years that Asmodeus got treated like a bitch by a mortal. Yeah, he was pissed. My shitty night was about to get spectacularly worse.

"Yeah, too bad you're going to get banished at sunrise. So you better get to torturing because it looks like you've only got about two hours left," I said.

There went that laugh again, and when he was done cackling, Asmodeus gave me a grin that may very well have made me piss myself a little. "What do you think all the souls were for, Harker? With this much soul energy stored in Cain's little memento of brotherly love, I can stay on this plane forever. Whenever I feel the summoning breaking, I can just send a soul to Hell in my place. As long as I don't run out of humans to slaughter, I've got all the time in the world. And that's the best thing about you breeders. No matter how many I kill, you just keep making more."

Fuck. He was probably right. The collapse of a summoning meant that a soul had to go back through the Gate into Hell, but I had no idea if it *had* to be the specific soul that came through the first time. For all I knew, any soul would do. I'd never summoned a demon when there was a spare soul around to condemn to eternal torment. But if anybody would know the loopholes, it was Asmodeus. He could likely dupe the magic forever, as long as he kept killing people. And with a Prince of Hell running around the United States, a high body count was certainly a given.

"Hey, excuse me? Mr. Asmodeus? I'm ready to go now. But how are you going to send me to Hell to see my friend if the Gate is closed?" Charlie was down off the bar now, standing next to Asmodeus looking up at the Prince of Hell like a kid begging his mom for a toy in the store. It was heartbreaking in a way, looking at this broken shell of a man, made that way by a manipulative prick of an adult years ago, now responsible for so much death and destruction.

Asmodeus looked down at Charlie, who still had Cain's amulet floating above his head. The demon plucked the artifact from the air and smiled down at Charlie. "Well done, my good and faithful servant."

Even my blood ran a little cold at that particular level of blasphemy. Or maybe it was running cold at the smile on Asmodeus's face. Or maybe both.

"I will indeed send you to Hell, Charles Welch, just as you asked." Then he reached out with a huge clawed hand and snapped Charlie's neck like a twig. The gaunt ghost-hunter dropped to the floor, his eyes wide as the life flooded out of him. With all the magic floating through the air, I could *see* Charlie's soul as it fled his body, and I watched as the Demon Lord aimed Cain's stone at it, wrapping the mottled black and green soul in bright red power, then pointed the stone straight down, sending the soul to plunge through the floor, presumably to Hell.

Asmodeus grinned at me. "I promised him I'd send him to Hell. I just didn't tell him I was going to do it the old-fashioned way. Now, Quincy Harker, where shall we begin?"

39

Well, fuck. Here I was again, staring a Prince of Hell in the face and trying to come up with a way that I walked out of this mess. I didn't have an ace up my sleeve this time, no get out of Hell free card hiding behind a rock. Nope, I just had what passed for wits in my house, whatever power I could call up, and my two fists.

That's when I realized that I was free from the binding spell Charlie laid on me. Poor, stupid Charlie, who just got tossed down into Hell like a discarded fast food wrapper. Nah, that's not even true anymore. With all the laws against littering, fast food wrappers get way more respect than Charlie got.

"That's right, Harker," Asmodeus said, and his voice sounded like a thousand bees all bussing around while they dragged their stingers down a chalkboard. "You're free. I don't need you tied up to kill you. I just need you within reach."

I got to my feet, called up enough power to shroud my fists in purple magic, and gave Asmodeus my best "go fuck yourself" grin. "Well come on then, dickbag. Let's dance."

Piece of advice: don't ever enter into single combat with a demon of any kind, but if you have to brawl with a denizen of Hell, and you have any choice in opponent whatsoever, don't pick one of the highest-ranking Princes in the joint. Asmodeus wasn't just a demon. He wasn't even *just* a Prince of Hell, if there is a run of the mill Lord of the Pits. No, he was Lucifer's wingman in the War on Heaven. Asmodeus was one of the angels who followed Lucifer when he stormed the Gates of Heaven, and he fell right alongside the Dawnbringer.

So outside of staring Lucifer dead in the face again, I was about to go mano-a-demon-o with the most powerful creature to ever swing a pitchfork. I was fucked, and I knew it, but if I could buy Glory and Zeek enough time to kill a dragon, maybe I could weaken Az enough before he killed me so they could take him down after I died. So I put up my dukes and got ready to rumble.

Asmodeus took one look at me and my fighting stance and laughed that bone-splitting cackle again. "You really think you can fight me, Harker? Come *on*. I stood toe to toe with *Gabriel*. Now I'm supposed to be afraid of *you*?"

"Not afraid, asshole, just aware." I threw half a dozen bolts of pure energy across the room at the demon while I sprinted to my left at top speed. I had no fucking idea what I was trying to run to, just that I didn't want to be standing still. Good call, too, since Asmodeus didn't even bat an eye at knocking my magic missiles out of the sky and sending several of them right back to where I stood seconds before.

I leapt into the air, pushing off a table and springing up a good twelve feet, spun around, pointed both palms at Asmodeus, and shouted, "*GLACIO!*" at the top of my lungs. Blue power streaked from my hands and enveloped the demon, wrapping him in ice. I continued to pour power at him until he was encased in a block of ice two feet thick on every side. I landed in a crouch on top of the bar and looked over to see if I'd even made him hesitate.

I hadn't. The stone in his hand flared red, and the ice prison shattered outward, turning into ice missiles streaking out in every direction. Including right at me. I dropped behind the bar as a chunk of ice the size of my head flew past. I heard a *crack* from behind me and looked up just in time to see the huge aquarium behind the bar shatter, dumping a couple thousand gallons of water and a huge fish on top of me.

The force of the water knocked me to the floor, and I rolled over and scrambled away on my hands and knees from the worst of the devastation, ignoring the fish flopping around behind me. A little animal cruelty was the least of the cruelties Asmodeus was going to inflict if I didn't come up with some way to stop him. I grabbed a bottle of Bacardi 151 off the shelf as I stood up, thinking that even if flames didn't hurt him, I might be able to distract him if I set him on fire.

I stood up, ready to fling the booze at him followed by a fireball, but Asmodeus was standing right in front of the bar as I came to my feet. He swatted the rum out of my hand, then slapped me across the cheek with what looked like barely any effort to him but felt like someone had just driven a taxi into the side of my face. I spun in a circle, my vision blurring from the impact, and came around into the path of an oncoming demon fist. I dropped, but not quick enough.

His fist grazed the top of my skull as I went down to my knees, and I swear just that much contact left me dizzy and nauseated. He'd barely touched me and given me a fucking concussion.

"Come here, Harker. This is getting tedious." The demon leaned over the bar and scrabbled for me, but I was already scurrying away on my hands and knees. One claw got the back of my leg, dragging a line of fire all the way from my thigh to my heel. At least now both legs were fucked up, so I wouldn't limp. I couldn't really walk much, but I was at least balanced.

I pulled myself to my feet and kinda threw myself up onto the bar. I called power, but it was hard to focus with my vision blurred and both legs screaming at me, so the energy flickered around my hands instead of giving off a steady light.

Asmodeus came around the bar, dragging one claw along the polished stone top, sending a white-hot knife of agony through my ears and making my stomach do even more cartwheels. I did my best to stand without weaving too much and made a "come here" gesture with both hands.

The demon smiled as he approached. "I thought you'd be more challenging. I thought the big, bad Reaper would at least be able to land a punch. But you're just as pitiful as the rest of these mortal trash. Lucifer was right. Father was a fool for creating you, and a fool twice over for valuing you over the Host. If you're the best of humanity, this will be no challenge at all. I shall rule this plane for a thousand years with no one strong enough to stop me."

"I'm not the best of humanity, Az-hole," I said. "I'm probably one of the worst examples of the species. But I swear this to you, Fallen One," I poured a little power into my words and wove the energy through the space between us, tethering Asmodeus to me, "as long as there is a single breath left in my body, I will fight you with everything I've got." Then I poured power down the lines of magic tying us together, sending as much elemental power as I could draw straight into Asmodeus's heart.

He didn't even blink. He just raised one long claw to his chest and scratched idly at the point that connected us. "Itchy," he said, and with a flick of a finger, severed the magical bond tying us together and pouring all that energy back into me. The power streaked back along the severed lines and flooded into my soul, picking me up bodily and flinging me across the room. I crashed into a table for four and went down in a jumble of white linens and splintered wood.

He didn't hurry to finish me. He didn't have to. Something low in my back broke when I landed, maybe my pelvis, and I couldn't move my right leg at all. I watched the grinning demon walk toward me, licking his lips at the thought of tearing me to shreds, and I knew I was about to die.

I went deep inside myself then, because I knew what was about to happen and knew I couldn't stop it. All I could try to do was fix the worst broken thing I'd done in my long life. I had only seconds to do it, but I had to try. I peered deep inside myself and found the wall I'd built up between myself and Rebecca Gail Flynn over the last six months. It was a thick wall, meant to keep her out forever, to never force her to be part of my world again. But right then, with death staring me in the face, I knew that she deserved better. She deserved to know how much she meant to me.

So I tore down that wall and felt the bond between us flare to life. It was as strong as ever, as strong as if I'd never been a selfish, cowardly fuck and walked away from her.

Harker? I felt her wake up. Felt the confusion, the joy, then the anger and the pain.

Flynn, I "said." *I'm sorry. I'm sorry I left, sorry I hurt you, and sorry I wasn't man enough to explain why. I'm a fucking idiot, and I'm probably going to die any second, but I wanted you to know without a shadow of a doubt, that my last thought on this earth was how much I love you, how special you are, and how much I wish I could see you just one more time before—*

Before what, Harker? Where are you? What's happening?

I love you. I'm sorry. Then I shut down enough of the link that I hoped she wouldn't feel my death in her head, but kept it open enough for me to feel her in my last moments. It was selfish as fuck, but that had been my M.O. for more than a century, and I wasn't going to learn anything new in my last ten seconds.

I looked up at Asmodeus's grinning face. "Did you tell her good-bye? Good. But don't worry, Harker. I'll tell her hello from you tomorrow." Then his clawed hand swung down, and I braced myself for him to rip out my heart and show it to me.

But a streak of white light blasted him in the chest, and he flew back across the room, slamming against a metal beam and falling to the floor, dazed. I looked up, and standing where half a second before was a Prince of Hell ready to murder me with his bare hands, stood a guardian angel in gleaming white armor with a sword blazing fire in one hand, and the other hand reaching down to help me to my feet. Again. I reached up and took her hand, gasping as the healing energy flowed into me, making me whole again instantly.

Glory pulled me to my feet. "Hey," she said.

"Hey."

"So, there's a demon over there."

"Yeah," I replied. "Big one. I can't beat him."

"Me neither," Glory said. "Looks like a good thing I brought help." She gestured to her right, and I looked over to see three figures walking in from the observation deck. Zeek was in full djinn mode, all dark skin, topknot, and magical sand whirling around his tree-trunk legs. Beside him strode a slim figure with jet-black skin and a wry smile on his face.

"Quincy Harker," Faustus said. "You and I have *got* to stop meeting like this."

"How did you get here?" I asked.

"I made a deal with the demons you sent me to make a deal with. Not only will they never bother the Robbinses again, but they also gave me a lift here. When I saw the light show, I figured this was probably the place to be tonight. And you know how I hate to miss a good party."

I let any other questions slide because at that moment, Asmodeus struggled to his feet and shook his head. "Well, if it isn't little Glory, the overachieving guardian suck-up. You know I hated you even when I was in Heaven, don't you?"

"Hello, Asmodeus," Glory said. "I think this is actually a good look for you. White wings and happiness just never seemed to suit you somehow. You always looked like you needed to suffer. Glad we could oblige."

"We? Oh, child, you had *nothing* to do with my pain."

"I didn't then. But I'm sure as hell going to now." Glory raised her sword and pointed it at Asmodeus. "Kill him!" She took off flying at the demon, with Zeek hurtling across the room from the opposite side, his magic allowing him to float over the scattered tables.

The third member of their group was a woman with golden-brown skin and a long braid stretching from the cornrows on her head halfway down her back. She wore leather pants, a shimmering golden armored shirt that rippled like scales with her every movement, and no shoes. She leapt into the air and flew straight at Asmodeus, a pair of eight-foot leathery golden wings appearing from her shoulder blades as she did. She flew all the way to the ceiling, pulled up, and unleashed a narrow stream of white-hot flame from her mouth, right at the demon's face.

I didn't know how they did it, but it looked for all the world like instead of killing the dragon, Glory and Zeek had recruited her to our cause. We might have a snowball's chance of living through this yet.

40

Asmodeus looked up, momentarily distracted by the fire bath, even if he wasn't hurt by it. That gave Zeek a chance to slam into the demon, knocking him back into the glass wall overlooking the Memphis skyline and the slowly brightening horizon. Dawn was coming, and if we could keep Asmodeus off-balance, we might be able to get the stone off him and use the dawn to send him back to Hell.

If we could keep fighting him for the next few minutes while the sun crept over the horizon. And if we could get Cain's murder rock away from him before that. A couple of big "ifs," but they were the only way I could think of to keep from being stuck with one of Hell's most powerful demons walking down Beale Street this afternoon.

Dragon Lady stopped breathing fire at the demon as Glory flew in from his right and took a big slice out of Asmodeus's thigh with her flaming sword. Az-hole lashed out with a fist, clipping Glory's wing and sending her pinwheeling ass over teakettle across the restaurant. Zeek stayed in close, throwing heavy punches and shifting his form completely to sand when Asmodeus struck back.

"Nice trick, wish I'd thought of it," I muttered, my legs still a little stiff from Glory's rapid healing.

"Shot?" Faustus said from my left elbow, and I turned to stare at him. The demon was standing behind the bar with a bottle of Macallan 12 in one hand, a pair of highball glasses in the other. He raised an eyebrow at me, a little hard to see since his ebony eyebrows were barely distinguishable from his obsidian forehead.

"What the fuck are you doing back here?" I asked, incredulous.

"Not dying," the demon replied simply. "I know where my talents lie, Harker, and going toe to toe with Asmodeus is not them. I'm the negotiator. The...get things done guy. I'm the guy in every prison movie who can 'get stuff.' The spy who gets called in to take out the bad guy when he's surrounded by goons and sending in a team of shooters would be worse than the target just accidentally getting a half-pound of nightshade in his hamburger. I'm that guy. I'm not the punch people in the face until they fall apart guy. That's what you have those three for. You need someone persuaded, intimidated, blackmailed, extorted, hacked, or robbed? Call me. You need someone beaten to a bloody pulp? Try the Teamsters. They're way better equipped for the heavy lifting."

"So you're the guy who taught Fagin to Fagin, huh?" I grinned at Faustus and reached out a hand for the glass. He passed it over and I leaned on the bar. "Then let me tell you what we're going to do..."

A minute and half later, Asmodeus was screeching in rage, Glory was standing right in front of him laying into the demon with her sword, Zeek was still doing his best floating like a butterfly and stinging like a bee, and Smaugette was still buzzing around the ceiling like a really hot-headed wasp. I downed one more swallow of good whiskey and walked out into the middle of the room. I lined myself up right in front of Asmodeus and shouted, "Glory! Down!"

We've done this a couple times before, so she knew to hit the deck right away. I clapped my wrists together, thrust my palms out in front of my chest and sent tendrils of power shooting out at them to strike Asmodeus right in the chest. Instead of trying to hurt him, these beams struck him and *flowed off*, streaming to the sides of the demon like rivulets of water coursing off his body. The streams of power continued to pound at him, stretching all the way back to my hands, then began to morph into glowing blue chains of pure energy.

"Push him back!" I shouted, and all three musketeers rushed to help. Zeek and Glory each grabbed a shoulder and shoved, and the dragon flew down beside me and laid one hand atop my joined wrists and closed her eyes. I felt the power inside me surge, and it began to flow faster and thicker as she somehow supercharged my magic, like a boost of nitrous to my soul.

My eyes went wide, and I turned to stare at her, but she just stood there, a golden-skinned beauty with a little smile quirking up one corner of her mouth. "Holy shit, lady. How did those two ever beat you?"

She smiled bigger. "They didn't. When the idiot human who bound me to his service died, I was released from any obligation to battle your compatriots. Then the one with the jet-black skin said that if I helped you, I would be rewarded with gold. Dragons love gold. So I came to help."

I decided this would be a really bad time to mention my severe lack of any gold to her, so I kept my mouth shut. She saw the look on my face and threw her head back. The laugh that came out was rich and warm. "I felt the presence of the demon, Quincy Harker. They are abominations and must be destroyed. I could not leave this place and allow one such as he to exist."

"That's good," I said. "Because I don't have any gold." Then I turned back to the task literally at hand and concentrated on slamming more power into the demon's chest. By now he was pressed up against another roof beam and I was having serious doubts about the structural integrity of this pyramid, but I shoved those worries aside and filed them under "Shit we'll deal with if we're still alive in half an hour."

With Asmodeus writhing against my power, I gritted my teeth as my fingers twined the air. As I manipulated the energy, the chains of power wound tighter and tighter around the demon's chest, binding him to the beam and rendering him immobile. For at least as long as the dragon and I could keep pouring the power on.

"We only need to hold him for a few more seconds, gang!" I shouted. "Once the sun's up, this asshat goes back home, with prejudice!" Asmodeus redoubled his efforts to break free of my chains as the first rays of sunlight streaked across the floor. Another twenty seconds, and he'd be back in Hell where he belonged.

Too bad I only managed to hold the bonds for ten.

With a mighty roar, Asmodeus flexed, and the chains of energy holding him to the wall shattered in a shockwave that sent Zeek and Glory flying backward. I dropped to one knee, and the dragon lady sucked all the magical backlash from the shattered spell into herself, laying her out flat on the restaurant floor. Good thing, too. That much juice coming back into me would have shattered every bone in my wrists and arms, if not pulverized me completely.

"Fool!" Asmodeus shouted, the first rays of dawn stretching across the floor to his feet. "I told you, as long as I have this artifact, I can't be banished!" He held Cain's stone high above his head and grinned at me in triumph.

Which quickly turned to shock as Faustus sprang out from under a nearby table, vaulted over Asmodeus's head, snatched the stone from his fingers, and dropped into a perfect superhero landing on the other side. The inky-skinned demon turned around to the Prince of Hell and twirled the stone between his fingers. "You mean *this* artifact?"

Asmodeus howled in rage as the sun broke over the horizon, bathing him fully in the first light of morning. "I'll destroy you for this, Quincy Harker!" he screamed, then faded into nothing but a puff of dust on the carpet as the sun rose over Memphis. He was gone. The Prince of Hell was back where he belonged, and the good guys were still alive.

"Huh," I said, staring at the spot on the floor recently occupied by a giant demon planning to eviscerate me and subjugate all of humanity. "I'll be damned. It worked."

Faustus looked over at me, his eyes growing large enough to encompass almost his entire face. "You didn't know if that would work?"

"It was a pretty solid theory," I said, walking back over to the bar and pouring myself a drink.

Faustus almost sprinted to me and slammed the artifact down onto the bar. I heard a loud *crack* and looked down to see the bar top spiderwebbed with new fault lines from the impact. "You're telling me I just pickpocketed one of the most powerful demons in Hell on a *hunch?*"

I knocked back half a glass of Scotch and poured one more, then passed one to Faustus. "It was a good hunch." I looked around the room. "Anybody else day drinking, or just me and the demon?"

Everyone raised their hands and walked over to the bar. Zeek and Glory assumed their mortal forms, and I had a trio of glasses waiting for them when they arrived. I refilled Faustus's now-empty tumbler and held up my own.

"To saving the world," I said. "Again."

"Again," Glory said, drinking and setting her glass down on the bar.

"Again?" Zeek asked.

The dragon lady didn't say anything, just downed her glass and looked around. "I don't see any gold."

"Yeah..." Faustus said. "I might have exaggerated the earning potential for this job. Sorry about that."

"I got to fight a demon. That's a good day. I doubt I'll see you again, Quincy Harker. But if I do, I hope it shall be as friends." She held out a hand to me, and I shook it.

"Me too," I said, completely honestly. "Because you kinda scare the shit outta me."

She laughed and turned away, walking toward the elevator.

"Hey," I called. "What's your name?"

"Aurin," she replied. "With an 'au,' obviously." Then she stepped into the elevator and was gone.

"That was a good-looking lizard," Faustus said.

"How are you still here?" Glory asked the demon.

"What do you mean?"

"Demons are cast back into Hell at sunrise. So why are you still here?"

"Oh, that," he said. "Well, it's not exactly like that. It's not so much that *demons* are cast back into Hell at sunrise."

"No, I'm pretty sure we just watched that happen."

"No, you just watched an infernal creature without a tether to the mortal world get cast back into Hell." He smiled at the parsing of the language, and I remembered that this guy was essentially the original asshole contract negotiator.

"So you found a way to tie yourself to this plane," I said. "How the fuck did you do that?"

"It wasn't easy, and it wasn't painless, and it *really* cut down on my power, but I can watch the sunrise without tap dancing in a lake of fire immediately afterward, so I call it worth it."

I didn't expect him to say much more than that. After all, he was sitting at a bar with a demon hunter and an angel, two people pretty much dedicated to sending people like him back to Hell. And he obviously didn't want to go back to Hell.

"So how did you get the demons to lay off the Robbins family?" I asked.

"Oh, that? Yeah...I kinda promised them I'd meet them at one of the casinos this afternoon and I'd teach them to cheat at craps."

"But they aren't tied to this world, are they?" Zeek asked.

"Nope," Faustus said with a smile. Then he waved a hand in front of his face, and instead of an obsidian-skinned demon in a tailored suit, there was an overweight white guy with red jowls in a Hawaiian shirt holding a highball glass. He knocked back the drink and set his glass on the bar. "But just in case they show up, I'm going to the boats to cheat at craps. Hey, Harker."

"Yeah?"

"If you ever need somebody to assault a Demon Prince on a hunch again, make sure I'm last on your list to call." Then he gave a little wave and vanished in a puff of black smoke.

I waved a hand in front of my face, coughing. "You can take the demon out of Goethe, but you can't take Goethe out of the demon.

Little bastard will always be theatrical." It was about then that I noticed he hadn't taken the artifact with him. I picked up the stone from the bar and slipped it into a pocket. It felt warm against my leg, and I knew I really didn't want to keep it for very long. It definitely needed to be in way holier hands than mine.

"Hey guys," Glory said, pointing over my shoulder. "I think our ride is here."

I turned to follow her finger, and standing in the doors leading out to the observation deck was Rebecca Gail Flynn. I felt my heart leap at the sight of her at the same time my stomach plummeted at the ass-chewing I knew I deserved.

I walked over to her and gave her my best sheepish smile. "Hey, Becks."

"Hey, Harker."

"I'm—" She held up a hand to cut me off before I could really even get my grovel going.

"Later. We've got a *lot* to talk about, and I've got a lot more to yell about. But that's after. Now get in." She stepped to one side, and I saw a helicopter-shaped vehicle hovering just off the observation deck. It was matte black, with no visible rotors, and made not even a whisper of sound as it floated in the morning air.

"What the fuck is that and where are we going?"

"It's a hex-drive helicopter, powered by magic. It's on loan from Homeland Security," Becks said. "We've got a serious problem."

"What's up?" Glory asked. "Oh, this is Zeek. He's a friend. He's also a djinn. Used to be Harker's boss, but he kinda fired Q. At least we think he fired him. You never can tell with these two."

"Not surprising. I know the kind of trouble you two can get into without adult supervision," Flynn said, then reached forward and gave Glory a hug. "Thanks for the updates. I owe you."

"Updates?" I asked, but Flynn held up her hand.

"You're still in time out. Let's go. Zeek, I'm afraid we can't offer you a ride back to your place, but thanks for not letting my idiot fiancé get killed."

"Not a problem," he replied. "I'll just wiggle my nose and pop back home."

"You can really do that?" I asked.

"No, dumbass. Now give me the keys to your truck. I left my wheels back at the bar."

I tossed them to him and gave him a nod. "Thanks, Zeek. For everything."

"You're welcome, Harker. If you're ever back in Memphis, don't ask to crash at my place."

I turned to Flynn and said, "Okay, let's go. So what's the rush? And when did we get back in the good graces of Homeland Security?"

"I'll explain it all on the way, but basically DHS decided we were the lesser of two evils when a different secret government agency tasked with policing the paranormal went rogue and started attacking and kidnapping known friendly cryptids and supernatural beings."

"Another...?" I asked as we walked out on the deck and boarded the "chopper." The whole no engines thing was weird. It was quieter in the helicopter than in most cars.

"DEMON," Becks said, her face grim. "Someone or something has taken over DEMON and turned them rogue."

"Fuuuuck," I said. "Those guys have a shitload of resources and ties to all those Hunters. And they're connected to the Church in a lot of places, too."

"That's not all," Flynn said. "They hit Charlotte, Harker."

I stared at her, trying to get a read through our link, but I couldn't make sense of the jumble of thoughts and emotions whirling through her head. "What are you saying, Becks? What happened in Charlotte?"

"They raided every known supernatural being in the city. Rounded them up and murdered the less-powerful ones. The more powerful ones...they took them somewhere. We haven't been able to find out where yet."

My blood was ice. A ball of lead formed in my stomach, and my mouth went dry. I felt fear like I had never known. Not even when I was standing in Lucifer's throne room staring down the First of the

Fallen had I been as afraid. "What are you saying, Becks?" The question was almost a whisper.

One tear rolled down the side of her face, but her jaw was tight and there was as much fury in her eyes as pain. "They got Luke, Harker. I'm sorry. I couldn't fight them off. They took out me, and Cassie, and Jo, and they kidnapped Luke."

I sat there for a second as everything tumbled around in my head and my gut. Then it all locked into place. "So the federal government decided to come into my house and fuck with my family, huh? Well, let's go kick some ass and save Count Dracula."

To Be Continued...

AFTERWORD

Welcome to the very first Quincy Harker novel. I hope you've enjoyed it, and like this change in format. After four years of successful sales, and the publication of sixteen novellas and four collections, I decided to change things up a bit. instead of four novellas annually, there will now be one or two Quincy Harker novels each year.

Why? Well, there are a couple of reasons, but it mostly boils down to storytelling. The last three Quincy Harker collections have really been serialized novels, with *The Cambion Cycle* telling one story, and The Quest for Glory books (*Damnation & Salvation*) telling an even longer one. The fact is that the characters in the Quincy Harker series need more room than a novella affords. Their stories have gotten too complex, with too many layers, for me to tell in 100-150 pages. I need more room to stretch my legs, and more time to explore what's going on with these people I've invented.

In short, I'm getting wordier as I get older, and I wanted to present the stories the way I want to tell them, and that means getting more content less frequently. This ended up being a long books for me, almost 90,000 words, or the length of three of the previous Harker novellas. That meant I got to explore some things more deeply, and really dig into the characters and their emotions. I think the extra length is worth it, and I think I've laid the groundwork for some really interesting things over the next few months and years. I hope you also enjoy the new format, and I look forward to taking you on a continuing journey for a long time.

Thanks for reading, thanks for loving Harker and the gang as much as I do, and my cat thanks you for buying these books. He needs the kibble. :)

John Hartness
June 20, 2019

ACKNOWLEDGMENTS

Thanks as always to Melissa McArthur for all her help, and for trying in vain to teach me where the commas go.

The following people help me bring this work to you by their Patreon-age. You can join them at Patreon.com/johnhartness.

Sean Fitzpatrick
Missy Walston
Vikki Harraden
Amanda Justice
Mark Ferber
Andy Bartalone
Sharon Moore
Wendy Taylor
Sheelagh Semper
Charlotte Henley Babb
Tommy Acuff
Larry Morgan
Delia Houghland
Sarah Ashburn
Noah Sturdevant

Arthur Raisfeld

Jo Good

Andreas Brücher

Sheryl R. Hayes

Amaranth Dawe

Butch Howard

Larry Nash

Travis & Casey Schilling

Michelle E. Botwinick

Leonard Rosenthol

Lisa Hodges

Patrick Dugan

Michelle Kaylan

Patricia Reilley

Diane Jackson

Chris Kidd

Mark Wilson

Kimberly Richardson

Matthew Granville

Candice Carpenter

Theresa Glover

Salem Macknee

Pat Hayes

Jared Pierce

Elizabeth Donald

Andrea Judy

Leland Crawford

Vikki Perry

Valentine Wolfe

Noella Handley

Don Lynch

Jeremy Willhoit

D.R. Perry

Anthony D. Hudson

John A. McColley

Dennis Bolton
Shiloh Walker/J.C. Daniels
Andrew Torn
Sue Lambert
Emilia Agrafojo
Tracy Syrstad
Samantha Dunaway Bryant
Steven R Yanacsek
Rebecca Ledford
David Hess
Ray Spitz
Lars Klander

ABOUT THE AUTHOR

John G. Hartness is a teller of tales, a righter of wrong, defender of ladies' virtues, and some people call him Maurice, for he speaks of the pompatus of love. He is also the best-selling author of EPIC-Award-winning series *The Black Knight Chronicles* from Bell Bridge Books, a comedic urban fantasy series that answers the eternal question "Why aren't there more fat vampires?" In July of 2016. John was honored with the Manly Wade Wellman Award by the NC Speculative Fiction Foundation for Best Novel by a North Carolina writer in 2015 for the first Quincy Harker novella, *Raising Hell.*

In 2016, John teamed up with a pair of other publishing industry ne'er-do-wells and founded Falstaff Books, a publishing company dedicated to pushing the boundaries of literature and entertainment.

In his copious free time John enjoys long walks on the beach, rescuing kittens from trees and getting caught in the rain. An avid *Magic: the Gathering* player, John is strong in his nerd-fu and has sometimes been referred to as "the Kevin Smith of Charlotte, NC." And not just for his girth.

Find out more about John online
www.johnhartness.com

STAY IN TOUCH!

If you enjoyed this book, please leave a review on Amazon, Goodreads, or wherever you like.

If you'd like to hear more about or from the author, please join my mailing list at https://www.subscribepage.com/g8d0a9.

You can get some free short stories just for signing up, and whenever a book gets 50 reviews, the author gets a unicorn. I need another unicorn. The ones I have are getting lonely. So please leave a review and get me another unicorn!

ALSO BY JOHN G HARTNESS

The Black Knight Chronicles - Omnibus Edition

The Black Knight Chronicles Continues - Omnibus #2

All Knight Long - Black Knight Chronicles #7

Scattered, Smothered, & Chunked - Bubba the Monster Hunter Season One

Grits, Guns, & Glory - Bubba Season Two

Wine, Women, & Song - Bubba Season Three

Monsters, Magic, & Mayhem - Bubba Season Four

Born to Be Wild

Shinepunk: A Beauregard the Monster Hunter Collection

Year One: A Quincy Harker, Demon Hunter Collection

The Cambion Cycle - Quincy Harker, Year Two

Damnation - Quincy Harker Year Three

Salvation - Quincy Harker Year Four

Histories: A Quincy Harker, Demon Hunter Collection

Zombies Ate My Homework: Shingles Book 5

Slow Ride: Shingles Book 12

Queen of Kats

Fireheart

Amazing Grace: A Dead Old Ladies Detective Agency Mystery

From the Stone

The Chosen

Hazard Pay and Other Tales

FALSTAFF BOOKS

**Want to know what's new
And coming soon from
Falstaff Books?**

Try This Free Ebook Sampler

https://www.instafreebie.com/free/bsZnl

**Follow the link.
Download the file.
Transfer to your e-reader, phone, tablet, watch, computer,
whatever.
Enjoy.**

CPSIA information can be obtained
at www.ICGtesting.com
Printed in the USA
BVHW042255061222
653556BV00016B/75/J

9 781645 540069